MW00883249

Only the Beginning

Book One of the Rockin' Country Series

By Laramie Briscoe

Edited by: Lindsay Gray Hopper
Cover Art by: Kari Ayasha, Cover to Cover Designs
Proofread by: Dawn Bourgeois
Formatting: Paul Salvette, BB eBooks
Cover Models: Jack and Ashley Edmund
Cover Photo: Mandy Hollis of MH Photography

Dedication

To the songs and musicians that make writing so much fun! If I could one day be a rockstar, I totally would!

Summary

Princess of Country Music
America's sweetheart
Survivor of the scrutiny that comes with it all

Hannah "Harmony" Stewart has lived most of her adult life in the spotlight. It hasn't always been easy. One heartbreak almost ruined her. Some days it's hard to keep a smile on her face and stay positive, but there are a lot of people counting on her to keep it together. Just when it seems like she's at the pinnacle of her career, her life takes a turn. She meets a man who challenges everything she knows about herself and makes her question if the life she's living is for her or for the Nashville machine.

Heavy Metal's bad boy
Hair trigger temper
Struggling to deal with pressure of the industry

Garrett "Reaper" Thompson is tired. Touring and keeping up appearances with his band "Black Friday" is beginning to wear him out. He's ready for a change, ready for something different. When he meets Hannah at an awards show, he knows that she's the one; he knows that he can't live without her.

The problem?

Their own insecurities, their fans, her ex-boyfriend, and the media themselves. Can they look past it all and come through on the other side? For their story—this is only the beginning.

Chapter One

The crowd screamed loudly, causing her palms to sweat and her heart to race. Harmony Stewart inhaled deeply and then exhaled, letting the breath flow through her. The relaxation technique worked. Shoulders that had been so tight she couldn't even roll them were now loose. It was always like this, she realized. Right before she went on stage, the nervous energy started, causing her to tense up—not fully being able to appreciate the life she was living. Closing her eyes, she breathed again, feeling her muscles loosen up even more.

"Harmony, you're up next."

She nodded, glancing at the production tech. "Thanks." Her voice was thin even to her own ears. This was just something that she went through, no matter how many millions of albums she sold or awards she garnered.

Looking out onto the stage, she saw the rock group, Black Friday, finishing up. A fan of the band, she tried to still the heart that threatened to beat out of her chest as they finished their song and walked towards her. The lead singer was the personification of hotness in her opinion. She had always wanted a meeting, but had never been able to approach him when they had been in the same space. This time he would have to walk right by her—not that she had deluded herself to think he would know who she even was. Pulling her shaking hands to her body, she gripped them hard as the group approached.

"Good job, guys," she smiled as they passed her. One by one, they nodded and accepted her smile until she came face to face with Reaper, the lead singer. She only knew his stage name. What she wouldn't give to know his real one.

"Thanks. Good luck out there, sweetheart," he smiled widely. His teeth were white and straight, the dimples that she had caught glimpses of in pictures deepened widely in his cheeks. He was tall, much taller than she had originally thought. He towered over her 5'6 frame (with heels, thank you very much), and the tattoos that traveled down his arms were a feast to her eyes. They were intricate, and she wished she had the time to study them all.

Harmony opened her mouth to tell him something else, but he was already gone. Disappointment hit her stomach hard and fast. But at least it had been a start. With any luck, she would see him at some other award show. She heard her cue as she looked back to where the rock band stood, debriefing with some of their management. For just a split second, her eyes met Reaper's and goose bumps appeared on her arms. If only they'd had more time.

Reaper sat with his head back, eyes closed. The night had been long. He never really liked doing these awards shows, but their fans were amazing. Even though they didn't have what others called "crossover" success, they had some of the most rabid fans in the music industry. That, however, didn't change the fact that he was lonely and tired of not having someone besides the members of his band to share his life with.

"Who was the cutie that smiled at us as we walked by?"

"That was Harmony Stewart," he answered, moving only his lips.

"Country singer?"

"Yes, dude," he sighed. "The country singer."

"She's cuter than I imagined. I've only seen her on TV a few times."

Reaper sighed again. "Seriously Train, you're getting on my fuckin' nerves. Do you have to talk all the time?"

"What's your problem? Do you need to get laid?" Train asked, having a seat next to his friend.

"Do you ever get sick of all this?" He lifted his long arms and big hands up; gesturing to the backstage green room they sat in.

"Sick of what? The free pussy, the free booze, the amazing trips overseas and around this great nation? Playing the music we love every night? I'm ready to do this the rest of my life. Why aren't you?"

Reaper lifted his head up and opened his eyes, staring into the eyes of his friend. "I'm burnt out. Not with the music, but with the lifestyle. I need a change, something different to shake things up."

"Burnt out? How can you be burnt out?"

"It's just…" he ran his fingers through his hair. "We've been on the road for a year. I need something new and exciting in my life. I'm sick of the same girls, the same bus, and the same hotel rooms."

"You're bein' a moody fucking pansy is what you're being. Do you know how many guys would give their left nut to be where we are?" Train slapped his friend on the shoulder, the disbelief showing on his face.

Reaper realized he would get nowhere with his friend. Train dealt with his demons in unhealthy ways and perhaps tonight wasn't the best time to approach him about this. He couldn't rightfully explain his feelings if he didn't fully understand them himself. Better to just pretend that everything was peachy. "You're right. I'm crazy. I just need some good alcohol and a good cigarette. Let's get to the after party."

"Now that's what I'm talkin' about," the lead guitarist said, grabbing his friend by the arm and ushering him out of the room.

Reaper realized that nobody seemed to care what he thought, how he felt, or just how lonely he was. He might as well make the best of what to him was an unbearable situation.

"Harmony? Are you changing into the dress that new designer sent you for the after party?"

"I think so," Harmony answered her best friend and assistant, Shell.

"You need to change now, then."

Harmony rolled her eyes and grabbed the hanger from Shell's hand. "Yes ma'am."

Used to bossing her friend around, Shell had a seat while Harmony changed. "So tell me, did you meet anybody interesting at this awards show?"

"I did. Did you see any of the show?"

"I didn't get a chance too, no. I wish I had, but there was a lot going on back here," Shell answered from behind the door that Harmony had closed to change.

"I'm so sorry, Shell. I know how hard you work, and you'll never fully know how much I appreciate it. You'll be excited to hear that I finally met the guys from Black Friday."

Harmony heard the squeal and couldn't help the smile that spread across her face.

"I am so damn jealous. That lead singer—was he as hot as he looks on TV?"

"Even more so. I actually said a few words to him. Top moment of my life this year—for real."

She finished changing and let herself out of the dressing room. Coming out, she turned around in a circle, making sure everything looked okay. For the show, Harmony had wanted to keep it classy and her dress had been very Old Hollywood. This dress, however, was young and fun. Sparkles and glitter reigned. The hot pink color showed off the tan she had been able to get during a short vacation before awards season ramped up.

"Does this look okay?" she asked, turning around again so Shell could see her from every angle.

"You look really good. Hoping to meet anybody at this party?"

"You never know," she shrugged. "Maybe the guys from Black Friday will be there, and I'll be able to say something else to them. I was kind of a blabbering fool earlier. Are you coming with me?"

Shell wrinkled her nose up at her friend. "I don't know. This hasn't been a stellar day for me."

"All the more reason for you to raid my closet, find something hot, and come out on the town with me."

"Why are you trying to corrupt me? Usually it's the other way around. You're the belle of the country ball, and I'm the one trying to get you to do Jager shots," Shell laughed.

"Maybe I'm ready to let my hair down. It's time. I am twenty-four years old, and I'm not gettin' any younger. If I keep goin' at this pace with the music, I'm not goin' to be married before thirty, and that's never who I wanted to be. I'm the type of girl who wants a boyfriend, wants to be in love. I'm gonna have to make that a priority."

Shell knew that Harmony was telling the truth. She was one of those women who were made to be in love, but she wasn't for sure that her friend had ever felt those feelings. Her one serious relationship hadn't ended well and left her feeling disconnected. It was nice to see that she was beginning to look past that time in her life. "Okay, okay. If I need to be there to keep you from asking the first man you meet to marry you, I'll be there to save you from yourself."

"You, Shell, are the best friend a girl could ask for." She reached over, kissing her on the cheek.

"You sure we can leave in an hour?" Reaper asked he unfolded himself from the backseat of the limo they had taken to the party location.

"Yes, I'm sure," Train answered with a huff. Reaper didn't miss the way he wiped the back of his hand over his nose. It was a sure sign that some things never changed. He raised his eyebrows as Train admonished him. "Dude, when did you become such a fucking killjoy?"

"I told you already, I'm just not feeling this tonight."

They got into line with the rest of the celebrities and the other members of their band to walk the red carpet that lead into the venue that housed the party for the night.

"Hey." Train hit his friend's elbow. "Isn't that the little country girl from earlier?" He pointed further up the carpet.

Reaper couldn't see for shit, so he squinted his eyes together, trying to bring the person in front of them better in focus. "Fuck," he mumbled, pulling the wrap-around sunglasses he normally wore on stage up to his eyes. They were part of his persona, but in actuality they were prescription and without them—he really couldn't see. "Yeah, that's her."

"Cute, isn't she?"

"Seriously man, we already talked about how cute she is."

At that moment, they walked onto the main part of the carpet. Flashbulbs went off as they plastered smiles on their faces. Photographers called their names from all around. A little further down the aisle a photographer yelled at Reaper.

"What sweetheart? Didn't hear you." He cupped his hand over his ear.

"Take a picture with Harmony. It'll be a good photo op."

Harmony heard the exchange from where she stood and laughed. "He might not want to be seen with someone like me," she smiled as she glanced back at him.

He couldn't tell if she was flirting with him or not, but he figured he would seize the day. "Nah, darlin' maybe you don't wanna be seen with someone like me."

A blush covered her face, and she turned around so that she faced him. "I'm a fan, seriously. I'd love to take a picture with you."

The smile she gave him made his stomach dance. He had faced huge crowds before overseas. Hundreds of thousands of people he had performed in front of and not been nervous. Approaching this woman with the smile on her face made his legs shake. He strode over to her and easily put his arm around her waist. Even wearing heels she only came up to his shoulder.

"Where do you want us to look?" he asked.

The amount of people screaming at them was so deafening neither one of them could understand what anyone was saying. "Let's just start looking to the left and then look to the right," she said as she gripped his waist.

They stood there for long minutes as everyone got their pictures—and when it was over, the two of them were reluctant to let go of each other.

"Thanks Reaper and Harmony," the original photographer told them.

"You're welcome," Harmony answered. She pulled her arm from around his waist and turned to face him. "Thanks for taking a picture with me. I guess I'll see you inside and maybe, just maybe, I'll learn what people call you besides Reaper?"

"If I tell you that, then I'd have to kill you. It's highly classified." He put his hands in the pockets of the pants he wore and rocked back on his heels.

She wasn't sure if he was flirting with her or not because she couldn't see his eyes, but she knew that they were staring right at her. "Well then, I guess I better figure out how to work on my security clearance." She gave him a flip of her hair as she turned from him and walked towards the entrance of the club.

The pictures were already making their way all over the world.

Chapter Two

"I so wish I was able to get his real name before the end of the night," Harmony groaned as she looked at the cover of a gossip magazine. She, like everyone else who passed the magazine rack at this grocery store, could see the picture of her and Reaper together. It was featured prominently along with a headline that made it seem as if she and the lead singer of Black Friday were dating.

"I wish you had too," Shell commiserated with her friend as she took the magazine out of Harmony's hand and looked at it. "The two of you make a striking couple."

That was the truth. Harmony had even taken the time to read the internet gossip sites on her plane ride home to Nashville. Everyone made a comment about how hot the two of them looked together—didn't seem to matter that they were polar opposites on the musical genre stick, something that surprised her.

"Is this an obsession? I may or may not have made that picture of the two of us my lock screen," Harmony admitted, her face burning.

"Girl, you do have it bad."

It was their turn in line next, and on impulse, Harmony grabbed the magazine out of Shell's hands and threw it in with her other purchases. In this affluent section of the city, it wasn't unusual to see stars out and about, so neither one of them had to worry about photographers or gossipers overhearing their conversation. With their groceries purchased, the two of them made their way outside to Harmony's Land Rover.

"You wanna drive?" she asked, Shell, holding the keys up to her friend.

"You bet. Did you get an email from your producer?"

"Nah, but I have a total of 200 emails since last night, so I need to go through some of these. You know I tend to do that best riding in a car," she grinned.

"I've never understood that either," Shell shook her head. "If I'm letting someone drive me around, I want to be watching. If I'm gonna die, I wanna know it beforehand."

"That's the difference between optimistic and pessimistic," Harmony laughed. "I just have a better outlook on life than you do."

As they merged into traffic, Harmony giggled loudly.

"Do share."

"My mother…my mother emailed me about that picture with Reaper. She asked me—who is that hot man with all those tattoos and why haven't I met him yet?"

"Why didn't she just call you?" Shell giggled along.

Harmony rolled her eyes, an indulgent smile on her face. "I got her an iPhone for her birthday a few weeks ago. She's been working hard on getting tech savvy, so now she thinks she doesn't have to call me. She either texts or emails just to show me that she can do it. Oh or she Facebook's me. It's cute."

As they talked, her phone buzzed again.

"That thing is blowin' up," Shell commented.

"No crap. I wish my love life was exciting as everyone else wants to make it out to be." Harmony got quiet as she looked at what had buzzed on her phone. "Oh my God!" she breathed.

"What?"

"This text message I just got. I don't recognize the number, but it's a California one. It's the same area code as my producer, who lives out there. It says *Sorry we didn't run into each other again. Just letting you know – it's Garrett.*"

Not catching on, Shell screwed up her face. "What the fuck does that mean?"

"You know I hate when you use that word," she wrinkled her nose in disgust.

"Girlfriend, if you wanna hang out with Black Friday, I'm thinkin' 'fuck' is going to be the least of your worries. Anyway, what did that text mean?"

"I think its Reaper. We talked about knowing each other's real names. How did he get my number? Why did he go to the trouble to get my number? What do I say?"

"Calm down there, Sparky. First, make sure it's him."

Harmony's fingers actually shook as she texted back. *Who is this?*

Within seconds, another text dinged and she saw that it was a multimedia message. She opened it and smiled as a picture of him flashed through. He smiled wide, his dimples showing, a warmth in his eyes.

"It is him." She turned her phone so that Shell could see.

"So his name is Garrett? That's much nicer than Reaper."

The phone rang as the two gazed at the picture. "That's him," Harmony grinned.

"Well answer the damn thing!"

Shushing her, she put the phone up to her ear. "Hello?"

"So, I see you got the picture, and now you know who I am." His voice was much deeper than it had been the night before, or maybe it was just easier to hear him without all those people around.

"I did. How did you get my number anyway?" She was very curious about that. It wasn't like she gave it out to a lot of people.

"We know mutual people," he commented mysteriously. "Anyway, the reason I called you is because we're doing a secret show in Nashville tonight at the arena. I have a few hours before I have to do anything, and I know you're in town too. Would you like to have a late lunch or an early dinner?"

He was asking her out? Was this real life? This kind of stuff never happened to her.

"Sure." Harmony's voice was high-pitched, even to her. "Where do you want to meet?"

"Where are you right now?"

"I'm in Green Hills."

Shell sat to the side, trying to get Harmony's attention by slapping her on the arm.

"Stop," she whispered.

"I'm not too far from there. I'll meet you in the mall parking lot? How's that?"

"Sounds good. I'm in a Land Rover. It's silver with black tinted windows. We'll park in the back so that you'll know it's me. My friend, Shell, is with me, but I'll just let her drive my car home."

Harmony hung up and hit Shell in the arm. "We're going out to lunch, dinner...whatever you wanna call it. We're going."

"It's a good thing you washed your hair, put on makeup, and actually cared about what you dressed in today," Shell deadpanned as she merged into the turning lane that would allow them to get into the mall parking lot.

"You're right. This could have been very bad, but I do look cute today if I do say so myself."

"I feel like I should give you a talk about going on a date with an older boy who drives a fast car, listens to rock music, and talks back to authority."

"You're hilarious. I am twenty-four years old. I think we can agree that I know how to take care of myself. Besides, I carry mace."

The two of them stopped talking as a blacked out new Dodge Charger pulled into the parking lot and up to the SUV they sat in. The window rolled down slightly on the driver's side, and Harmony caught a glance of Garrett.

"That is one sexy car," Shell breathed. "You're birth control is up to date, right?"

"Oh my gosh. Are you serious right now? I don't sleep with men on the first date."

"I have a feelin' that man gets women to drop their panties way before they know his real name."

Gazing back at the car, Harmony had to admit to herself that Shell was probably right. Instead, she groaned and opened the door.

"Be careful. I'll have my phone on me if you need me," Shell said as she watched her friend hop down.

"I will be. I'll call ya."

Harmony's heart thundered in her chest as she walked around to the passenger side of the car. The door opened before she got there, and she smiled as she saw Garrett leaning over, holding it open for her from the driver's seat.

"Hey," he greeted her as she sat down and buckled up.

"Hey," she answered back, feeling nervous about being alone in the car with him. This was so unlike anything she ever did. Usually, she knew someone for a few weeks before she ever went out with them, but something about this told her that it would be alright. For the first time in her life, she decided to follow her heart and throw caution to the wind.

"First things first, I told you my real name, are you gonna tell me yours?"

She glanced over at him, feeling his eyes on her. "What makes you think Harmony isn't my given name?"

"Because most people I know in this business aren't honest about anything. I'm thinking someone as pretty as you; with as many admirers...you're not putting your real name out there."

She blushed and bit her lip. "It's Hannah Stewart. I just use a different first name."

"Nice to meet you, Hannah." He leaned over, shaking her hand.

"Same here, Garrett."

"Now that you know my name, does it take away any of my mystique?" he asked, messing with the keys that sat in the ignition.

"Not at all. The mystique is you, not your name."

That seemed to put him at ease. He took a deep breath and faced her. "So what's a good place to eat around here?"

"Depends on what you want. We have a large variety."

"I'm from California; I've never really had down home southern cooking before. How about I try it here?"

A smile tilted the corners of her mouth, and she clapped her hands together. "This is going to be so fun; I know exactly where we can go."

Hannah directed him through the city a few minutes up the road to a little diner that had grown to be an institution, at least for her.

"This looks like a hole in the wall," he commented as they pulled into a parking spot and got out of the car.

She waited as he came around to the passenger side so that they could walk in together. "It is, but it's some of the best home cookin' besides my own mother's you'll ever eat. It's usually busy, but I used to do songwriters' nights and they know me. It looks like we hit it at a pretty good time though," Hannah observed the parking lot.

"You sure they won't turn me away?" he asked, indicating the tattoos that peaked out under the arms of the t-shirt he wore.

"I think you'll be fine." She cupped her hand around his arm as they walked into the building.

Garrett could feel the eyes of the patrons and staff on him. He was used to it, but for the first time it gave him pause. She was so normal looking compared to him, they were surely questioning what she thought walking in here with her hand wrapped around his arm.

"Hannah." An elderly woman shuffled over to the two of them.

"Hey, Ms. Greta," Hannah greeted her, pulling the small woman into her arms and giving her a kiss on the cheek.

"How are you, sweetheart?"

"I'm doin' good. My friend here hasn't ever had any down home southern cookin'…he's from California. I knew just where to bring him too," Hannah winked up at Garrett.

He steeled himself against the look he just knew this woman would give him. Surprise wrote itself across his face as the older woman looked him up and down, gave him a saucy smile, and cupped his large hand in her small one.

"C'mon back here boy, let me show you how they butter these handmade biscuits."

The giggle that escaped Hannah's mouth was worth the blush that covered his. He wasn't exactly sure she was really talking about biscuits, but he followed her just the same.

Chapter Three

The two of them found themselves seated in a booth a little while later, both having ordered from the menu.

"I can't believe that I can get fried chicken and moonshine at the same restaurant. The guys are going be so pissed I didn't invite them," Garret said as he took a picture of the menu with his phone.

"Are you sending that to them?" Hannah asked, taking a sip of her sweet tea.

"Yeah, and I'm putting it on Twitter. If people can figure out where I am, then they'll know where we're doing the secret show tonight," he grinned.

"Secret shows? I've never done anything like that before."

He nodded and held up a finger while he hit a few buttons on his phone. "There. Posted. Hopefully we can fill the arena. That's always the goal with these secret shows."

"I'm intrigued," she admitted.

"We tour a lot, but it's still not enough all the time. There are still kids who don't get to come out because asshole scalpers buy a good portion of the tickets and sell them to the highest bidder. In markets that we don't always get to…usually the south and along the eastern seaboard, we do these secret shows. We only promote a few hours in advance, like I'm doing right now. But you'd be surprised how many fans find out and make it here. I'm assuming people are going to be looking for us to be in Nashville since it's all the rage we're 'dating' and all."

Hannah giggled and blushed. "My mom actually texted me to find out who you were. She was all 'I know we haven't met him before'."

"My mom did something like that too. I had to explain to her that we just took a picture for some reporters. Of course, now I'm sure there will be something about it since we're in Nashville tonight and the two of us are at lunch, but this was planned a few months in advance."

At that moment, his phone started blowing up with sounds. "Twitter," he explained. "Looks like the kids know where we are."

It amused her, the way he called fans the kids. "Are none of your fans your own age?"

"Are you calling me old?"

She shook her head. "I thought you were twenty-nine," she admitted. It was embarrassing to admit she knew as much as she did about him. "At least that's what I've read. It's just you're calling your fans kids, is throwing me off."

Garrett liked watching her squirm. It was obvious she didn't want to offend anyone, much less him. "I am going be thirty this year, but I feel older than that as far as worldly experiences go, so I tend to call the fans kids. Granted, they are normally younger than me, but there are a lot the same age and a few years older."

"You are an old man compared to me." She lifted her eyebrows, teasing him as she took a bite of the food that had been delivered to them.

"Ouch." He put his hand over his heart. "That kinda hurts. How old are you?"

"Twenty-four."

"That was a good year," he grinned, his eyes getting a far off look. "I dated a Playboy Playmate for a few months, and wow was that a crazy time in my life."

Hannah threw an unused napkin at him. "Seriously?"

"I don't have a filter; you'll learn that about me."

"I will?" she questioned. "You're assuming I'll see you again after this?"

He had the decency to squirm in his seat this time. "Well I figured, you have my number now, I have yours. We could be text, Twitter, Facebook, and Instagram buddies. I already follow your Instagram anyway."

"Really?"

"Hey, I'm a tech savvy kinda guy. I do all that stuff."

She wiped her mouth. "No, I mean why do you follow mine?"

He lifted a shoulder up and ducked his head slightly. "I've always thought you were kinda cute."

Hannah didn't know what to say to that, she was used to people telling her that she was cute, sexy, beautiful, and pretty—but they were all in the way you described someone that you looked up to. This man was her equal. "Well thanks; I've always thought you were too."

"But you're not following me on Instagram," he pouted, pushing out his bottom lip.

She couldn't help the giggle that erupted from deep within her throat. "You're a mess."

"Is that a southern saying?" he asked, genuinely confused.

"I guess so, I've never heard anyone else besides a fellow southerners use it."

He wrinkled his nose, and a smile spread across his face. "Kind of like how 'bless your heart' is southern for 'fuck you'?"

"Oh my goodness," she opened her mouth. "Not at all."

"Have I embarrassed you?"

She primly folded her hands in front of her plate, pushing it back now that she was done with it. "I just don't like that word."

"What word?" The way he bit his bottom lip told her he knew exactly what word she was talking about.

"The 'f' word."

"Oh, Hannah, you are going to be so much fun to corrupt," he laughed, reaching over to grab her hand. "Please give me a chance to do it."

She couldn't answer that question truthfully. Did she really want to be corrupted? What would that really entail? "We'll see."

Throwing caution to the wind, he kicked his leg out a little so that his foot touched hers. It caused her to lift her eyes so that they could see each other. "Let me start tonight? Come to our show…you're a fan right?"

He had a point. She was a fan and hadn't ever been able to make it to a show. "Do I get a backstage pass?"

Was she flirting with him right now? This woman was an enigma, and he wanted badly to figure her out, learn what made her smile, and learn what made her tick. "If you promise to be there."

"Then I'll be there. Should I wear my shirt that says Mrs. Reaper on it?" she asked, and he spit out the drink he had just taken.

"You have one of those shirts?"

The look on his face was worth the embarrassment of admitting that she did in fact have one. "I do. Along with one that reads 'Black Friday Groupie'...I just normally sleep in them."

For some reason, since she slept in them, he didn't want anyone else to see her in those shirts. Not until he could publically and privately make a claim on her. "Tell you what; I'll have something sent to you."

"Sent to me?"

"It's a prototype, but I think it'll fit you well. You can either pick it up when you show up tonight, or I can have it sent to your house."

"You can send it to my house. After all, you're gonna have to drop me off."

She had a point and he was very curious about where she lived.

Garrett checked his watch and whistled. "I hate to do this, but I have to go. I gotta get my workout in before the show, and we have a few radio stations calling in. I'll have just enough time if I take you home in the next little bit."

"I understand." She reached into her purse to grab her wallet.

"What the hell are you doing?" he asked as he saw her taking some bills out.

"Paying for our meal. I invited you here," she explained. She didn't want to tell him that she didn't know how to classify this. Had it been a date? Were they supposed to pay for their own portion of the meal? It was the part of dating she had never been sure about. Of course it didn't help matters that she had gotten her record deal the summer she turned eighteen.

"Put that shit away, you're hurting my manhood. No guy with the sense that God gave him would let a beautiful woman pay for a meal when he had the time of his life." He closed his hand over hers, pushing it back towards her purse. "I got this. It's the best time I've had in a long while, and it was my pleasure to have lunch with you."

Hannah felt her stomach flip from the words he spoke and the smile he bestowed upon her. "Okay then, next time will be my treat?"

He liked that. She was talking about a next time. "Sure thing."

"It's about time you made it home," Shell yelled as she heard Hannah make her way into the house.

"Sorry that took so long, but we were having a great time. In fact, I'm going to their secret show tonight at the arena."

"Yeah, they just talked about it on the radio. They said he put a picture up from the menu to the diner and everybody figured out where they are tonight. They're starting to line up," she explained as she sat at the counter, reading the magazine the two of them had bought at the grocery. "So, tell me…how was it?"

"Different from what I'm used to. He's a nice guy though—he's sending over backstage passes for me tonight and a shirt to wear. I'm kinda nervous, but I'm excited at the same time."

Shell looked at her friend. There was a glow there that hadn't been there in a while. Since an asshole had taken the light out of her. "Just be careful, Hannah. I don't want to see you hurt again."

"I'm trying to take this slow, but there's just something about him. He makes me feel like everything is gonna be alright."

"Just tell me that you're going into this with your eyes wide open. His lifestyle, his music, his whole being is completely different than yours," Shell cautioned.

"I know," Hannah nodded. "Maybe that's what I like about it. That my whole life won't be tied up with his because we don't live in the same city and because he doesn't do the same music as me. I won't have to worry if we decide to stop seeing each other that I'll see him every time I go down to Broadway."

Both of them knew that she was referencing her relationship that had ended badly over a year ago. It was still a sore subject with Hannah, and she, for the most part, refused to speak of it. Shell still wasn't exactly sure what had transpired—only knew that it had caused an ache so deeply in her friend that it had taken her spark away. That spark was back now, and she would help her do anything to keep it there.

The doorbell rang and Shell moved to answer it. "Want me to get it?"

"If you want to. You know you don't have to do everything for me."

"Yeah, yeah," Shell shook her head as she answered the door. "Can I help you?" she asked the courier on the doorstep.

"I have a package here for Harmony from Reaper."

"Yeah, I'm Harmony's assistant. I'll sign for it."

Within moments the package was in the kitchen and on the counter.

"I'm nervous to open it," Hannah admitted as she looked at it. She had her thumb in her mouth, worrying her nail with the sharp edges of her teeth.

Shell giggled. "Why? You afraid it's gonna bite you?"

"No, but it's like if I accept this gift from him and go to this show, it moves everything along."

"Well that's what you want right?"

"I just don't want to get in too deep, too fast."

"Hannah," Shell shook her head. "He's leaving tonight or tomorrow, and by then you'll know if you want it to continue or not, but you have got to start living your life again. Why not start here and now? If you don't want to wear whatever this is, you don't have to. If you don't want to go to this show tonight, you don't have to."

Hannah knew that her friend was right, but her hands still shook as she opened the package. Inside lay a couple of backstage passes and a black shirt. On the front was a picture of Garrett's face with the words 'Reaper's Girl' below it. The back was shredded so that whatever was worn underneath could be seen.

"That's sexy," Shell giggled. "I can't wait to see you, of all people, wear that."

Included were a pair of sunglasses that matched the ones Garrett wore on stage. "Are you making fun of me?" Hannah asked.

"No, I'm just saying modest little ole Hannah is gonna have a hard time wearing something where her bra can be seen, and I can't wait to see how you pull this off."

Pulling her bottom lip between her teeth, Hannah mumbled. "He did say he was going to have fun corrupting me."

Shell slapped her hand on the counter and laughed loudly. "Oh dear God, this is going to be so much fun to watch."

Chapter Four

Hannah turned this way and that in the mirror. "Do you think I look okay?" she asked Shell, her mouth screwed in a frown.

"You look great, girlfriend. Seriously. I didn't think you would be able to make yourself look like you belong with the Black Friday crowd, but you did."

Instead of smiling, Hannah looked at herself critically again. Her eyes took in the black leather leggings coupled with a pair of stiletto boots. The shirt Garrett had given to her was now on her body, a hot pink tank top underneath. When she moved a certain way, it gave soft glimpses and it covered everything along the shredded back.

"Are you sure this tank top isn't too bright?" she bit her lip.

"I know you're worried about this, but trust me. You look smoking'. I like what you did with your eyes and your hair," Shell complimented.

Finally a smile appeared on Hannah's face. "Really? It's way darker than I'm used to. I don't think I've ever worn this much eye liner in my life, even on stage. But I have to admit, it's really fun."

"I like the way it makes your eyes pop. That and your hair being super curly make you look like a completely different person."

She worried her lip between her teeth again. "I hope he still likes me like this. Ya know? Maybe he only likes good girls he wants to corrupt."

Shell laughed. "Trust me, you're still a goodie two shoes under all that makeup and hair product. That's not going to change who you are on the inside."

Hannah blew out a breath. She knew those words were true, but it still worried her. This was so different than what she was used to. While it was nice to branch out, it was also nerve-wracking.

"Don't wait up for me," she grinned at Shell as she grabbed her bag and walked out of the bedroom.

"You better call or text me."

Garrett's leg shook frantically as he checked Twitter on his phone. He was more amped for this show than he normally was. He tried to tell himself it wasn't because he hoped Hannah would be here. It wasn't because he wanted to put on an amazing show for her. No, it wasn't for any of those things at all.

"You sure she's coming man?" Jared, better known as Train, asked as he had a seat next to his friend.

"She told me she was."

His insecurities were beginning to shout in his head though. Garrett wondered what the hell he was thinking inviting her to this show. There was no way she would fit in with all of these people, and while he loved their fans, those same fans would eat her alive. Still though, he hoped she would show up. Messing around on his phone, he saw a new alert. It was from Hannah's Instagram, and he immediately clicked on the icon. There was a picture of her smiling face, her makeup much darker than normal, her hair a curly mass hanging around her face. He could see the top of the shirt that he knew read 'Reaper's Girl' on it. The picture was captioned.

On my way to @BlackFriday show! My first! Wish me luck!

Immediately the feed filled with people questioning whether they were dating or not—wanting to know exactly what was going on between the two of them. How did they explain to these people that they were normal? They were two people who had admired one another, and now they had decided to get to know each other. Not for the first time, he cursed his celebrity status.

"She's on her way," he told Jared. "Just posted a picture to her Instagram account and said she was coming to see us."

"That'll be fun to read about after the show."

Garrett couldn't help but laugh. "You know my mom's probably gotten her Google alert that our name has been used by another celebrity and now she's planning children. You should have seen the fucking text message she sent me after that picture of us showed up yesterday."

Jared grinned. Garrett's mom had been on him for years to settle down and give her grandchildren with a nice girl. He was pretty sure the woman was probably picking out which spare bedroom in her house she would be turning into a nursery as they spoke.

"I don't envy you, man, but I do love your mom. When she gets something in her head, she goes for it. No stopping Marie Thompson."

Garrett reached over and slugged Jared in the arm.

"Ouch, that's my playing arm, fucker," Jared groaned as he rubbed his bicep.

"Whine a little more for me."

The two of them were just getting going when their tour manager, Rick, came in. "Garrett, they told me to let you know. Hannah's here."

This was it. He would see if she could hang out at the rock show or not. If she couldn't then there was no reason for them to continue a friendship. But if she could, he planned to see how far he could take it.

Backstage at concerts were all the same. People ran around doing this or that, trying to beat the clock for that moment when the artist would step out in front of the hordes of fans and give them the show of a lifetime. The only difference between this one and her concerts were the way the people looked. Most of her employees were very clean cut. Here, almost everyone wore a t-shirt with the arms cut off and had tattoos covering their arms. She had been directed to this corridor and told that Garrett would meet up with her here.

She did what most everyone did when they didn't want anyone to know they were nervous. She took her phone out and began going through the comments that had appeared underneath her post about being at this show. Hannah was surprised as most of them were positive and wished her luck. That was unexpected. With the two of them being part of two totally different worlds, she had expected some horribly bad comments. It appeared that she had been spared—this time anyway.

"Hannah."

She glanced up as she heard her name and saw Garrett walking towards her. "Hey," she smiled as she walked up to him. It wasn't awkward at all as he put his arms around her. Instead, it felt right to put her own arms around his waist and squeeze tightly. "Thanks for inviting me."

"Thanks for coming. And thanks for wearing that shirt," he grinned. "Turn around; I'm interested to see how you handled the back."

He really was hoping to corrupt her, she realized. "I think you'll find that I have a pretty sharp mind." She turned to let him see the rest of her outfit.

"You are good," he told her as he put his hand at her waist. "I do have to admit, I'm glad you're not the type of woman to be showing her bra on the first date."

She couldn't tell if he was joking or not, so she just chose not to comment. "Did you see all the comments I got on my Instagram? I know you follow me," she teased.

"I did. C'mon, let's take a picture together and let me put it up. That way I can be popular too. Who knows, maybe I'll be popular enough that someone by the name of Harmony will follow me," his dimples were prominent as he grinned, teasing her.

"Fine, I'll follow you if you tag me in it." She rolled her eyes.

"You roll your eyes, but I know you do want to follow me."

"You're so right. It will completely make my life," she told him dryly.

He pulled her close and posed with his head against hers, taking the picture quickly. "I didn't realize you had such a sense of humor."

"I don't get to be dry a lot of the time. People expect me to be perky, happy, almost cheerleader happy, Harmony all the time. Hannah though, Hannah is a little darker, a little more dry, but I'm usually a pretty happy woman. It's not much of a stretch, but I have moments just like everyone else does," she shrugged.

"People seem to think we should always be on all the time, just because of what we chose to do for a living. I'm with you. Sometimes I can't smile. Sometimes I've been up for almost two days straight and I haven't had a shower and I just want to be alone."

"I hope this isn't one of those times you've gone a few days without a shower," she pulled back slightly from him.

"Ha ha."

"Garrett, we're going on."

He grabbed her hand and pulled her through the crowds and maze of people as they made their way to where they would take the stage. "I had hoped we would have a little bit more time together before the show, but it is what it is," he said by way of apology as he put in his inner ear monitors.

"Believe me, I understand. Is it okay if I stand back here?" she asked.

"Very. I hope you enjoy," he told her as he went out on stage.

There were flames and flash bangs, and then there was the roar of the crowd. Above all of that, she heard the smooth tone of Garrett's voice. "How the fuck you doin' Nashville?" he asked the crowd. They answered him with loud screams. "I hope you're ready to have a good time tonight."

Hannah observed the concert through the eyes of someone who did this for a living but also someone who loved to see other people perform. The band was a well-oiled machine. They knew what worked well for them, and they knew exactly how to play off one another to get the desired response from the audience. At some point, Garrett had taken his shirt off and thrown it into the audience. She realized he had more tattoos than she originally thought, but rather than turning her off like she figured would happen, she loved them. His skin was red and wet with the flush of heat from the lights of the stage making the tattoos stand out in sharp relief. Another thing she hadn't anticipated was how muscular he really was. His biceps were huge, his ab muscles cut. Hannah knew almost immediately that she was way out of her league, and she wondered exactly how she was going to be able to keep up a friendship with this man. He was something completely different than what she was used to. In a moment of uncertainty, she texted those exact words to Shell.

Almost immediately, Shell texted back. "Different can be good. You won't know until you try."

Maybe her friend had a point, Hannah rationalized. You didn't ever know anything until you gave it a shot.

Lifting her head up and giving the stage her full attention, she noticed they had slowed things down and they all now sat on stools. A few members of the band had what looked like acoustic guitars in their hands. The melody was familiar as they started to play, and she had to smile. It was one of her favorite songs. She loved the tone of Garrett's voice on this one. As he started to sing, he glanced over and saw her mouthing the words in the wings of the stage.

"Would it be alright if a friend of mine came out to help?" he asked the crowd, over the sound of the guitars.

They answered with another loud scream.

"C'mon out Harmony Stewart. Show this crowd how a country girl can rock."

She took a deep breath as she stepped out there. This was either the best or worst idea she had ever had in her life.

Chapter Five

Hannah walked out onto the stage, a smile plastered on her face. This was part of her persona, the ability to be cool under pressure. Never before had she relied on the Harmony part of her personality so heavily. This crowd, out of any she had performed for, made her nervous. She had been handed a mic before she'd walked out from the shadows. "How's everybody doing?" Her voice seemed so small amongst this room, but she had performed at this arena numerous times, and there was no reason she should be feeling this way. She had sold it out the last time.

"Give her a hand," Garrett instructed the crowd.

It was less enthusiastic than Black Friday's welcome had been, but at least she didn't hear any boos and that was something. She looked around, wondering if she was supposed to stand there or if there was another stool sitting somewhere. Just as she was about to ask, the guy she recognized as Train slapped Garrett on the arm.

"Dude, you're slippin'. You invite a beautiful woman out here on stage—wearing a 'Reaper's Girl' shirt that I might add goes on sale next week at our webstore—and you don't even give her a place to sit. Hang on sweetheart, I gotcha," he said as he got up off his stool and walked over to the wings and grabbed another.

The crowd booed and yelled at Garrett. "Now, don't turn on me," he told them. "I wasn't sure she'd accept my invitation."

"Likely story," she said quietly in her own mic.

The guys laughed along with the expressive crowd.

"Wow, I see how it is now." He rubbed his hand along his jean-clad thighs. "Invite a woman out to the show to try and impress her, and it's ruined by not offering her a seat. I'll have to remember that."

She could tell by the tone of his voice that he was teasing, but Hannah couldn't help but respond. "I accept gifts as expressions of apology. Carnations are my favorite flower, and anything coconut will make me forgive you on the spot."

Train, who had brought the stool out and sat it next to his, clapped the empty spot. "C'mon and sit next to me. I know how to treat a woman."

Hannah giggled as she walked past Garrett and had a seat next to the other man. She crossed her legs and looked up at the guitar player. "Hopefully, he took notes from you," she grinned.

"Hopefully, he did…actually he always does. I've been getting him laid since 1997." The crowd roared as Train held his arms up in a victorious gesture. "That's really my claim to fame. Has nothing to do with this band."

Garrett cleared his throat. "If we're done talking about me like I'm not here. The reason I invited Harmony out was for her to sing. So whatcha say? You want to sing with me?"

An immediate blush covered her cheeks. She normally didn't sing with other people, and this felt so intimate compared to anything she had ever done before. The truth, however, was that she wanted to. She wanted to sing with him badly. "I'd love to. As long as you continue with *Lonely Road*." That was the song that had gotten her interested in the band. It sounded more country than rock, but the lyrics were so heartfelt that Black Friday fans loved it just the same.

"Then that's the one we'll do," he grinned. "As long as it's okay with the kids," he gestured to the audience.

They were met again with loud screams. "I think they're good with it," she told him.

Train began the opening chords to the tamest song they did. There was nothing hard rock about it, but it was a haunting ballad about leaving a loved one behind. It could be interpreted many ways—whether the being alone was because of touring, a job, or death. Whatever the original cause for writing the song had been, she loved it. Hannah's voice wasn't as strong as Garrett's, but she was a very good harmonizer, and she harmonized perfectly with him as they shared the chorus and alternated on the verses of the song. Everyone in the room probably figured they had sung it with each other before—that was how effortlessly it came across. When they were done, Harmony stood up and took a small bow before waving enthusiastically at the crowd. She thanked the band and turned to Garrett, keeping the microphone down next to her leg so that it wouldn't pick up what she was saying.

"Thanks for inviting me out here, it's been pretty awesome," she told him, looking back out at the crowd.

He leaned down; hugging her like he would do with anyone else that had come out to sing with his band. "It was my pleasure. Enjoy the rest of the show, and I'll see you in a bit."

As she went back to where she had been watching the show earlier, she didn't miss the fluttery feeling in her stomach. It had been a long time since she had felt that way from one little touch from a man. She knew from past experience that this could either be the best thing ever or it could end badly. The last time may have ended badly, but like Shell had said, you never knew until you gave it a try.

The dressing room area for Black Friday was decidedly different than her dressing room area was. Lots of people milled around, many of them women. Most of those women had little to no clothing on, and it made Hannah a little uncomfortable.

"We haven't met."

Hannah looked up and saw the lead guitarist, Train, standing in front of her. "We haven't, but I wanted to thank you for the seat out there. I'm Hannah."

"Not a problem," he told her, holding out his hand. "Sorry I'm sweaty. I figure you're used to it. Jared."

"So you're not really Train, and he's not really Reaper. If people knew that your real names were so normal, they might not find you so fascinating," she teased.

"Like Hannah is so much more exciting."

"You got me there," she laughed. It didn't escape her that Garrett hadn't made his way to this room, and she looked behind Jared's shoulder.

"He got stopped by the local rock station. He's giving a quick interview, and he'll be here in just a few minutes."

She blushed. "Sorry, I didn't mean to be rude."

"Honey, I don't think you could ever be purposely rude."

"No," Hannah shook her head. "I can. I don't like to, but I can. Sometimes you have to protect yourself from people who want to take advantage of you."

Jared immediately liked this girl. She had a smart head on her shoulders, but she had a naivety that maybe Garrett needed. Especially since he had expressed boredom with the way their lives were going.

"You got that right. You have to look out for you. Nobody else in this business is going to do it for you. It took us a long time to realize that."

Hands clamped on Jared's shoulders, and she saw Garrett's face. "Stop monopolizing her time," he chided.

"I'm just keeping her preoccupied while you fuck around with the radio stations. Can't leave a woman that looks like her alone backstage, somebody will scoop her up if you aren't careful."

Garrett sighed. "Just go drink some whiskey and find a groupie."

Jared laughed loudly. "I love getting under your skin." He turned to Hannah. "It was very nice to meet you. I hope to see you again sometime."

"I hope so too. Thanks for my seat and thanks for the talk."

After Jared left, the two of them stood in silence. Neither one of them wanted to say anything to break the spell of this night. When Hannah finally felt too awkward, she raised her eyes to meet his. Gone were the sunglasses he performed in, and she was taken aback by how green his eyes were. "Thanks for inviting me," she spit out lamely.

"Thanks for coming," he grabbed her hand on impulse. "We got to load out of here in the next hour. It's a long drive overnight to Cincinnati."

That was something she understood. As an artist, trying to stay relevant and trying to reach as many people as possible kept you busy. "That *will* be a long drive."

He wanted to say something else, to let her know that he had enjoyed their time together today. "Do you mind if I call or text you? Hell, I have Skype. If I get bored or I have insomnia or whatever?" He finished the question in a rush. It seemed like he was worried she would say no.

"Sure, I'd love that. I'm in Nashville for the next couple of days, but then I leave too. It'll be nice to have somebody to talk to that understands the craziness of this life."

"It's hard isn't it?" He rubbed his thumb along her knuckle. "When no one really gets why you're burned out, tired, or hyped up."

"It is," she agreed, biting her lip. Her heart had kicked up a beat, thumping in time to the cadence of the rubbing of his thumb across her skin. "It's also hard to explain to people who have no idea what the rush of a crowd can do for you. What it can make you push through or even forget."

"Yes. You're so right." He finally let go of her hand and rubbed the same hand along his forehead.

He was sweaty and his skin was still red with the heat of being on stage. This close, she could see every tattoo, every hair, the slight stubble on his cheeks and chin. She liked him like this. Maybe if she played her cards right she would get to see it more often. "Well, I guess I better get going. You obviously need to take a shower before you head out."

"I do, but I wish we had a couple more days to spend here," he told her truthfully.

"Like you said, it's our life. At least we understand each other."

There was that, they did understand each other. "Let me at least walk you out. You parked in the band lot right?"

"I did."

He grabbed a shirt and put it over his torso, and she almost made a sound of disapproval. Guys like him just didn't come along in her life that often. Especially not in the circle of friends she had. She wanted to know everything about him and what made him so different compared to everyone else. Why did he get her attention when no one else seemed to be able to?

"Let's go," he told her as he grabbed his pass and motioned to a security guard that he was walking her out.

Jared saw her leaving and called out a goodbye to her. The rest of them followed suit even though she hadn't been able to officially meet them. The women who had gathered in the room appeared to breathe a sigh of relief that she was leaving. She wondered—even though she knew she had no right to—if one of them would try to have a good time with Garrett before he got on his bus to ride to the next city. He did need to take a shower, and *she* had even been propositioned by male groupies in a shower setting before.

"Don't worry," he told her as they walked into the hall. "None of those women back there interest me."

She wondered how he knew what she was thinking. Was she that transparent?

"I've seen that look before," he explained to her. "But to be honest with you, the fact that you're so different from what I'm used to is what makes me so interested in you. I've been bored lately. With everything. You're like a breath of fresh air." He opened the door to the parking lot and ushered her outside.

"So, I'm just an experiment?" She didn't like that.

"Not at all," he said quickly, walking her over to the Range Rover he'd seen her drive earlier in the day. "I'm just explaining that you have nothing to worry about with those other girls in that dressing room. They're part of what makes me bored. They're the same old, same old. I don't want the same thing that I've always had. I want something different."

That's what this all boiled down to. Both of them were looking for something different.

"I want something different too." She reached up and kissed him on the cheek.

"I'm glad," he grinned as he opened the door to her car and waited for her to get her seat belt fastened. "I'll call you later."

"I'll do my best to answer," she teased.

He chuckled. "I'll just call until you do. I'm persistent like that."

She laughed and shut her door, waving to him as she pulled out of the parking lot and into the flow of traffic leading down Broadway. Her mind was going a million miles a minute, and she wondered just what in the world she'd just gotten herself into.

Chapter Six

Hannah lay in bed, flipping through late night TV, wondering if Garrett was going to text or call her. Late nights were nothing new for her, and usually this would be the time when she would get most of her songwriting done, but she couldn't seem to do that in her house. She had to be in a hotel room, lonely, wishing for the type of life that all her friends from high school had. For some reason, she never could get into that mindset when she was in her own bed, in her own house. Just as she was about to give it up and set the sleep timer, her phone beeped.

You still awake?

It was a text message from Garrett. The smile that spread across her face couldn't be helped. She realized quickly it was a good thing that no one could see her. If they could, they would see the giddiness of a new relationship, that feeling of wanting to talk to or be around the other person all the time. It was scary how fast that had happened. Never before had it been like this.

I am, she texted back.

In just a few moments, there was a request to FaceTime. Technology was an amazing thing. As soon as she accepted the request, she saw Garrett's face. It was dark where he was, but she could make out his features.

"Hey." She waved and leaned her head back against her pillows.

"Hey yourself," he yawned, covering his mouth with his hand.

"You tired?"

"Tired, but wired, ya know?"

She nodded because she did know. It took her a long time to come down from being on stage, even if she was exhausted. "It takes me a few hours."

"Me too and I truly hate sleeping on this bus. It's one of my fears that we'll be in a wreck and I'll never know what hit me," he admitted.

Hannah laughed. "It's funny that you mention that. Shell and I had a conversation about that earlier today. Me, I'm better off just not knowing. If it's gonna happen, I don't wanna see it coming. Apparently the two of you have something in common."

"I like to be in control."

His voice was dark and smooth as he said the words. They caused goosebumps to appear on her arms.

"Some people do and some are willing to let others take control for them in certain aspects of their lives."

"Are you the type to let others take control?" he asked, his eyes sparkling with humor.

"I guess it kinda depends," she squirmed. "There are some things I don't want to make decisions on. There's others, like my career, my personal life, that I really do want to have control over."

Garrett wanted to get further into this with her, but their relationship was so new that he didn't want to scare her off. Instead, he switched topics. "Did you have a good time tonight?"

She smiled at him. "I did. Your show was awesome."

"You're just saying that because I invited you, and you feel the need to be nice to me," he scoffed.

"No…I don't blow smoke up people's butts. If I don't like it, I just say 'bless your heart'."

He laughed loudly. "Which we've already discussed as being the equivalent of 'fuck you' in southern speak."

She frowned and he chuckled again.

"You hate that word, right?"

"I seriously do." She ran her hand through her hair.

For the first time, she realized she looked a mess. She had taken a shower as soon as she had come home, and then she'd gotten ready for bed. Her hair was a tangled mass, and she knew she had dark circles under her eyes from the breakneck pace she had been keeping over the past few months.

"You look great," he told her.

"How'd you know what I just thought?" His ability to know what she thought before she told him was unnerving to her.

He ducked his head and then ran his tongue over his bottom lip. "I have a lot of experience with women. Most have the same insecurities. But trust me. When I said you were cute earlier, I meant it. You don't need to look the way you did when you came to the show for me to think you're hot."

"So you didn't like it?"

"No, I'm not saying that at all," he was quick to protest. "You really did look hot. I'm sorry I didn't get to tell you that earlier, but things were a little rushed. What I'm saying is that you're cute with no makeup and tired circles under your eyes. I have the same ones," he leaned closer to the phone, and she focused in on his eyes. "See, I have the same ones. It comes with the territory."

She laughed as she got an up close and personal look at his eyes and pores. "Move the phone back, that's freaky. It like magnified everything a thousand times."

"Awesome," he grinned. "Let me take my pants off real quick and then I'll really get to magnifying."

"Garrett!" she blushed. "I can't believe you just said that to me."

He laughed, a deep belly laugh. So hard that he had to put the phone down. When he brought it back up, he was brushing his eyes. "You are so easy to rile up. I can't believe how innocent you've been able to stay while in this business."

She bit her lip. "I always had people around me that didn't let me get involved in the sex and drugs side of it." Should she admit to him her darkest secrets?

"Really? Do you wish that maybe you had? Some of my best times were in my early twenties. I pretty much screwed anything that walked," he admitted. "But now that I'm almost thirty, I'm much more selective. It's not as fun as it used to be."

Steering the conversation away from her, she asked him. "What about the drug part?"

"I experimented just like most young people do. Granted, I probably did it on a larger level because of our position. We did a lot of rock festivals back then where drugs were very easily accessible. I didn't ever have a problem, but I did become a little too dependent at one time. Luckily, I have family who doesn't want to see me go down that road. I don't want to go down that road. So I stopped. I still drink; every once in a while I'll have a cigarette or smoke some pot, but for the most part I'm through experimenting. That's not to say other guys in the band aren't, but I can't tell them how to live."

He was so honest with her and she loved that. "I like that you're honest with me. My last relationship…The guy wasn't so honest, and it's hard for me to trust now."

"Well that guy was a dumbass then. I can't help but be completely honest with you. There's something about you that makes me want to be honest."

She smiled tiredly. "I'm glad, because I want you to be honest with me—even if it's not the easiest thing—it's something I appreciate."

Garrett yawned again. "I'll mark that down in my file labeled 'Hannah' in my head then."

"You have a file?"

"Oh yeah," he ticked off facts on his fingers. "You like carnations, anything coconut, and now I can add to that honesty."

"Yet, I know almost nothing about you. I don't even have a file named 'Garrett' in my head."

His mouth hung open in shock, and he brought his hand up to his chest, holding it over his heart. "Ouch. Damn, girl. You know how to bring a guy down a few pegs."

"Somebody's gotta keep you on your toes. I have a feeling you get what you want just a little too easily."

She did have a point there. He usually did get what he wanted, but not because it was easy. "I work for everything I've got and everything I want. If I decide that I want you, trust me. You're going know it and you're going say yes."

Hannah could hear the promise in his voice. "Then I guess I'm just gonna have to figure out if you want me or not."

"If you haven't guessed by now, then I'm not doing my job right."

That warmed a place within her. The last man she had tried to have a relationship with hadn't worked at it. She had done all the working, all the sacrificing, everything. This time around, she promised herself that it would be equal opportunity and she wouldn't lay her whole heart on the line without him laying his heart on the line too. "You're doin' just fine," she yawned on the end of her sentence.

"You're tired, I'm tired. I'm going to let you go."

It was true, she really was tired, but she didn't want to let him go. "You'll call me again?" she questioned.

The smile that spread across his face was bright and wide, showing his dimples. "You bet, but you know you could call me too. I do like getting phone calls from beautiful girls."

She rolled her eyes.

"Text messages too, nudie pics, whatever," he grinned to show he was teasing.

She laughed. "You are way too much."

"I like to keep things interesting, what can I say?" He made no excuses.

"Just say 'goodnight, Hannah'."

"Goodnight, Hannah. Have sweet dreams, and I'll talk to you tomorrow."

She waved at him. "Goodnight, Garrett. You too. I am glad I got to go to your show tonight."

"I am too."

With those words he disconnected the call, and she lay back against the pillow, a smile on her face. That fluttery feeling was back in her stomach. "Hannah, you can't go into this like you did the last one," she chastised herself. The last one had almost been the end of her—it had devastated her when it ended. She had a feeling this one would decimate her. Looking up at her ceiling, she whispered. "God, please tell me I'm doing the right thing here."

"Are you sure that's all you want?" Hannah asked Shell as she hurried into a deli the next morning. She was running late picking Shell up for a meeting with a new production company. Luckily for all involved, the company was located in Nashville, so she could enjoy her time at home and still get work accomplished too.

"Yeah," Shell said on the other end of the phone. "I ate late last night, but please make sure you get me a coffee. You'll be here right after that?"

"I will. Shouldn't be more than thirty minutes. We should be right on time for the meeting even if I am running late getting you."

"Okay, see you when you get here."

Hannah disconnected the call and stepped up to the counter, ordering the meal for herself and Shell. After paying and being told how long it would take, she moved to stand over to the side, browsing the magazine rack. One of the most prominent magazines had the picture of her and Garrett from the after party on it. She took a picture of it and texted it to Garrett, along with a 'good morning'. She figured it would probably be a few hours before he saw it, but it would be something nice for him to wake up to. As she scrolled through some of the emails on her phone, she felt someone come up behind her. People in Nashville were used to seeing stars out and about, so she didn't turn around, she just continued about her business. For long minutes, the person stood behind her before she felt them lean in.

"Is that your new boyfriend?"

She stiffened automatically, shying away. That voice had caused her so much heartache, so much anger, so much hurt, that still affected her. Each time she was home in Nashville she hoped she wouldn't see him, that just maybe she could go a few days without running into him. This was a big city, after all. It never seemed to fail, whenever she came into town, she ran into him. It would feel good to turn around and tell him exactly what she thought of him, but she had been raised to be polite, and every time she had stood up for herself, he'd knocked her down. Sometimes physically and sometimes mentally. Plastering a smile on her face, she turned, coming face to face with the last man who had not only broken her heart, but her spirit.

Hannah hadn't seen him in a few months, not even on TV, and he had been in the studio making his new album from what she had heard around town. He had let his blonde hair grow longer than it ever had when they were together, the tips of it just brushed the edges of his shirt. Being unkempt wasn't something he'd allowed her to do while they were together, and she wanted to say something about the unshaven beard that covered his face, the dark circles under his blue eyes. It was obvious he had partied hard the night before. She knew that some women liked that look, but it only reinforced the fact that she didn't even find him attractive anymore.

"Ashton." She did her best to not let him see just how much he ticked her off. "Not that it's any of your business, but he's a friend."

"That's how we started out right?"

He was cocky, and that was one of the many things she realized too late she hated about him. Which was small in the grand scheme of what he had actually done to her, but it helped to focus on the things that hadn't given her nightmares. She ignored him as her phone beeped and they called her name.

"It was good to see you," he called out as she walked away.

She couldn't say the same to him. Her appetite was gone when she got back to her car, but she was glad to see a text from Garrett.

We look pretty damn good on that cover! Not sure what you're doing today, but hope you have a good one. Call me when you have time.

That was exactly what she needed. As Ashton walked out of the deli, she put her car in reverse and backed away, not looking at him again.

Chapter Seven

"You look like somebody pissed in your Cheerios," Shell observed as she got into the passenger side of the vehicle. "What happened after you called me?"

Her normally cheery friend wore a frown on her face, her eyes drawn together with unhappiness. It wasn't a look that Shell had seen on her in a long while. It was definitely cause for alarm.

"I saw Ashton," Hannah said in a clipped tone.

"Oh shit."

Hannah visibly swallowed and gripped the steering wheel tighter. "Yeah."

"That's the worst thing about this town, huh?"

Shaking her head, Hannah couldn't help the dry laugh that escaped her throat. "It really is. Every time I think I'm over it, I run into him again, and all the anger and fear comes rushing back."

"Maybe it would help you if you just talk it out," she pressed. "You've never even told me what happened between the two of you. You dated for two years, and then he was gone. I didn't give you a hard time because I knew that it hurt you. But now, maybe you need to tell me exactly what happened."

"We don't have time." Hannah checked her watch and sighed.

"Hannah, if it's bothering you this much, you seriously need to make the time."

She knew that her friend was right. It would make her feel better to tell someone about what had gone on between her and Ashton, but that would also require that she open up a spot in her that she had closed with a padlock. She would have to re-open a wound. But really it wasn't closed, not if it still made her this angry. Maybe she should have done what all the websites had recommended and sought professional help, but either way, she had to tell someone something. "Do me a favor." She handed her phone to Shell. "Call them and tell them we're running late…that's it's an emergency. I don't care how you do it; just get me out of this meeting. You do that and I'll tell you what happened."

This was a change of pace for Hannah. She never cancelled or made excuses about being late. That's what told Shell just how important this was, just how much this bothered her.

Making a turn and going in the opposite direction, Hannah half listened to the conversation going on between Shell and to the person on the other end of the phone. This was so unlike her, but she did need to get this out. Garrett made her want to trust someone again, made her want to be open to a possible relationship. If she didn't get through these feelings of anger and distrust, she would never be able to give him a true chance. It wouldn't be fair, and she was nothing if not fair.

"Okay, I bought you a day. Tomorrow you're going to have to make it to this meeting. Today you're going to have to tell me just what happened between you and Ashton Coleman."

Just hearing his name caused her stomach to flip. As if the universe was in on the joke, the radio even began playing his most recent hit song. She reached over and shut it off quickly, the thin tone of his voice that all women loved wearing on *her* already thin nerves.

"By the way, you have a text from Garrett."

"I'll get it in a few minutes. I don't want to talk to him before I do this. I would much rather talk to him after."

They pulled into a public park and grabbed their breakfast, taking it to the picnic tables to eat. Once they sat, Shell gave Hannah as much time as she needed. After long minutes, Hannah finally opened her mouth.

"I trusted Ashton with everything. You know that right?"

Shell nodded. Ashton had even been given some control over her public persona and had tried to change her into a person that just was not Hannah Stewart.

"I was comfortable with that for a long time just because I was young." She licked her lips and played with the paper her muffin sat in. "I was twenty-one years old when we got together. I had been doing this for a few years, and I was just ready to be an adult. I thought that letting someone that I loved handle everything was being an adult. We were a couple, and I was content to let him be the man."

"I hated that," Shell laughed. "Remember the arguments you and I got into about it when he tried to tell you how to dress?"

"I do," Hannah nodded. "And that should have been my first clue. But I was stupid."

She stopped for a long time, and Shell wasn't sure that she would go on. She got a far-off look in her eyes as she watched kids playing in the park, couples jogging or bike riding, older people walking. It seemed as if she didn't want to continue, or maybe she was just arguing with herself. Trying to figure out how much she wanted to reveal.

"You weren't stupid," Shell coaxed. "You were in love."

"No, trust me, I was stupid," she shook her head, a self-deprecating smile on her face. "It was good up until a few months before we broke up. Him telling me what to do was really startin' to get on my nerves. At one point he even told me I needed to learn to talk without my accent."

"What?"

"Yeah, he wanted me to go to voice lessons to get rid of it. I'm Nashville born and bred. It's not just gonna go away. You might as well make me learn to write right-handed. It just ain't happening."

"Where was I through that?" Shell knew that there was a time in her and Hannah's friendship where they hadn't been as close as they were now, but for the life of her, she couldn't remember Ashton being that damn controlling.

"I kept everybody away and at arm's length, just because I didn't want anyone telling me what an idiot I was being. It was around the time you dated 'he who shall not be named'...so you were kind of not paying a whole lot of attention to me and my relationship. You had stars in your eyes too."

"Oh yeah." Shell wrinkled her nose in disgust. "We were both dumbasses."

"Pretty much. Anyway, touring was getting to be a lot of work. I was doing it more than normal, and Ashton and I were in different cities most of the time. His sales were starting to pick up, and his record company had him doing a radio tour. I was hearing rumors of him being with other girls, but you have to understand, I heard that the whole time we were together."

Shell knew that the rumors about the country golden couple had run the gamut of good and bad. A lot of it had been lies, so there was no reason that Hannah should have believed anything other people were telling her.

Her face burned as she admitted the next part. "I did ask him about it. One night when we were in a hotel room in Chicago, I asked him because I noticed a weird mark on his back. He was my first, and I'm not what one would call wild in bed. I'm not a scratcher or anything like that. The mark on his back looked like fingernails, and I asked him what it was. Of course he said he got it working out."

Holding up a hand, Shell stopped her. "That makes me sad for you, honey. That no man has ever made you want to be wild enough in bed to scratch his back. Please give me your phone so I can text Garrett."

A laugh bubbled up from Hannah's throat, and she let it out, glad that Shell had broken the tension of the conversation. "You will not be texting Garrett anything. This is me being honest with you."

"We'll keep it between ourselves, but seriously, if a man doesn't make you want to scratch his back, he ain't doin' it right."

Hannah ignored her friend and continued. "The next week, I got some pictures text messaged to me from a number I didn't recognize. It was Ashton with another woman. I could see everything. There was even a video with it." Her eyes were bright with tears, and her chin trembled slightly. "Trust me when I say he was way more into her than he ever was me. That was pretty apparent in the way he responded to her and the things he asked her to do for him. I called him and broke up with him that day. I couldn't do it. I couldn't be in a relationship that was a lie. But it's so embarrassing…to know I'm such a cold fish. That's what he told her on the video."

A sinking feeling settled in Shell's stomach. "Oh honey, please don't tell me you think this had anything to do with you."

"It did, don't you see? I'm just not that kind of woman. I don't think I'll ever be able to keep a man sexually satisfied, so I'm probably just destined to be forever alone."

"Get that thought out of your head right now. Promise me you won't base the rest of your relationships off that one. Promise me. Ashton was a dumbass. He's young, and he's in a position to sleep with anything that walks right now. He'll get sick of it, and then he'll realize what he threw away. Luckily for you, you have someone interested in you who's past that age."

Hannah's mind went back to the conversation she and Garrett had the night before. He had flat out told her he was done sowing his wild oats so to speak. Could this be different than what she'd had with Ashton? Could she trust him?

"He told me last night he was done sleeping with girls just because he could, when we FaceTimed after the show. He said it's gotten boring," she shrugged, pulling the sleeves of her long sleeve shirt over her hands.

"Then believe it, Hannah. These two men are completely different. Ashton liked to tell you what to do because he was threatened by your fame."

"He's famous too," she argued.

"But he didn't get there until after he started dating you. You were the star when the two of you got together. Garrett doesn't need you to make him popular or a success. I daresay in your different circles he is much more famous than you are. He doesn't need a damn thing from you. Don't let this experience with Ashton ruin what you could have with another man."

It was easy for Shell to say.

"I'm just having fun with Garrett. We're just talking on the phone and texting."

"If that's the only thing you think you're doing, Hannah, then you are naive. He brought you on stage, and you let him see you without makeup while you FaceTimed. You only FaceTime when you're lying in bed before you go to sleep. I'm not saying the two of you are going to get married, but you don't let a lot of men see you without your game face on because you are a proper southern lady. What I am telling you is that you're crazy if you let what Ashton did to you make you not have a good time with the hotness that is this man." She pulled Hannah's phone over and showed her the unlock screen. It still showed the picture of the two of them together. Shell had a feeling that Hannah hadn't been completely honest with her. There had been more than once there at the end where she had worn a lot more makeup than normal and she had hidden herself away, but if Garrett could bring a smile to Hannah's face, then Shell would overlook it for now.

"He is hot…and nice…and really sweet…and he went to all the trouble of finding out my number and inviting me to the show."

"He did."

"Okay," she exhaled. "I'm gonna do it. I'm gonna go for it. If and when the opportunity presents itself, I'm gonna give it everything I've got with Garrett Thompson."

"Good," Shell grinned. "Now if I could only get you to say a great big 'fuck you' to Ashton, we would be doing awesome."

A smile spread across Hannah's face, her cheeks going red. "Poor Ashton Coleman, I hope somebody blesses his heart."

Chapter Eight

"Dude, change the fucking channel. I'm not watching this stupid game show again," Jared yelled at one of the other members of Black Friday.

Garrett lay in his bunk trying to drown the rest of the guys out. They were getting stir crazy, having been on the bus for almost a full day. Their next stop was Omaha. Cincinnati to Nebraska was a hell of a drive. He wanted to be anywhere but here right now. Jared was being annoying, and none of the other band members wanted to face the fact that he was out of control…again. As Garrett turned over and shut the curtain of his bunk as tightly as he could, his phone rang. The ringtone was a Harmony Stewart song, and he hurried to answer it.

"You finally called me," he said by way of greeting.

"Yeah," she laughed. "Sorry I kind of flaked on you yesterday after sending you that text message, but I had some stuff happen that required my attention."

"Everything okay?" he asked, concern apparent in his voice.

"Just stupid emotional stuff, ya know?"

He did. He dealt with his emotions every time Jared acted out like he was now. Garrett could still hear him yelling at the other members in the back of the bus. "I know what you mean," he said softly.

"Are you okay?" she asked him on impulse. He'd questioned her, so it stood to reason that she could ask him the same question.

Garrett sighed deeply. "Just ready to get off this damn bus. We've been on it for almost twenty-four hours straight, and the guys are starting to get stir crazy. I've actually cocooned myself in my bunk."

"Wow, considering what you told me the other night about being scared of not seeing what's going on, that says something." She wondered if something else was going on. His voice wasn't as jovial as normal. It was quiet and subdued; tired definitely, but at the same time it seemed troubled.

"I know, right? I'd just rather be here than back there with the rest of them."

Wanting to get him talking to her, she decided to delve into his life the way he delved into hers. "So tell me about your band members. I met Jared, but what about the other two?"

His band was one of his favorite things to talk about. These men were his best friends and the closest thing he had to family that was not blood-related to him. "We have our drummer, Nightmare."

"What's his real name?" she questioned almost immediately.

"Who's to say that's not his real name?"

"C'mon Garrett," she stretched his name out with her accent, causing him to grin.

"Did you do that to emphasize that my real name is not rock-n-roll enough?"

"Maybe."

He could hear the grin in her voice. "That hurts, Hannah."

"So tell me his real name."

"Chris." He laughed when she snorted.

"You guys have the most basic names imaginable. Is the other one Bradley?"

"Are you sure you didn't read our bio?" he questioned her, his voice completely serious.

"I'm a fan, I have read your bio, but you know as well as I do that they keep your real names locked down. Did I seriously just guess it right?"

"You did."

"See," she cleared her throat, and he could hear the smile in her voice. "Most basic names ever. What do they go by on stage?"

"Bradley is our bass guitarist and he uses Raven. See, we're normal except for our death metal stage names."

She nodded, even though he couldn't see her. "I'm beginning to truly believe that."

As he opened his mouth to talk, he heard a loud noise from the back and then lots of yelling. "Hold that thought, I got to take care of something." He dropped his phone to the mattress with Hannah's call still connected.

Garrett jumped out of his bunk and went to the back where the TV and game systems sat along with a large couch and a table. When he got there, he saw Jared on the ground beating on Brad. Chris pulled at them, trying to get the two off each other.

"What the fuck?" Garrett asked loudly.

He was the tallest of the group, and because of that he carried more muscle mass than the rest of them. He had also been known to beat the shit out of people that even looked at him the wrong way when he was younger. In every sense of the word, he was their leader. They broke apart, and no one said anything, they all just stared at Jared.

"Where the fuck is it?" he asked, his voice calm as he approached the man he called his best friend.

"I don't know what you're talking about."

Jared was the king of liars when he was like this, and they all knew it. The only one that would call him on it was Garrett. "Don't make me go look for it and don't look at me like I'm fuckin' stupid. Where is it?"

"Why can't you all just leave me alone?" Jared scream, lashing out again, this time going for Garrett.

Sidestepping his friend, Garrett shoved him up against the wall and pushed his hands behind his back, holding Jared down. "Because we love you. Now tell me where the hell it is, and better yet, where the hell did you get it?"

All the fight went out of Jared's body as he nodded towards his bunk. Garrett walked that way, but before he went to the bunk, he picked up the phone in his own bunk.

"Hannah, hey. I have to call you back, we have a situation." He hung up before she could say anything or ask him any questions.

Throwing the phone down on his bed with as much force as he could, he stalked across the aisle to Jared's bunk and opened the curtain. In the corner sat a mirror and a razorblade. White residue still coated the mirror.

"Is this worth it?" Garrett asked as he stalked back into the area where they all sat. "For a twenty second high, is it worth it?"

"No, it never is," Jared told him, his voice quivering.

"Then you better do something about it because, best friend or not, I'm getting sick of this shit."

How could he bring Hannah into this group of people? She was the queen of country radio, and people loved her. How could he expose her to this?

Walking back to his bunk, he dialed her number, hoping that it went to voicemail but at the same time that she would pick up.

"Is everything okay? I heard a lot of yelling."

He debated on what he should tell her. So far he'd been honest with everything about his life. He should be honest with this. "No, it's not okay. Look, I have to be honest with you. I can't expect you to go into this without telling you the truth about one of the guys."

"Go into what?" Her heart thundered in her chest.

"I like you," he told her. "I know it's crazy. We just met and we've only hung out twice, but there's something about you that I like. I would love to get to know you better, but it's your decision if that happens. My band could hurt your public persona, and in your brand of music, that's everything."

"How could they do that?" She didn't want to comment on him liking her until she figured out just what he was trying to tell her.

He ran a hand through his hair, pissed that Jared was putting him in this situation. "Remember when I said that I'd experimented with drugs, but other members of the band kinda do their own thing?"

"Yeah."

"Jared, the guy who was so nice and polite to you the other night," he hated telling her this. "He just put one of the other guys down on the ground because he snorted a whole bunch of coke and didn't know what to do with himself. So if you can't handle that, tell me right now."

After a few moments of silence, his voice pleaded, "Hannah, say something."

"Can't you do something to help him?" she asked, her voice so small on the other end of the line. This scared her.

He sighed, blowing out a deep breath. "We've tried. His parents have tried. Jared is who he is. He's got the biggest heart of anyone I know, and he's everyone's best friend until he picks up that mirror and does a line off of it. It's his fatal flaw."

"But it's not yours," she told him softly.

"You're right. It's not. But Jared comes with me. He's my best friend. I would never turn my back on him. No matter what he does, I'm always going to be there for him. He's always been there for me. We've been in more scrapes together than I can even mention. We started this together. I'm not giving up on him because he has a habit that he can't kick."

As crazy as it sounded, she admired that about him. He obviously was persistent.

"Well, if you can handle me being so bad in the sack that my last boyfriend cheated on me and left me for a fling with another woman, then I can deal with your friend," she said in a rush.

"I'm sorry, what?" He couldn't help but laugh. "You're bad in the sack so your last boyfriend left you?"

"He cheated on me. I'm assuming I'm no good when it comes to sex."

She was young, and he figured that no matter what her stage persona said, she was also very self-conscious in her own skin. Especially in the business they were in. Everyone told you that you had to have a six-pack, straight teeth (the whiter the better), your hair cut just so, and never mention anything about the little tricks that got you that way. Garrett was more than willing to take a chance on her.

"Why don't you let me be the judge of that when the time comes?"

Her stomach fluttered. This man was talking like he already knew they would have an intimate relationship. "Okay," her voice squeaked, and she had to clear her throat.

"If you're okay with me, then I'm okay with you," he told her, glancing over to the bunk that held Jared, probably sleeping off his high.

"Then I guess together we're okay."

Garrett knew to make this work they had to see each other. Their relationship couldn't sustain on technology alone. "Where are you?" he asked abruptly.

"I'm in my hotel room fixing to leave for the airport."

"No, I mean what city are you in?"

"I'm flying to Kansas City to do a concert there in two days. I have a day and a half to lounge around. Well, part of a day and a half anyway."

Someone meant for this to happen, Garrett decided. "Awesome, we're going to be in Omaha within the next few hours. We're not too far away from each other. Do you want me to come get you or do you want to come to me? If this is going to work, we have to spend time together."

He was right and she knew it. Biting her thumbnail, she thought for a moment. "You can come get me. When is your concert?"

"We're performing tomorrow night."

She quickly looked at the calendar on her phone. "Great, I'm not performing until the day after tomorrow, and I don't have any obligations for the press or radio. How about you come get me, I'll hang out with you and go to your concert tomorrow night, and then I'll either drive myself or take a short flight back to Kansas City for my concert the next day. Does that work?"

"So you'd stay with me, right?" He wanted to be clear.

"Unless you have a roommate. I know some bands double up."

"No, this band doesn't. Trust me on that. Chris snores like a lumberjack."

She laughed, that fluttery feeling coming back to her stomach. She was going to stay with Garrett Thompson. Overnight. And a day. Stuff like this never happened to her. "So when should you hit Omaha?"

"A few hours. Probably right about the time you hit Kansas City, so you'll have to wait on me to get to you, but it shouldn't be any later than this afternoon."

"Okay," she told him, zipping up her suitcase. "I'll be waiting."

"I can't wait to see you," he told her softly. After dealing with Jared he needed some good in his life.

"Same here, I'll see you soon."

They hung up and Hannah screamed. She was spending the night with Garrett Thompson. Spending the night did not equal getting naked and doing the wild thing, but still this was big. What in the world was she going to wear? Quickly she dialed Shell's number, and before her friend could say anything, she blurted out, "We've got to stop at Victoria's Secret. I'm spending the night with Garrett tonight."

Chapter Nine

"Are you sure you're okay with me leaving you here?"

"Hannah, I'm not a child, and you're not babysitting me. I will be perfectly fine if I stay in a hotel room by myself for a while," Shell smiled indulgently. "I'll order room service, a movie, and enjoy your suite until you get back. I promise, I'm good."

"I still feel bad," Hannah worried her lip between her teeth.

"Don't." She put her hands on Hannah's shoulders and turned her so that they faced one another. "I don't have to be there every step of the way. I'm fine staying here by myself, but if it makes you feel better, next time just ask Garrett if it's okay that I tag along."

The two of them usually did everything together. It had been that way since Hannah and Ashton had parted ways. It felt odd for Hannah to leave Shell behind while she went off to start another chapter of her life.

"Go and have fun. Do you want me to pull up that picture that Garrett did for that magazine a couple of months ago? The one where he's shirtless in the rain?

You're spending the night with *that* man. Do not give it up because you're worried about me. I'm just gonna tell you now, I wouldn't think twice about it."

Hannah laughed, shocked. "Well thanks for nothin' BFF."

They heard Hannah's phone start buzzing with the ringtone she had assigned to Garrett. "There he is. Answer it, and go have fun!"

"Hello?"

"Hey," she could hear the smile in his voice. "I'm here, what room are you in? I'll come up there and help you grab your stuff."

"No, that's not necessary. I haven't unpacked anything, so I'll just meet you down there in a few minutes."

"I'll be waiting."

"Oh wait," she stopped him before he hung up. "What are you driving today?"

"I rented an Escalade. If the guys all want to go out later, they'll need a big vehicle. See, I'm a nice guy."

"That you are. I'll be right there."

Shell sat in a chair next to the door, her legs crossed, her foot swinging. "Did he offer to come up and bring your stuff down?"

"Yes, Mom, he did."

"Well that's more than I can say for Ashton—who couldn't even lift your suitcase, much less carry it down to his car."

Hannah couldn't help the snort that came out of her nose. "That was unbelievably mean, but oh so true." She reached down and hugged her friend before letting the door shut behind her.

Shell looked around the empty hotel room, and with a smirk, she said out loud to no one but herself, "I hope she took my advice and got that birth control up to date."

The day was beautiful yet cold as she stepped out from the hotel and onto the curb. She hadn't noticed earlier how chilly it was, and she rubbed her hands up and down her arms as she waited for Garrett to come around and pick her up. Her jacket was in her suitcase, and she made a mental note to remember to get it out.

She noticed an Escalade pull up with tinted windows. The passenger side one came down partway, and she saw Garrett inside. She all but ran over to the car and jerked the door open. She was that excited to see him.

"Did you not bring a jacket?" he asked as he pulled his sunglasses down to get a good look at her.

"No," her teeth chattered as she hopped into the passenger side.

Shoving the gear into park, he took his sunglasses off, setting them in the cup holder and then unbuckled his seat belt. It was on the tip of her tongue to ask what he was doing, but he pulled his hoodie over his head, leaving him in a long sleeve shirt. "Here, wear this. The heater is good, but if you're anything like me, you get cold and it's hard to get warm again."

"I am the same way, so thank you." She put the hoodie over her head and noticed that it swallowed her whole. The ends of the sleeves fell so far past her hands she could probably double them up, and she figured that when she stood it would probably look like a dress on her. Hannah couldn't help but pull the neck of the shirt into her nose and breathe deeply. It smelled just like him, and she knew that if given the chance, she would take it with her when she ultimately had to leave.

"You're welcome, now I have to figure out how to get the fuck outta here."

He glanced over at her, a smile playing at the corner of his lips.

"You said that just because you know I hate that word," she accused.

"Maybe. But it's one of my favorite words, so we're going to have to come to some sort of compromise about it."

Ignoring him, she checked his blind spot. "Do you know where you're going?"

"Kinda, and I've got the GPS," he pointed to the satellite map on the console.

"Are you one of those people who has to have complete quiet when it comes to finding your way out of a place you aren't familiar with?"

"Not really, but as soon as I make this turn, I'm on the main highway, so feel free to talk as much as you want," he told her as he merged into traffic and took the exit that would take them straight to Omaha.

"I meant to tell you something."

"Oh yeah?" He set the cruise control and moved to lean on the console, one hand on the wheel. "What's that?"

"I got myself a 'Garrett' file." She pointed to her forehead.

His dimples showed as he looked between her and the road. "You finally got enough information, huh?"

"I did," she nodded. "You're persistent, you love your fans, you like apple pie moonshine, and you love your best friend more than he probably even knows."

On impulse, he reached over and grabbed her hand, rubbing his thumb across her knuckles. "Thanks for listening to me by the way. I'm glad I didn't scare you off. I was scared I would."

"I'm not saying that it didn't scare me at all. I don't like physical violence, and I didn't like what I heard, but I understand that it was necessary. It takes a lot to scare me off of something that I want."

He liked the sound of that. "So do you want to hear about what we're going to do tomorrow?" It was getting a little too serious between the two of them, and he wanted it to go back to a fun date.

"You have something planned?"

"Well," he pulled his hand from hers and scratched the stubble on his cheek. "I wasn't going to have one, but I made the mistake of opening my big-ass mouth to my mother. I told her I was taking a beautiful woman out for the weekend. Of course she knew it was you, and then she hounded me for a few hours about what I had planned for us to do. When I told her I didn't have anything planned, she literally sent me a list of things that we can do in Omaha. I found something that I thought you would enjoy. Then I sent it to her for her approval."

Hannah laughed. "Oh my God, your mom and my mom could be BFF's. Mine's the same way. She's texted me a few times since that picture of us showed up together."

"Your mom texts? That would be nice if mine learned how to do that, but no, she calls me at 5 A.M., and then bitches when I'm not in the mood to talk."

"Oh yeah, my mom just learned how to do all the tech-savvy stuff like texting, Facebook, and Twitter. So she's cute about wanting to use it all the time. She would rather do that stuff to show me that she can rather than call me."

"Hey, don't knock that shit. At least then you can pretend like you didn't get the text or something. With a phone call, they know you at least got the voicemail."

She smacked him on the shoulder. "Do you really do that to your mom?"

He shrugged. "Sometimes. She's nosey."

"She's your mom, she's supposed to be."

"What about you? Are you nosey?" he teased.

"Not really. I mean I guess I kinda used to be back when I started in the business. I still read the gossip magazines and the blogs and all that stuff. None of them ever had anything about me in them, so it was okay for me to read it. Then it was like things changed, and overnight people cared about me, about what I was doing, and it wasn't so much fun anymore. I'm private and I don't care much for paparazzi," she admitted.

"But you do all the social media stuff."

"Yeah, because I can control it. I don't mind giving the fans a glimpse into my personal life, but I want to be able to show them on my own terms." She shifted in her seat. "Anyway, we got off topic. What are we doing?"

"We're going to the aquarium that they have in town. They also have a zoo, but I'm not sure how cold it'll be. I didn't have time to check all that out."

She grinned over at him. "Do you know that I've never been to an aquarium but I've always wanted to go. I'm excited now."

"Good, I'm glad. I was worried you would think it was lame or something, but I had limited time and resources to work with."

"No, you did good, I'm surprised you did so well actually."

"Grab my phone and thank my mom."

She laughed. Immediately, she thought that she would probably like his mom. As they passed a sign that told them they had 100 miles left to go, she watched their surroundings. "This is nice, driving in a car where you can see your surroundings."

"I know—you can see what's coming at you. Really though, I like to drive," he told her as he switched lanes and passed a slow moving car.

"That works out well, because I'm a rider. I usually text or check my phone while Shell drives."

"Speaking of her, what is she doing while you spend tonight and tomorrow with me?"

Again she felt the sadness about leaving her friend behind. "She told me she was going to rent a movie and get some room service. Ya know, enjoy her time alone," she bit her lip and looked over at his profile.

"I should have told you to invite her, but I never even thought about it," he admitted.

"She told me she's a big girl; she can take care of herself, so I'm going to do my absolute best just to have fun while we're together."

He wagged his eyebrows at her. "I'll be sure to help you however I can. I'll be whatever you need me to be."

A blush covered her cheeks. "Why do I get the feeling that you mean that in a completely different way than how I'm taking it?"

"Because I'm a guy, and you're not trustful of guys. It's okay though, I'll worm my way under your skin, and then you'll wonder how you ever lived without me. It's kinda what I do with people."

He was so confident that she had to laugh. "Is that right?"

"That's right. Ask anybody. The first time I asked any of the guys to be in the band, they all told me no. Yet here we are a decade later with millions of records sold, millions of fans, and sold-out tours wherever we go. I think they've learned not to doubt me and just trust that I can make the right decisions for everyone involved."

"So what decisions do you have for me? I'm curious."

He stuck his lip out, pretending to ponder her. "I think you should just learn to say 'fuck you' and have a good time."

"I don't know that I'll ever be able to do one of those things, but I think maybe you could show me how to cut loose and have a good time."

"I think I can too, if only you would let me."

She shifted in her seat, leaning her head against the window as they pulled off the main highway and went into downtown traffic. "I guess I could let you, and I guess this weekend would be a good a time to start as any."

They pulled up to the hotel, and he popped the lock on the doors to let the valet open them. "Then come on, Ms. Stewart, your good time awaits."

Chapter Ten

To say it was unusual for Hannah to be sitting back, letting a man other than a concierge carry her luggage, was an understatement. No man that she had ever dated, casually or seriously, had ever done things like that for her. In the back of her mind, she could hear Shell's voice telling her that she'd never dated a man before. It was exciting and it made her feel that much more like a grown up.

"We're on the top floor. I pulled rank with the guys and got the biggest suite they have. I now have to grovel for the next week, but after you see this place, you'll realize it was worth it," he grinned at her, putting a key card in the elevator and hitting the correct button.

"Garrett, you didn't have to do that for me. I would have been perfectly happy with whatever room you normally stay in," she protested.

"Nah, really. It was fine. Off and on we've done it for different people. I haven't done it in a while, and I wanted to do it for you. It's not a big deal," he assured her.

Well, that was kind of a lie. It had been a big deal. The guys had given him a ton of shit for it. They'd made fun of him in their vulgar way and then proceeded to make sweet kissing sounds for the remainder of their bus ride. When it had finally come to a stop in Omaha, he was looking forward to his drive alone. They did it out of love and because they knew it bugged the shit out of him, but sometimes they were just a little too much.

"I have a feeling you're making it sound much less annoying than it was, but thank you anyway." She went up on her tiptoes and kissed him on the cheek.

He didn't answer either way, just enjoyed that she was willing not to put up a fight about it. When the elevator dinged, it opened right into the suite.

"Here we go," he said, pulling her suitcase in behind him.

Hannah had never seen anything like this before. It looked to be two stories, had a kitchen, a fireplace, and a dining room table. "Garrett, this is amazing."

"It is pretty awesome," he conceded as he walked up the stairs to put her suitcase where the bed was. He had already been here and scoped it out for all of five minutes before he left to pick her up.

She glanced at the watch on her wrist and realized that it was getting to be early evening and she was getting hungry. "So what are our plans for tonight?" Her stomach picked that moment to growl, loudly.

Garrett cracked up and leaned over the banister to look at her. "First thing will be getting you some food. When was the last time you ate?"

"Early this morning. We've been on the go since then, and I have to admit, I was a little nervous about coming here."

It had really been a lot nervous, but she didn't need to tell him that. Her nerves were her own thing, he would learn about them soon enough.

He finished walking down the stairs and came to a stop in front of her. "There isn't any reason for you to be nervous. I promise. I'm not going to ask you for something that you can't give."

She exhaled loudly. "I know, but this is all so different and new to me that I'm just nervous about it. You should be flattered."

"I am, kinda," he grinned.

Her eyes couldn't help but follow him as he walked around the room. She wasn't sure what he was doing, but when he picked up a piece of paper and handed it to her, she wanted to get down on her knees and thank him. It was a menu to room service.

"It all looks so good." She bit her lip as she studied what was offered. "Are you hungry?" she looked up at him.

"I'm starving, to be honest. So why don't we eat and then figure out what we want to do."

"Sounds like a good plan to me."

After mulling over the menu, the two of them made their choices, and he called it down so that it would be delivered to them. Just as he hung up the room phone, his cell phone rang and he hurried to answer it. "Yeah?"

Hannah did her best to not listen, but it was hard when they were in the same room, and when he glanced over at her and said 'let me see what she wants to do', she figured this included her as well.

"What's going on?" she asked as he hung up the phone.

"The guys found this bar they want to check out. It's supposed to be nice, and it's in the west section of Omaha. They heard that it has good drinks and a rock-n-roll atmosphere. They want to know if we want to go with them."

He watched as her eyes narrowed. She probably wasn't used to this at all, so he hurried to smooth things over.

"We don't have to if you don't want to; they were just trying to be polite. They know it's important to me that you like them."

"Then we'll definitely go. I just hope I have something to wear," she assured him.

It was obvious that he was worried about this. "If you're sure."

It hit her almost out of left field what the problem was. "If Jared gets out of hand, know that I won't think it's your fault or that it reflects badly on your band. He's his own person, okay?"

"Okay, and I'm pretty sure you'll be able to find something to wear. That suitcase was fuckin' heavy."

He had to give it to her; she didn't even give him a hard time about using that word.

"At least you're strong enough to pick it up."

She had a point there. He had kind of shown off for her. If that's what it took to win her trust and heart, then he would keep doing it. No matter how long it took.

Hannah scrutinized her appearance in the bathroom's full length mirror. She hadn't wanted to dress up, but she hadn't wanted to dress down either. She wanted to look nice. This was the first time she would be going out with a rock band. One that she had read stories about in the past. For a while, there had been a little blurb about them in every gossip magazine she picked up. Most of it had to do with them getting drunk and out of hand—usually in a strip club. The first time she would be hanging around the men that Garrett called best friends. To say she was nervous was an understatement, and she wanted to look perfect.

Facing the mirror, she took a picture with her phone and texted it to Shell.

Do I look acceptable for a night out with a bunch of rockers?

Within seconds, she got a reply.

You look hot! Go have fun for the both of us!

Hannah closed her eyes and took a deep breath before walking out of the bathroom. Garrett sat on the bed watching TV, but his eyes lifted up when he heard the door.

"Wow!" he breathed, his mouth opening and closing a few times.

"Do you like?" she turned around in a circle.

Did he like? The woman in front of him was so hot he was about to combust. She wore a little black dress with what looked like lace overlay. One shoulder was bare while the other sleeve went below her elbow. But what made the outfit were her hair and her shoes. Her hair had been curled into corkscrew curls, and her shoes were a bright aquamarine blue glitter with a black ribbon on the top. He normally wasn't a shoe man, but these shoes made her legs look a mile long.

"I fucking love, and I say that with the utmost respect."

She giggled. They were going to have to come to an agreement about that word. "Thanks. So you think I'm presentable for a night out with rock stars?"

"You are very presentable." He stood up and stalked over to her. The heels gave her enough height so that she actually came up to his collar bone. Reaching out, he rested his hands on her hips and pulled her towards him so that they touched.

The quick movement he made caused her to stumble slightly against him. She tilted her head up so that she didn't hit her nose on his chest. When she did, his eyes caught hers and they stared at one another for what seemed like forever. Hannah didn't want to let him go, she dug her hands into the leather of the jacket he wore, not bringing him closer, but not allowing him to get away either.

"You look beautiful," he said softly as he lowered his head, moving his hands around to the back of her neck. He picked up the mass of curls with his hands and buried them into her hair, pulling her mouth closer to his.

She didn't want to tear her eyes away from his, but she had to close hers as his lips met hers. The kiss was much softer and sweeter than she had anticipated. Once their lips met, he didn't try to coax them apart; he just softly stroked her hair and gave her light pecks. Hannah wanted more, but she was afraid that if she tried to take more it would run them headlong into a place she wasn't sure she wanted to go yet. Removing her hand from his jacket, she ran it along the arm that held her head, stopping at his elbow and tightening her fingers there.

"Thanks," she whispered as he pulled away, a smile tilting at the corners of her lips.

Her lipstick was smeared slightly, and he used his thumb to repair it then moved away from her body. "We got to get going. We're meeting the guys downstairs. Remember, we don't have to stay with them if they do something that makes you feel uncomfortable."

She grabbed her jacket, a leather one that had been a gift from Shell for her last birthday. "I know...I don't want you to worry about me. Things will be fine, let me just make sure I have my ID," she told him as she rifled through a clutch that she carried.

"Got everything?" he asked as he stood next to the door.

"Sure do, I'm ready whenever you are."

They got on the elevator, and he pressed the button for the ground floor. They didn't say anything, and it wasn't uncomfortable. She stood in front of him, leaning back against his body. He ran his hands along her sides. The elevator dinged as they reached the bottom floor, and they stepped out, Garrett grabbing her hand as they exited.

"The guys should be over here waiting for us in the bar," he told her as they walked in the direction a sign pointed.

He could feel her hand shaking as they approached the hotel bar. "You okay?" he asked again.

"Just nervous. It's something that happens when I get nervous. It's hard to hide when you're standing in front of thousands of people, but I can't figure out why I can't hide it with you," she admitted.

"You don't ever have to hide anything with me," he assured her as they rounded the corner and he moved to open the door.

"I'll try not to from now on," she told him walking through the open door.

As she did, she heard wolf whistles from a group of guys sitting in a booth. She recognized them as the other members of the band. She might not been formally introduced, but she knew exactly what they looked like.

Garrett couldn't help the grin that spread across his face and the chuckle that rumbled up in his throat. "That would be my friends. Classy, aren't they?"

"They sure are. Before we go over there, I feel like we should commemorate this night. Take a picture with me."

With him having the long arms, he pulled her to his side and stuck her phone out, taking a picture as they smiled. He handed it back to her and looked to see how well he had done.

"That's a good picture, tag me in it," he told her.

She nodded as she pressed a few buttons and uploaded the picture. The caption read.

My first time partying like a rock star with @ReaperBF! Wish me luck!

If people had been wondering about their relationship before, then they were wondering about it now. Sooner rather than later, Hannah knew that they would have to make some sort of statement. She figured after these next few days they would know for sure.

Never had a few days meant so much.

Chapter Eleven

"**G**uys, you know who she is, but you haven't been formally introduced. Hannah, this is Jared, Bradley, and Chris."

She nodded at each of them as they raised their hands when they were introduced. "It's good to meet you guys, I hope you don't mind that I'm crashing your party."

"A beautiful woman like you? You're not crashing it at all. You're giving us a much better time," Jared grinned up at her from where he sat.

"Don't believe a word he says, he flirts with all the ladies," Garrett said, running his hand down her back.

"Somehow, I think you're telling me the truth," she winked at Jared.

"So when are we leaving?" Bradley asked, running a hand through his black hair. She could see how he gotten his nickname of Raven.

"Whenever you want to." Garrett pulled the keys to the Escalade out of his pocket and threw them for someone to catch them. "Whoever wants to drive, be my guest."

Bradley caught the keys and threw some money on the table to cover the drinks they had while waiting. "Let's roll, gentlemen and lady."

The group of them made it to the Escalade and got in, Garrett taking a spot in the back that was extended. Only two people could sit there, and he brought Hannah along with him. The small space and his big body made them sit pressed up against each other.

"I hope you have a good time tonight," he smiled at her. His voice was deep and intimate against her ear, the timbre causing goose bumps to form along her arms.

"I hope I do too."

There was a silence in the vehicle, and she couldn't help but feel that it was partially because of her. Hannah didn't know these men well enough to break that silence. Just when she was about to say something, Jared turned around in his seat and faced her.

"So tell me, how much of a dick is Ashton Coleman?"

It took her by surprise, and she could hardly do anything but laugh. "I can't believe you just said that to me," she continued to laugh, but she was in shock.

"Oh c'mon. You dated the guy for like two years. You were obviously too good for him. If we're going to accept you into the group, you've got to give us something," Jared chastised her.

"You don't have to answer anything you don't want to," Garrett told her, hitting Jared on the back of the head. "Dude, some people don't talk shit about everybody like you do."

"No, it's okay," she said. He was right. If there was anybody she could discuss how much of a jerk Ashton

Coleman had been to her, it was these guys. "He really was a jerk."

"No, honey." Garrett put his arm around her. "Jared called him a dick."

"Yeah, a dick and a jerk are two very different things," Jared nodded.

"A dick is a straight-up asshole. Somebody that makes you or the people you care about cry. A jerk just makes you want to cancel his porn account. So, what was this guy?" Bradley asked from where he sat behind the steering wheel.

She chewed that around for thought. "Then he really was a dick," she said the word softly, causing all the guys to crack up.

"It's okay, you can say that around us," Chris told her from his place beside Jared. "We're not gonna run tell all the tabloids that you said a bad word."

"Dude, don't make fun of her," Garrett piped up. "She lives a completely different life than we do."

"No, it's okay," she told him, laying her hand on his thigh. "My life is kind of a joke compared to y'all's. I can take it."

"Yeah, Garrett, let her stand up for herself," Jared needled his friend. He loved to get Garrett's back up.

"Shut the fuck up, man."

"No, he's right." Hannah rubbed her hand along his thigh this time, trying to calm him down. "I can stand up for myself, but I don't because usually other people do it for me. But yeah, Ashton Coleman is the biggest dick to ever walk the planet."

Garrett couldn't help but watch her mouth as she formed the word. Hearing it come out from between her lips was doing things to him that he didn't want to look at too closely.

"That's so good to hear, because my last girlfriend was totally in love with him," Chris told her. "She had his poster up everywhere. I hated that douchebag."

"She probably slept with him. Everyone else did," Hannah said before she could stop herself.

"Ohhhh," she heard as all the guys hit Chris on the arms, in the stomach.

"That was harsh, Hannah." Chris held his stomach where Jared had hit him the hardest.

"I'm so sorry," she apologized. "I meant that more as a dig on him than on the women he cheated on me with."

"He cheated on you?" Bradley asked.

"Yeah." Her tone was clipped, and it was obvious that she didn't want to talk about it, but one thing she didn't know about these guys was the fact they gossiped like old women. "He sure did."

"He's crazy."

"He's a douchebag."

"I hope you cheated on him with someone else."

"He really is a dick."

The last phrase came from beside her, and she smiled up at Garrett. "Thanks, you're right, he is. I appreciate the support, guys," she laughed as she took in everything they had said.

Pulling up to the valet parking at the bar, Bradley turned around. "Well if you're with Garrett, then you're one of us, and we take care of our own. Welcome to the family."

This bar was like nothing that Hannah had ever seen before. It was decorated in shades of black and red, and heavy metal played over the speakers. People sat in groups at tables along one side of the room, while the other side held a large group dance floor.

"We're going up here," Garrett said into her ear as they took some stairs and arrived at what she figured was a VIP area.

It overlooked the whole bar and she stepped up to the railing to have a glance. Some people noticed her and pointed at her. She smiled and waved as pictures were taken. It was only when she went to turn around that she noticed Reaper had come up behind her as well.

"What do you want to drink?" He had to lean in close to be heard over the loud bass of the rock beats.

Water wouldn't do with this crowd, so she told him the one drink she liked. "Crown and Coke."

"You like the hard stuff?" Surprise was evident on his face.

"Not everything about me is goodie-two-shoes. I have my moments," she said as she stood on her tiptoes to reach his ear.

"I'd like to figure out how to get to those moments," he flirted with her.

She had taken her jacket off when they entered the club, and he trailed his fingertips down her bare arm. "Hopefully, you'll find out one day."

Hannah watched as he went over to the private bar in this area and placed their order. Taking a deep breath, she smoothed her dress down her thighs to calm her nerves. These guys had been wild in their younger years, and she hoped that they had calmed down enough that she could hang with them. If she couldn't hang with them, she wasn't sure she had a future with Garrett. She plastered a smile on her face when he walked back over towards her, drinks in hand.

"You look hot standing here with the lights of the club behind you. It's like you're starring in my very own music video," he told her as he handed her the drink she had requested.

Wanting to fortify herself, she took a gulp from the glass. "I don't know how to flirt back with you," she admitted. "You're much better than I am. I'm so far out of my league with you, it's not even funny."

"You aren't out of your league, you just need to relax."

He pulled her over to the table, and they had a seat. She sat back, crossing her legs, and listened to the group. There was never a dull moment in their conversation, and she had a hard time following along. They were close, and there were a lot of inside jokes that she wasn't privy to, but she was still having a good time nonetheless.

"So who's your friend that I always see you with?" Jared asked when there was a brief lull in the conversation.

"My friend?" She was genuinely confused.

"You know, that blonde that's always hanging around with you. I've seen her in the background all the time."

"You mean Shell?" She raised her eyebrow in surprise.

"He's talking about the one that was in your car the other day, so I think you said that was Shell?" Garrett confirmed.

"What do you want to know about my friend for?"

"She's kinda cute," Jared grinned over at her.

Hannah leaned into Garrett, her lips touching his ear. "Is he serious right now?"

Lazily he leaned back against the seat, pushing his arm in between her and the seat. His hand rested softly against her hip bone. "You never know with him. Why don't you bust his balls about it?"

"Why would I give you my friend's number? I've read womanizing stories about you in the tabloids. Are you crazy?"

"Damn, man," Chris laughed, putting his drink up to his lips. "She's got you there."

A blank look overtook his face before he took a drink from his own beer. "That was a long time ago," he argued. She'd obviously inadvertently hit on something that pissed him off.

Garrett stiffened next to her before talking. "She's just joking, you know that, right?"

Jared got up from where he sat and stood next to the two of them. "Don't talk shit about me unless you know me, and honey, just because you might be laying on your back for him doesn't mean you know me." He took off, walking towards the main level of the bar.

She was shocked. No one had ever talked to her like that before in her life.

"I'm really sorry about that," Garrett told her, grinding his back teeth together. He wanted to rip his best friend apart with his bare hands.

"Not your fault. I told you I wouldn't hold anything he did against you, but I will tell you he makes me nervous."

Garrett made a mental note to have a conversation with him later.

"Sorry I asked." She leaned over to the group. "Didn't mean to be such a Debbie Downer."

Chris took a drink from his bottle again. "Don't worry about it, he's different. You never know with him. He's not going to ruin our good time, so don't even think about it. I'm about to go find me a woman," he stood up and flexed his arms.

She couldn't help but breathe a sigh of relief. She thought that maybe she had ruined their night and that had scared her. If there was one thing she wanted, it was for these guys to like her.

"You didn't do anything. Seriously, none of us know what will set him off. You can't be careful of something you have no idea about," Garrett assured her.

Glancing around, she saw that they had been left alone at their table. "Glad that I didn't ruin it, but it looks like everyone left us alone."

"Good," he said, turning around so that they faced one another. "They were imposing on our alone time," he shouted over the loud music.

"So what do you want to do?"

"First, I'm gonna take this shot, and then I think I'm going to do something that I've thought about doing since you climbed into the backseat with me."

Hannah watched as he tipped his head back, swallowing the liquid in one gulp. Her eyes watched his Adam's apple bob up and down as he pushed the liquid past his throat. "That shit's strong," he said as he set the shot glass down on the table.

Now what was he going to do? He had taken the shot, and now he looked at her with the strangest glint in his eyes. She had a moment before he buried his hands in her hair and pulled her mouth to his. This kiss was different than the one from before. This time he coaxed her lips open, lightly running his tongue along her bottom lip. The promise it held was enough to keep her coming back for more.

Chapter Twelve

"We're heading out guys. Keep the car, we're gonna take a cab," Garrett told the rest of them as he helped Hannah up and put his arm around her.

"Bunch of wusses!" Bradley heckled as they turned to leave.

Garrett flipped him the bird as the two of them walked out the exit door. He had already asked the bartender to call them a cab and was pleased to see that it was waiting for them as soon as they stepped out onto the curb. Also outside was a line of people waiting to get in.

"Reaper! Harmony!"

People called out to them as he popped the back door of the cab open. Hannah was nice enough to turn and wave at everyone, he did the same. Carefully, he ushered her into the cab and told the driver where to take them. His phone buzzed in his pants, and he took it out, holding it very close to his eyes.

"Are you okay?" she asked as she saw him holding the phone so close to his face.

He blushed. "Something I haven't told you about me. The reason I wear those sunglasses on stage?"

"Yeah?" She had always thought it was part of his onstage persona, but apparently this was something a little more personal.

"They're prescription. I can't see for shit."

Hannah laughed. "Are you kidding me? I wondered why you always wore them. You don't wear anything else?"

"Every once in a while I'll wear contacts, but I have astigmatism, and they hurt after a while. I thought that going to the bar; it'd be a bad idea because if there's smoke in the air, they hurt worse."

"So you haven't seen me at all tonight? You have no idea exactly how I look?" she asked, putting her hands on her hips.

"No, I took them out while we were driving to the club. It was dark enough in the SUV that you didn't see me. But I didn't have any solution, so I just threw them in the cup holder. Now I can't see, and I'm getting all kinds of notifications. I think one is from my Mom too, damnit."

She giggled so hard she had to grab her stomach. "This is crackin' me up."

"Seriously? Me not being able to see is this funny to you?"

"It's just that," she bit her lip and scooted over closer to him so that he could see her, "you're this badass guy who looks like he could kill somebody if they looked at you the wrong way, and you're telling me you can't see. Do you wear glasses at night? Like real glasses?"

"Yeah," he sighed. "I do have regular glasses, and I'll be putting them on as soon as we get back to the suite. I'm starting to get a headache."

"It's cute," she told him, running her hand along the back of his neck. "Really."

His shoulders shook as he blew out a deep breath. "So much for looking like a badass, huh?"

"If it makes you feel any better, old-timer, I have glasses for when I read."

He glanced over at her, his mouth wide open. "Old-timer? Oh my God, you've hurt me so much." He held his hand over his heart. "You aren't that much younger than me. Damn, Hannah." He shook his head.

"I'm sorry," she apologized as she wiped at her eyes. "That was mean and I'm sorry. You're still sexy, even if you can't see me."

"Oh yeah?" He put his arm around her shoulders and pulled her close. "There, I can see where your lips are now," he whispered as he dove in, brushing his lips against hers.

"So how do I look?" Garrett asked as he walked down the stairs and into the living area of the suite.

The two of them had headed in different directions when they arrived. She'd gone to one bathroom and removed her makeup, putting her hair up in a ponytail. She debated on which pair of pajamas to wear. At Victoria's Secret she had purchased sweatpants and a tank top as well as a nightie. Hannah had debated with herself for more than ten minutes about what she should wear. In the end, her insecurities won out, and she put the sweat pants and tank on, cursing herself the whole time.

While she waited on him, she started the fireplace and got comfortable. It was warm by the time he walked down and faced her, modeling his glasses.

"You look distinguished," she told him honestly. The wire-rimmed glasses gave him a little bit of a Clark Kent/Superman vibe.

He laughed when she told him so. "I'd much rather have a Bruce Wayne/The Dark Knight vibe."

"Why does that not surprise me?" she grinned, moving her feet so that he could sit next to her on the couch.

"I am who I am," he shrugged, checking his phone as it went off. "Hell, it's my mom. If I don't answer this, she's just going to keep calling."

She waved her hand that she was fine with it and grabbed her own phone, she had a ton of notifications from the picture she had posted with him before going out for the night. Reception seemed to be pretty good among both her and his fans. There were quite a bit of new followers on her Instagram, and she had a couple of private messages on some of her accounts. One of them was from a Marie Thompson. She wondered if this woman was related to Garrett. To the side, she could hear his conversation; she would have to ask him later.

"Hey mom." He smiled indulgently over at Hannah, making a talking motion with his hand.

"What?" he asked, holding the phone away from his ear. "Where'd you hear that from?"

Hannah couldn't hear the other side of the conversation, but she could tell his mom was giving him an earful.

"She's here with me right now. Trust me we aren't shacking up at the moment. Right now I'm on the phone with you. You're cockblocking my game."

Hannah smacked him in the arm. "I can't believe you just said to your mother."

He laughed, putting his mom on speaker phone. "She's used to me, right mom?"

"Unfortunately, I am used to you. I take it this is Harmony?"

"Her name's Hannah. I thought I told you that," he told her, holding the end of the phone up towards his mouth.

"You might have, but let's be honest, son. You tell me a little bit of what you want me to know and then a lot of BS. I have to figure out what's the truth and what's not."

"What can I say?" He looked over at Hannah. "She knows me so well."

"Hopefully, I raised you with some manners," his mom quipped over the phone.

"You did, I promise. Hannah, this is my mom, Marie Thompson. Mom this is Hannah Stewart, better known to the world as Harmony."

"Nice to meet you," Hannah grinned, even though the other woman couldn't see her. She scooted over to sit next to Garrett. "Question, did you just friend me on Instagram? I have someone by that name who sent me a notification tonight."

"I did, it's the only way I can seem to get pictures of my son. I think he's posted more with you in the past few days then he's posted for the last year. I hope you don't mind."

Garrett interrupted. "She likes to think she's social-media savvy."

They ignored him. "It's fine; you can friend me on whatever you want."

"Be careful what you tell her. She'll be sharing pictures of me as a baby on Throwback Thursday. She has no shame."

"No matter how old you are, Garrett, you're my baby," Marie told him through the phone.

"If you don't need anything else mom, we have an early day tomorrow. I'd like to get some shuteye."

Hannah blushed involuntarily, she couldn't help but think about what getting shuteye would include. They would be sleeping in the same bed. It made her just the least bit uncomfortable mentioning it in front of his mother. With Ashton, they had never spoken about anything like that in front of other people. They were never affectionate or posted any kind of pictures of each other. He always had to appear to be the single country singer turned movie star. Now she could see exactly what she had been missing. A real relationship was so much different than what she was used to, and Garrett wasn't threatened by anything. He wasn't scared to let others know how he felt. He really was who he was, and you either liked it or you didn't.

"Alright, the two of you have a good time tomorrow. Garrett, you better be on good behavior, and Hannah, I can't wait to get to know you better."

"Me neither," Hannah piped up from where she sat next to him.

"I will be, Momma. Love you," he told her, his finger over the end call button.

"Love you too," she told him before he disconnected.

"Do you always hang up on her?" Hannah pointed to the phone. "That's not nice."

Garrett defended himself. "Either you hang up on her or she hangs up on you. She doesn't say 'bye'. You're still sittin' there talking, and then you hear a damn dial tone. It's become a game now. To see if I can hang up on her before she hangs up on me."

"What if she has something else to say?"

"She'll call back; she's had to do it before. It's just kind of how we are."

"That's so funny. You compete with your mom to see who can hang up on each other first."

He lifted his shoulder up in a shrug. "Sometimes I'm just happy to get her off the phone. She was on good behavior tonight because you're here."

"Are you going to be on good behavior because I'm here?" She couldn't believe she had just asked him that question, couldn't believe that she flirted with him now, even though she hadn't been able to before.

"I don't want to, but I think I should." He grabbed her hand and held it against his leg. "And that's the truth. I don't think you're ready for what comes with me."

"What does that mean?" she asked, enjoying the feel of his fingers as they made patterns on the palm of her hand.

She watched as he ran his tongue along his bottom lip. "I'm an intense kinda guy. I think someone like you will have to be eased into my bed," he told her honestly.

"What do you mean intense?"

"Answer me this, what was the craziest thing you did with Ashton?"

She didn't exactly know what he meant by that question. "I'm not sure I know what you mean."

"That's my answer right there. If you knew what I meant, then you would know what kind of lover I am and what kind of a man I am. I'm not going to scare you off; I'll be patient with you," he told her very matter-of-factly.

Just when she thought she got a bead on him, he surprised her and changed directions.

"Am I going to be able to keep you?" she asked quietly. "If we do get into this kind of relationship, who's to say you won't think I'm a cold fish like Ashton did."

"I can tell just by the kisses we've shared and just by looking in your eyes that you're going to be perfect for me." He used his other hand to move behind her neck and cup her jawbone, forcing her to look him in the eyes.

"I wasn't perfect for Ashton."

"But you are for me. He didn't know what to do with you. He didn't know how to let you know what he wanted. I do."

"You seem very sure of yourself," she told him, not believing entirely what he said.

"I am and I haven't been wrong when it comes to a woman yet. You've got it, Hannah. You just need to tap into it, and I can show you how to do that."

She sighed heavily and let her eyes drop.

"But like I said, that's for another night. Let's go get that shuteye. It'll be time to get up and have our adventure before we know it."

His easy smile stilled her heart, but the worry that she wouldn't be able to keep him was there too. It nagged the back of her mind, even when he pulled her into his arms and hugged her tightly, pressing a kiss to her temple. Would she be able to keep this man? She just wasn't sure.

Chapter Thirteen

"I can't tell you how excited I am about this."

Garrett glanced over to the passenger side and grinned at Hannah. "I'm glad that you are. Sorry it's so cold today. I'm not even sure that there will be anything in the zoo, but at least we'll be able to check out the aquarium," he told her, taking a drink of the coffee they had stopped to get.

"Either way, it doesn't matter. I've never done either before," she admitted, sitting up taller in her seat as they approached the exit for the aquarium.

It was nice to see the world through someone else's eyes. None of the guys would ever be excited about going to a zoo or an aquarium. He had to admit because she was so looking forward to it, so was he. They pulled into the parking area, both breathing deeply as he turned the SUV off.

"Are you nervous?" he asked. They were going out in public by themselves in a town that wasn't home to either one of them on a date for the first time.

"Just a little bit," she admitted as she got out and put her hood over her head. The wind was chilly, and she was glad she had grabbed some gloves to go along with her jacket.

Hannah watched as he walked over to her, pulling his hooded jacket up over the hat he wore. With his sunglasses on, he looked especially dangerous. Something about that caused her to want to shout to the world that this man was on her arm today.

"You ready?" he asked, holding his hand out for her.

"Sure am," she told him as she zipped her jacket up and grabbed his hand.

Garrett loved the feel of her smaller hand in his. It brought forth every protective instinct in him. He had never been the type of person to get all caught up in having to protect the woman in his life. She was different—this woman made him want to do a million things he had never thought of before.

There weren't a whole lot of people making their way to the entrance on this cold, sunny day. Most appeared to be couples skipping work on a weekday. He and Hannah stood in line together, her body tucked against his as they waited their turn to pay.

"You okay?" Garrett asked. "You got quiet."

"I'm fine, just thinking about how lucky I am to be with you today. Let's go have some fun." She pulled him over to the side and watched as he opened the map.

As he heard her words, his dimples deepened and he smiled so wide she could see his teeth. "Well thanks; I'm glad you appreciate the fact that I take my mom's advice."

He would have to remember to thank his mom later. When she had suggested the zoo and aquarium, he'd thought she was crazy, but apparently his mom knew girls like Hannah a lot better than he did.

After walking around for a few hours, they were tired and very hungry. "Let's go in here," Hannah pulled him into a restaurant that had a cafeteria feel to it.

"I'm starving." He rubbed his stomach as they stood in line. "I haven't done this much walking around in a while. I need to get back on my workout schedule."

She cut her eyes at him, knowing how large his biceps were. "I think you're doin' just fine."

"Damn, you're going to make me blush," he grinned, moving her in front of him.

She leaned back against his chest, enjoying the warmth flowing from his body. He put his hands at her hips and pulled her so that they stood flush with each other. So concentrated on the menu, he didn't even notice that she had pulled her phone out and taken a picture of the two of them.

"Sneaky, sneaky." He pinched her side through her jacket.

"You were so serious there for a minute. I've not seen that side of you before. I like it."

Garrett realized for not the first time that she was very observant. Most people wrote her off as being flaky and sweet just because of the music she liked to make, but there were so many layers to her. Layers that he sincerely hoped he would be able to peel back and get to know.

"There's a lot to me just like there's a lot to you."

For the first time, she felt like someone saw behind her persona and was starting to get to know the real person that lurked there. It was a good feeling—scary, but good at the same time. If there was anything that Hannah was sick of, it was being misunderstood and pigeonholed. "Thanks for realizing that." On a whim, she leaned up to kiss his cheek.

Recognizing an opportunity, he smoothly turned his head and grabbed her lips with his own. His hand buried in her hair, still curly from the night before, and he allowed himself to play there for a few seconds, brushing their lips against one another. He pulled back and licked his lips, and she knew that even though he wore those sunglasses, he was looking directly into her eyes.

"You're welcome." He pressed his hand against her hip. "It's our turn."

In a daze, she ordered her food as did he. When she pulled out money to pay for it, he brushed her hands away, insisting again that this had been his idea and her money was no good.

"When we go out next time, it's my treat," she told him, crossing her arms over her chest.

"You're right, it will be a treat when we get to see each other again, but you may as well get used to the fact that I'm kind of an old-fashioned guy when it comes to you."

That shouldn't have made her stomach warm and a smile spread across her face, but it did. It wasn't about him treating her like she was a piece of china that would break; it was about him caring enough to treat her like she mattered. With Ashton, it had never been that way. Looking back now, she saw just how different it was. It had been about what she could do for him not what they could for each other.

"I'll do my best. It's just that…" She licked her lips as they had a seat at a table and took their jackets off. "I've never been treated this way before. It doesn't unnerve me, but I'm just not used to it."

"And that's a damn shame is what that is."

A smiled played on her lips. "Are you going to take your glasses off? Will you be able to see?"

"Laugh it up." He flicked a napkin at her. "Just for your info, these aren't the ones I wear on stage, these aren't prescription. I put contacts in this morning, thank you very fucking much."

"You're cute when you get all huffy." She reached across the table and grabbed his hand.

"I'm used to the guys making fun of me, but you...you're breaking my heart here," he teased.

She took a drink of her water and a bite of the chicken she had ordered, chewing thoughtfully for a moment. "Would it make you feel better if I confessed something about myself?"

"There's nothing wrong with you. You're obviously perfect," he deadpanned quickly, gaining a snort from her.

"I'm so far from perfect it's not even funny. But here ya go...ya ready?"

From across the table, he squinted at her and pursed his lips. "You're willing to break the mold on yourself to keep me from feeling like I'm defective? This I gotta hear."

Hannah took a deep breath, she couldn't believe that she was about to confess this to someone who she had only met a few days before. Not many people knew this about her, but if they were practicing truth in their relationship then this would be the perfect time to tell him.

"Okay." She scooted around in her chair. "Back when I first started in the business, I was eighteen and they really wanted me to be a pop sensation, even though that's not what I wanted to do. They wanted me to be a dancer and look sexy and have blonde hair—all of that. I wanted this so badly that I did everything my first record company told me to do. I puked up my food, dyed my hair blonde, and got," she leaned forward so that she could whisper and he could hear her, "breast implants."

His eyebrow kicked up, and he tucked his chin into his chest. "You shitting me right now?"

"Nope. Not even Shell knows that about me. We met right after my nineteenth birthday when they hired her to be my makeup artist. We became friends, and she morphed into my personal assistant, but yeah. These," she pointed to her chest, "are fake."

"But they aren't huge," he said, wanting to kick his own ass as the words came out of his mouth.

"Nope, I didn't have a lot to work with, but I was at least able to keep them from going up too much. And the kicker," she shook her head, "is that first record label dumped me right after I had the surgery. So it was a blessing in disguise. I'm not that girl that sings and dances on stage. I write my own music and I sing from the heart. There's not one thing about that original deal that would have made me happy."

"Wow!"

She waited a few moments for him to say something, and when he said nothing, she teased. "Did I make you speechless?"

"You actually kind of did. Out of anything you could have told me…that is so not what I expected. But thanks for sharing that with me."

"It's only fair, right? Now we know secrets about each other. We have a reason to keep this all together."

He didn't need a reason, but if it made her feel better, then that was fine with him. "Wait, Ashton never saw the scars?"

Hannah took another drink of her water and shook her head. "They aren't huge or anything, but let's just say sex with him was way different than what I imagine it would be like with you." Her face burned as she finished that sentence.

She imagined what it would be like with him? Oh hell yeah. He couldn't wait to get past the newness of the relationship so that they could just move on with the rest of their lives. Instead, he cleared his throat, the corner of his mouth tilting up. "Never did it with the lights on, huh?"

"Umm, no."

Reaching across the table, he grabbed her hand again, pulling on it to force her to look into his eyes. "It is a lot different with me, and I'm going to be patient with you. I'm not going to force you to do anything that you don't want to. You know that, right?"

She did and above all she trusted him. Something that she hadn't been sure she would be able to do after Ashton, but for some reason this man was able to get beneath all the defenses she thought she had set up for herself.

"I know and I trust you."

Those were the best, most powerful words Garrett had ever heard in his life.

Chapter Fourteen

"You sure it's okay for me to come along to the show?" Hannah asked as she followed Garrett out of the hotel room that night.

"Yeah, I definitely want you there, unless you need to leave before it's over. I hate that you're driving back to Kansas City tonight by yourself."

She smiled, although it held a little bit of sadness. "It's okay; I think I'll need some time to myself after you leave."

He could relate. The time they had spent together, he wasn't going to forget. "How are you getting back? You want to take back the Escalade with you and turn it into the rental car company? They have a location right outside the hotel you're staying at."

"Sure. I'll call Shell and talk to her on the way back. Like you said on the drive here, it's just a straight shot once you make the exit."

"Enough of that." He grabbed her hand and her suitcase as they took the elevator down to the main level.

"Where is everyone else?" she asked as they hit the lobby and saw no other members of the group.

"They left an hour or so ago, I wanted some more time with you. We need to get there ASAP though, I have a couple of interviews with radio stations that I need to do."

She nodded, holding tightly to his hand as they made their way out to where the SUV awaited them. Fans must have figured out where they were staying because a large throng gathered outside. He stopped at different intervals to take pictures with people, and Hannah did her best to fade into the background. These fans were much different than her own. Not to mention how well liked he was by women, this might not be a great place for her to be right now. Some people recognized her, and they shouted out her name. Waving and smiling, she acknowledged them without taking any of the spotlight away from Garrett.

"You handled that well," he complimented after they had gotten into the SUV and were on their way to the venue.

"Thanks, but I'm kind of out of my element here."

"Well," he took one of his hands off the wheel and grabbed her hand, "I guess we're both learning as we go. I've had girlfriends before, but none of them were anything like you. Only one other even accompanied me out on the road. That's how much I want to get to know you, and I can't put my finger on why, but I really do. My mom always told me that I would never know when it would happen, but when it did I'd be knocked on my ass."

"When what would happen?" she asked him.

He laughed. "When there would be one woman I was more interested in getting to know than getting in her panties."

"Gotta love your mom, huh?"

"She's something else alright."

"The two of you seem to have a good relationship," Hannah observed.

"We do," he nodded. "It wasn't always like that. Especially when I was a rebellious teenager getting brought home by the cops. She and my dad…damn, they had their work cut out for them with me. I'm lucky they didn't send me off to military school. It was that bad."

"Got into fights, huh?

"I'm the fighter of the group," he confirmed.

"I wouldn't have thought that," she deadpanned.

He ran his hand through his hair. "I've calmed down a lot over the years. But if I get into a mood, I'm kinda hard to get along with, and I throw punches first, ask questions later."

"I can't even imagine that about you," she admitted and hoped that he had never raised a hand to a woman.

"Believe it. I can be a bastard." He glanced over at her, trying to get a read on her. "That doesn't mean I am all the time, as evidenced by the time we've spent together. But I do have my days just like everybody does."

"There are days when I'm not nice at all," she confessed.

"I have a very hard time believing that. So next time you're having one give me a call, I'll talk you out of it."

Hannah had a feeling that just remembering the times they had spent together in the past few days would be enough to wipe that kind of day from her memory. She would hold this time they had been able to etch out for each other close to her heart.

Garrett stood on stage, chest heaving, sweat pouring down his back. As the crowd chanted "Black Friday" he couldn't help the grin that covered his face. This was where he felt most alive. He fed off the energy of the crowd, and for an hour and a half a night he felt completely invincible.

"We're gonna slow it down for a second, Omaha. Is that okay with you?" His words were met by a huge roar from the crowd. "Now, you know a few days ago I invited a lovely young lady on stage to sing with us in Nashville. Who was that?"

"Harmony," the crowd shouted back at him.

"That's right," he grinned and motioned towards where she stood in the wings. "She came to visit me for a few days, and she's here tonight. Would some Black Friday fans like to hear her sing again?"

Hannah cringed. At least in Nashville, people really knew who she was. Surprise didn't even begin to describe her feelings when the crowd roared with pleasure. Garrett motioned for her to come out.

"Do I have to get her a seat again?" Jared asked from where he sat across the way. "That shit made it online. You better get your game straight," he talked to his friend.

Garrett flipped him off. "There's a seat right here with her name on it." He slapped the chair beside him.

As she made it out to the group, he handed her a microphone. "Everybody say 'hi' to Harmony."

She smiled brightly and waved at the crowd who responded to her just like they had to him. "I hope everybody is having a good time tonight at the show, I know I am," she told them as she had a seat and crossed her legs. Turning in her seat, she moved to face Garrett.

"You want to sing the same song we sang a few days ago?" he asked, grabbing her hand.

She couldn't believe he was being so touchy-feely with her in front of his fans, but she couldn't deny that she liked it. "Sure," she told him softly into the mic. "If they don't mind."

"Nah, they don't mind." He pointed out to the crowd. "Do ya?"

Jared started playing the opening chords of the song and the crowd screamed, pulling out cell phones and recording devices. This time Hannah was more in control of the situation and not so caught off guard, her voice was much surer and much stronger than before. In a matter of minutes the song was over and everyone was screaming for them. Hannah went to get down from the stool when Garrett appeared in front of her, grabbing her around the waist and lifting her down. She reached up and gave him a hug.

"Thanks for inviting me out here," she told him.

"Thanks for coming." He settled his hands on her hips and spread his legs, leaning so that he was more on her level. Before she knew what he was doing, he leaned down, kissing her in front of all the fans. The screams were deafening, even to the two of them. When he pulled away, he tapped her hip slightly. "See you in about thirty more minutes."

When she got back into the wings, her phone was already buzzing. One message was a text message from Shell.

So you have so much to tell me! I just read that Garrett kissed you on stage at his concert. I'm expecting all the details!

Hannah knew she had been neglecting her friend for the past few days, but it had been needed.

I'll call you when I'm on my way to Kansas City. I'll need your help to stay awake anyway.

Not knowing when she would have the chance to do so again, she took a picture of Garrett on stage, standing in front of the drum kit. From where she stood, it was of him with the crowd behind him. She knew that everyone would love it, so she uploaded it to her Instagram and tagged him in it.

@ReaperBF doing what he does best! Look at that crowd behind him! Thanks for having me out!

Putting her phone in the back pocket of her jeans, she decided she would enjoy the rest of the show and worry about the rest later.

"I can't believe you have to go. I kinda wish we sang the same type of music, and then I could bug management to let you stay on my tour." Garrett pushed her hair back from her face as they stood outside the venue.

He had her boxed in at the SUV, one hand at her hip, one hand at her hair. She was doing her best not to show him just how much she was going to miss him. This had become so normal for her in such a short amount of time. It scared and thrilled her all at once.

"I know, I wish that too, but maybe our differences are what make us want to be together so much," she told him, leaning her head against his shoulder.

"And she's smart too," he whispered, putting his hands at her neck and pushing her head up so he could see her eyes. She rewarded him with a small laugh that tugged at him. "I really think I'm gonna miss the hell outta you," he told her truthfully.

"I think I'm gonna miss you too. You have that way about you, Garrett Thompson." She played with the shirt that covered his chest.

"Oh yeah," he flirted. "What kind of way is that?"

"The way that makes just about every woman you come into contact with want to fall at your feet. You smile with those dimples of yours and the whole population just wants to tell you 'yes' to anything you ask. You're kinda funny too." She tilted her head up, placing a kiss at his jawline.

"You have that way about you too, Hannah Stewart. That's why I'm going to miss you so much. I really wish I could drive down with you to Kansas City, but we gotta be out of here in just a few minutes," the apology was in his voice.

"I understand. Sometimes this relationship isn't going to be easy, and I think it would be good if we realized that now." She put her arms around his neck and hugged him. She squealed as he tightened his arms around her, lifting her off the ground with the strength of his embrace.

"You're right, we're going to have to get used to this. I'll call you later?" he asked as he let go of her, setting her back on the ground.

"I'll be waiting on it. We can always FaceTime, and you know how I love to Instagram." She did her best to smile brightly for him.

He could tell that she was sad, even after their short amount of time together. "We'll see each other soon," he promised. "Have a good show tomorrow night, and be careful tonight. If you need anything, just call. I'll pick up, no matter what time it is."

"Same here," she told him, walking over to the driver's side and popping the door open. "Tell the guys thank you for welcoming me so nicely. I meant to say something, but I completely forgot about it."

"I'll be sure and let them know," he told her as he watched her buckle her seat belt before pulling out into traffic.

For the first time in a long time he went back to his bus and onto the next city with a very heavy heart.

Chapter Fifteen

"Why in the world do I have so many notifications?" Hannah asked out loud a few days later as she and Shell sat at dinner.

"I have no idea. You know I don't follow that social media crap that you do. Your hot boyfriend probably posted something about you," Shell quipped.

Even though her face flushed, Hannah shook her head. "He's not my boyfriend. We haven't put a label on it. More than likely it's that Rocker's Edge magazine that's been posting crap about me the last few days. Our fans are okay with us being together, but this magazine hates that one of their own is fraternizing with the 'enemy'. Garrett told me to ignore it, but they keep tagging me."

"Whatever about the magazine. Just block them and move on with your life. Back to Garrett. You stayed with him for a couple of days and you kissed. The two of you text, talk, and do all kinds of other stuff all the time. He's your boyfriend."

Leave it to Shell to cut to the heart of the matter and decide to stop beating around the bush. "Like I said, we haven't put a label on it, but I do talk to him every day."

"You tell yourself what you need to, but you do need a label for it."

Hannah checked her phone and saw that she had been tagged on a picture from Instagram, but it was one of her with the entire band.

We miss you @HarmonyStewart! Come hang on with us again soon! BF

"Aww, that was sweet. The guys from the band posted a picture we all took together and told me they miss me." She turned her phone around so that she could show Shell.

"Which one is that?" Shell asked, pointing to Jared, who was pictured sitting beside Hannah and Garrett in the booth.

"That's Jared."

"He's cute," Shell commented.

Did she tell her friend about what Garrett had confided in her? "He is and he's nice, but he's got some...issues," she finally said.

"Don't we all?" Shell mumbled.

"His are a little bit more complicated than other people's, but he did ask me for your number. He said he thought you were kind of cute."

Hannah bit her lip. She shouldn't have said that—now Shell would be interested.

"He did?"

"Yeah, but seriously, I don't know if I want you involved with him."

Shell regarded her with keen eyes. "What do you know that you aren't telling me?"

It wouldn't be breaking Garrett's confidence if she was just trying to warn a friend, Hannah reasoned with herself. "According to Garrett, he's had and continues to have some substance abuse issues. I get the feeling he gets clean and can stay there, but then things happen in his life and he falls off the wagon."

"Have you ever seen it?"

"Not the using, but I did witness some very dramatic emotion switches," Hannah answered. "I was only around the group for a small amount of time. I did hear him and Garrett get into an argument one day when I was talking to him. It was pretty heated."

"Well, I guess it's my decision then on what I want to do," Shell sighed.

"That it is. I can give him your number if you want me to, and then it'll be your decision on if you want to answer the phone." Hannah stopped and looked at Shell, a small smile playing on her face. "I have a feeling I'm going to be hanging out with these guys a lot, so I want you there with me. Having said that, I don't want you in a place that's going to hurt you. You're my best friend."

Shell pondered that for a minute. What would be the problem if she was friends with someone who obviously needed one? While it had been fine for her to be by herself for a few days, did she really want her friend to go off and have a life that didn't include her? Since becoming Hannah's assistant, the time she had for herself had become very little. If she didn't take advantage of the opportunities that presented themselves to her, then she might not have a life at all.

"Oh what the hell? Give him my number, and then I'll decide if I want to answer it if he decides to call."

"You're sure about this? I don't want you to do something that you feel like you have to because of me."

"How long have you known me, Hannah?"

"Too long," she joked.

"You're so funny, but really, when have I ever done something I didn't want to do?"

She had a point. Usually it was Hannah doing things that she didn't want to because she felt like she had to. It was never Shell. Shell had no qualms about telling anybody no.

"Okay, I'll give the number to Garrett to give to Jared."

"This has been the longest damn day ever," Garrett sighed.

He unfolded his body onto the couch that had been set up in the backstage area of the venue they were at. He coughed loudly, putting his hand up to his forehead. Thankfully, their show was done for the night, but that didn't make him feel any better.

"You alright?" Jared asked as he walked by him. "You sounded like you were losing your voice out there."

"I feel like shit," he blew out a breath and rolled over on his side. "Grouchy as fuck too."

To be honest, he didn't feel like dealing with anyone. This was the part he hated most about touring. You did it until your body wore down and you were so tired that you couldn't fight off the sickness anymore. What he did want to do was go collapse in his bunk and sleep for the next twenty-four hours. Better yet, sleeping in his own bed at home would be magnificent.

"Do you want us to leave you alone?" Jared asked, having a seat in the chair opposite the couch.

This was exactly why they were best friends. Jared could be one of the most compassionate people in the world. They had been through a lot in their lives together. In their teen years, Jared was the one usually getting hauled home with him in the back of a squad car. *This* was his best friend.

"When we get on the bus, yeah. I'm in a foul-ass mood."

"Well you hid it pretty damn good out there on stage," Jared complimented him.

"I didn't start feeling bad until about the third song from the end. It hit me like a fuckin' brick wall. My head hurts, I feel shaky, I'm hot then I'm cold."

Jared took a drink of water from the bottle he carried in his hand. "That's what you get for walking out in freezing ass cold weather to try to impress a woman."

Flipping him the bird required way too much work, but Garrett was able to do it. "It's worth it if I'm sick because of that. That day was one of the best I've had in a long time."

The fire in Jared's eyes dampened, and he cleared his throat. "I'm glad, man; you deserve it. I know I gave you a hard time a few weeks ago about the free booze, the free pussy, but I get what you're saying about it being lonely. I don't know…it just hit me hard the past few days. It's a lonely life we live. Not many people could put up with it."

"I miss this," Garrett whispered from where he lay on the couch. "You talking to me like this."

"Don't grow a vagina on me now." Jared bounced from one foot to the other.

"Seriously, you're my friend. My best friend. No matter what you have going on in your life, I'm here for you. I get frustrated because I know that you could do so much better and I know that you're not a dumbass."

"Believe it or not," Jared reached down and grabbed Garrett's hand, helping him sit up on the couch, "I appreciate where you're coming from, and I'm a lucky bastard to have you in my corner, but I've gotta get out of my own head. That comes on my time, not anyone else's."

"I know," he nodded. "But I wouldn't be your friend if I didn't at least tell you how I felt. I'm scared for you. I don't want to bury your ass, so don't make me."

Those last words affected Jared. He could tell by the way he stiffened and got quiet for a few moments. If one word that was said to him could change the course of his life, Garrett would say whatever he needed to—whenever he needed to.

"Let's get you on the bus. You really do look like shit."

A bus with three other people could sometimes be the loneliest place in the world, Jared decided a few hours later. Everyone else had crashed, and they had quarantined Garrett as best they could. For a group of men, they'd done a pretty good job of figuring out that he was indeed running a fever, and he had the disposition of a woman delivering a child. They were giving him a very wide berth. For the third time in the past three hours, he heard

Garrett's phone go off and again saw Hannah's name on the ID. Making a decision, he picked it up.

"Hello?"

"Hi, I was trying to reach Garrett," Hannah started. The voice on the other end of the line wasn't Garrett, but it was familiar. Hannah bit her lip, wondering if she had called the right number or not.

"Yeah, Hannah, I know. It's Jared."

"Oh hey," she said. Why was he answering Garrett's phone? This was beyond weird.

"Sorry to confuse you like this, but Garrett's sick, and he left his phone out here so he could get some sleep. I saw that you've called a couple of times and figured you'd be worried since you two talk every night," Jared explained, hoping that he didn't sound as jealous as he felt of their ability to talk to each other the way they did.

"He's sick? Is he okay?" she asked quickly.

"He's got a fever, and he was complaining of body aches. He's not the happiest of people right now. Trust me when I say you're lucky that he left his phone out here."

She could hear the laughter in Jared's voice. Settling in, she bit her lip and wondered if she should just go ahead and talk to Jared. Telling Garrett to relay the message now was pretty stupid. This was Garrett's best friend. They would learn to be friends and get along themselves.

"I hope he gets better soon. When he wakes up, will you tell him I called?"

"I sure will. If he doesn't break his fever by morning, we'll get him to a doctor. He's our frontman, he can't be out of commission for too long."

There was a small silence, and he could hear Hannah's voice over the line. "Jared?"

"Yeah?"

"I know I told you the other day that I wouldn't give you Shell's number, but you came up in conversation and she said that she wouldn't mind if you had it. If I give this to you, I'm trusting you not to hurt her." She held back what she really wanted to say, and he could tell by the tone of her voice.

"Just go ahead and say what you want to. If Garrett trusts you enough to tell you my secrets, then he really cares for you, and if he cares for you that much, you're a really good person. I should go ahead and say that I'm sorry about what I said to you. Sometimes my mouth gets me in trouble, and I should know better at my age but I obviously don't sometimes."

She blew out a breath. "He did tell me, and I want you to know that I don't think badly of you, at all. Things happen in life, and people react to them in different ways. What I do care about is if you hurt my friend and if you hurt Garrett."

"I'm trying to be better…"

She cut him off. "Why not just *be* better instead of trying?"

The no-nonsense tone of her voice wasn't degrading; it was simply asking a question.

"It's hard for people who don't live the addict lifestyle to understand, and I don't expect you to. Just know that I am doing the best I can with what I have. I'm going to kick this one day. I have too."

"As long as you're making progress," she relented. "I'm giving you this number, and I warn you—she is my very best friend in this whole world. Please don't make me regret it."

"I could say the same to you. Garrett is my very best friend in the whole world, don't screw him over. Don't play with his head."

They were quiet for a moment, both of them weighing what the other had said. Curiosity got the better of Hannah.

"Does your telling me this have anything to do with the other woman he brought out on tour with him?"

He laughed, but it was a hollow sound. "We never got along, she and I. I like you. You don't make him choose between us, you let him make his own decisions. Just like you coming out to the bar with us, you chose to do something fun. I respect that. He's never had a girlfriend like that."

"We're not putting labels on it," she told him quickly.

This time he laughed flat out. "Yeah right."

"Well there ya go," she told him dryly. "You and Shell have something in common already."

A few minutes later, Jared hung up the phone, happier for his friend and himself than he'd been in a very long time.

Chapter Sixteen

Garrett groaned as he rolled over in his bunk. His body ached and he was freezing. His head pounded as he fought to lift himself up, causing his vision to swim.

"You alright in there, man?" he heard Jared ask as he pushed the curtain back.

"I feel like death, I mean literal death. What time is it?" He saw bright sunshine; it definitely wasn't the middle of the night anymore.

"It's almost noon. I was just coming to check on you. We just pulled into Dallas. Did you want to see a doctor? Rick said if you do, we need to go now. If we're gonna have to cancel the show, we'll need to do it as soon as possible."

"Cancel the show, my ass," Garrett grumbled as he flung his feet over the side of the bunk and attempted to stand. He swayed and Jared reached out, grabbing him around the arms.

"You need to see what a doctor says first before you start talking out of your ass," Jared scolded. "Do you need help or what?"

"No." He stood for a second and gathered his bearings. "I got it."

"If you're sure." Jared stood behind him, following him up the narrow hallway.

Jared watched as Garrett grabbed a blanket and put it around himself before collapsing on the couch. "Can you tell Rick that I do need to go to the doctor, but he's got to give me a minute."

"Sure, I'll be right back."

Garrett saw his phone lying on the side table and grabbed it. Frowning when he saw missed calls from Hannah, he noticed someone had spoken with her for fifteen minutes the night before. He'd have to figure out who jacked his phone. It appeared he had notifications and a couple of texts from his mom and one from Hannah too. Scrolling through, he immediately clicked on one that showed it was from Instagram from Hannah's feed. What popped up was a picture of her smiling, making a heart with her hands in front of the camera. She wore the 'Reaper's Girl' shirt and what she had put below it made him crack a semblance of a smile.

Really hoping @ReaperBF feels better! The boyfriend needs to not be sick!

Boyfriend? So she had finally done it. She had finally allowed herself to put a label on it. He liked that. He liked that a lot. Flipping back to his texts, he saw more of the same from her, telling him that she hoped he felt better.

Your boyfriend feels like shit. I'm going to see a doctor here in a bit. I'll let you know what they say. Cute pic btw!

Knowing what time it was, he didn't expect a response from her very quickly. Country radio was different than rock radio. Most of his interviews were done at night, most of hers done in the afternoon. Not even bothering to read the text from his mom, he just dialed her number.

"How are you? I saw Hannah's post that you're sick."

"Hey to you too, mom," his voice was rough, even to his own ears.

"You sound like crap there, son. You going to the doctor?"

"Yeah, I'm trying to get up the energy to put on clothes so that I can," he admitted to her.

"Do you have a fever?"

"Pretty sure I do. I've had the chills off and on all night, and my whole body hurts. My throat feels rough, and my head is so heavy it feels like it could fall off my neck," he complained. Even though he complained, it felt so good to complain to his mom, didn't matter how old he got.

"Sounds like you have the flu. Have you been keeping hydrated?"

"No, I haven't. I slept forever, and I just woke up…I feel really weak, so I think I'm dehydrated."

She whistled. "Do I need to come out there and help you out?"

He smirked. "Mom, I'm twenty-nine years old."

"You would prefer your girlfriend be there?"

Garrett grinned, that woman didn't miss a damn thing.

"I would like it if she was here, but I wouldn't want to infect her either. I'm a grown man; I can deal with this on my own."

Marie laughed. "You've never been able to deal with that kind of stuff on your own, but if you think you can this time, you go right ahead. Let me know what the doctor says. Your dad says hi, and he hopes that you feel better. He's out golfing today."

"Jealous!" Garret grumbled into the phone. "You need to get him to start using that cell phone I bought him."

"I would have better luck convincing him to pierce his nipples."

"Mom!" He ran his hand over his aching forehead and closed his eyes. "Seriously? Did you have to go there?"

"It's the truth. You and I both know it. He hates technology."

Someone walked into the living area and Garrett glanced up, seeing Rick. "Hey, I gotta go. Rick's here, and I'm going to go see a doctor. Love you and tell dad that I love him too."

"You feel better, and if you need anything you can call me. Love you, be careful, and do what the doctor tells you."

They hung up and Garrett threw the phone on his stomach. "I guess I have to get dressed, huh?"

"As much as I know you want to just lay around here, I got you an appointment, and we need to get over there. I don't like how pale you're looking there, buddy. You were knocked out last night, and that's really unlike you," Rick told him as he put his hand out to help Garrett up off the couch.

"I know. I missed all kinds of stuff on my phone, and you know I usually have that thing up my ass. It's my lifeline."

Rick grinned. "You gotta keep in touch with the fans and that girlfriend of yours."

"Who talked to her last night? Do you know? She talked to somebody for like fifteen minutes according to the call log. Makes me nervous."

"The only person back here late last night was Jared. I'm sure he was just telling her how you were doing."

Garrett hoped that was all they were talking about.

Hannah rolled her neck on her shoulders to release the tension that had built throughout her long day. Visiting radio stations could be fun and draining at the same time. This being her third one for the day, it was starting to be a drain. She sat in the booth, answering questions from fans and the male and female DJ.

"We have another question from a caller. You're on the phone with Harmony Stewart, what's your question?"

"Hi Harmony." She heard the voice of what sounded like a young girl.

"Hey, whatcha got for me?" Hannah asked, smiling at the upbeat voice.

"I never would have thought that you and Reaper would be together. He seems like a completely different type of person than you. What attracted you to him?"

Hannah had been waiting for something like this all day. Somehow she had the feeling that fans would want to ask questions about her relationship.

"She's blushing," the DJ teased her. "But you have to admit, you two don't look like you run around with the same crowd."

"I agree," she nodded, even though only he could see her. "But he is a really good guy with a good heart."

"A guy named Reaper?"

She giggled, and the DJ kept going.

"Listen to her giggle. I wish y'all could see her now."

"No, seriously, he's a really nice guy, and it's not like Reaper's his real name. But yeah, he's got pretty awesome green eyes too."

"I personally like his tattoo's," the female DJ added. "I don't like them on everybody, but on him they work."

"That they do," Hannah agreed. "While we're at it, there's a slim chance he might be listening. I hope he's feeling better."

"We saw your message on Instagram this morning," the male DJ told her. "What's wrong with him?"

"I'm not sure. When I called last night, I ended up talking to one of the other band members, Train…"

The female DJ interrupted. "He's my favorite. I'm officially jealous."

"I'm jealous of them all because they get to hang out with Harmony!"

"Now that's something to be jealous of." Hannah grinned, thankful that he had taken the heat off of her relationship with Garrett.

"Thanks for hanging out with us today, Harmony."

"It's been my pleasure." She felt her phone vibrate in her back pocket and wanted to fish it out, but she had been ingrained to display good manners around all members of the press since she had started in the business.

"Y'all be sure and check out her show tonight. There are no tickets available, but we will be giving away two pairs tonight…we'll leave you with the newest hit by Harmony Stewart, and we'll keep them rolling."

They shut off the switch that broadcast them to the airwaves, and Hannah stood up, stretching her arms over her head. "Thanks for having me today. I appreciate it."

"Thanks for coming. We're lookin' forward to the show tonight," the female DJ told her, giving her a hug.

When she was finally out of the building, she pulled the phone out and scrolled quickly, seeing a text from Garrett.

Flu, on an IV, this sucks!

Accompanying the text was a picture of his hand taped up, an obvious IV there. She dialed his number as she walked to her transportation for the day.

"Hey."

The voice that answered did not sound like the one she associated with him at all. "Garrett?"

"Yeah, I know I sound rough. Feel pretty rough too. Sorry I missed you last night."

"It's okay. I had a good talk with Jared anyway."

"With Jared? Really? What did the two of you talk about?" It was nice to talk to her, to hear her voice soothed him.

"Believe it or not, you and Shell, but mostly you."

"What did you have to say about me?" He coughed and she cringed.

"It wasn't me; it was Jared telling me I better not hurt his best friend."

That was nice to hear after everything that had gone on between him and Jared. Trying to get Jared to clean up had driven a wedge between the two of them. They were still close, but not as close as they once were. To hear that he cared enough to tell Hannah that gave Garrett hope that maybe they could work past everything.

"That's a bromance for you."

"It sure is," she agreed. "So how are you feeling?"

He put his arm over his head, trying to get comfortable with the IV in his arm. "Pretty shitty. We're having to cancel the next few shows. I might be in here overnight, depending on if my counts go up."

"Really? I didn't realize it was that serious," she told him, biting her lip.

"I was running a pretty high fever when they got me here, and I ran one all last night. I haven't been able to keep much liquid in me, so I'm dehydrated and I'm just feeling bad right now."

"I'm so sorry that you're sick."

"It's okay. I don't get sick often, but when I do, I do it up. Pray that you don't get it. You were around me." He cleared his throat, and she could hear him moving around.

"I'm sure I'll be fine, I took my flu shot." she wanted to say more, but her car pulled up to the Fort Worth Auditorium and the door opened. "I gotta go get ready for my show tonight, but I'll talk to you later," she told him.

"Yeah, it's not like I'm going anywhere. Every time I stand up, the room does a nice spin for me. Needless to say, I'll be here. I have my computer so maybe we can Skype?"

"Definitely," she agreed.

They ended the call, and she put her game face on. It was time to go do some work.

Chapter Seventeen

"**A**re you sure this is goin' to be okay?"

Jared glanced at Hannah again. "Have you never broken a rule in your life?"

His face was so sour, she had to laugh. "I don't like having other people mad at me," she protested, walking closely behind him as they entered the hospital.

"You're going to have to get over that. At some point you're going to make people mad. You get over it, they get over it, and then you move on."

She admired that and wished she could be more like that. All her life she had hated to disappoint anyone or make them unhappy in any way. "I'll work on that," she told him as they got onto the elevator and he pressed the button for the floor Garrett was on.

Visiting hours had yet to start, but Jared assured her that he'd spoken with Garrett and he was definitely awake. She was hoping they didn't get busted.

"This is the slowest damn elevator ever," Jared cursed.

"I know," Hannah said as she looked up at the floors numbers as they increased. A flash caught the corner of her eye, and she snapped up to see Jared holding his phone.

"What did you do?" she asked, putting her hand through her hair.

"I'm gonna show everybody what a rule breaker you are, Ms. Stewart," he laughed.

She watched as he pressed buttons on his phone, obviously uploading the picture somewhere. "Did you put that on Twitter?"

"Yup, and Instagram. Told everybody you were breaking the rules to see your hot boyfriend."

Hannah rolled her eyes. "You're going to get something started, mark my words. At some point, y'alls female fans are going to hate my guts."

"Don't worry." He put his arm around her as they stepped off the elevator. "We like you, so we won't let them be too mean to you."

She cut her eyes over at him. "You obviously know nothing about women. We're meanest to each other and, good grief, can we backstab."

"Glad I'm not a chick," he smirked, directing her to the room that Garrett was occupying. He knocked lightly before pushing the door open. "You still alive in here?"

From the bed, Garrett flipped Jared off.

"Now, be nice to me, I brought somebody to see you."

Garrett opened his eyes and turned his head to face the door. "Hey," he grinned, seeing Hannah standing behind Jared.

"Hey, are you feeling better?" she asked, stepping forward and walking over to his bed.

"I am," he told her, reaching his hand out as far as it would go with the IV still there.

"I'm going to meet Shell for coffee," Jared mentioned. It was so nonchalant; the both of them almost didn't hear him.

They stared at him open-mouthed.

"What? I called, she answered. While Hannah's up here checking on you, I'll be across the street having coffee with Shell. Just let me know when you're ready to leave," he said to Hannah.

"That wench, didn't even tell me," she laughed as she watched Jared's back disappear out the door.

Having a seat on the chair next to the bed, Hannah took a good look at him. "You look like crap."

He laughed and coughed at the same time. "Gee, thanks. That makes me feel so much better."

"I say that in the best way possible. At least we know that you aren't playing hooky," she teased.

"I haven't played hooky since my senior year of high school, thank you very much," he told her, rolling around in the bed to get himself situated.

"So you had to cancel some shows?"

Having someone to talk to about the business side of things was going to be interesting, he decided. No one else in his life, as far as a girlfriend, had ever been able to understand what he went through. It felt good not having to explain everything.

"Yeah, we're going to pick them up on the backend of the tour. The insurance won't allow us to cancel completely and refund the money, so instead of getting done in April, we'll be done the first week of May," he sighed.

"It's not your fault, you know?"

"I know, but I hate that some of the crew will have to cancel vacations. A lot of them don't see their families much as it is, and I just hate that they're having to let their families down because of me. I just feel bad." He had to stop and cough loudly, causing her to cringe.

"But listen to you; you can't go on stage like that. You have an obligation to the fans too. You can't please everybody, Garrett." She reached out and grabbed his hand. "If you're not there to sing, then most people don't even wanna go to the show. Let's be honest here. You're the hot frontman that all the women come to see and all the men want to be like. You have to be there to make the money so that the crew can take those vacations. It's a double-edged sword, but I do understand where you're coming from."

He put his hands on his forehead. "It feels like I'm letting everybody down."

"Now you're just being dramatic," she laughed.

He side-eyed her and crossed his arms over his chest before cracking a smile. "You're right, I am. I just don't wanna be here. I'd much rather be hacking a lung up on stage."

Hannah opened her mouth to say something when someone knocked on the door. They looked at each other wide-eyed.

"Give me just a sec," he told the person on the other side. He motioned for her to go into the bathroom.

Giggling, she grabbed her stuff and went inside, shutting the door quietly. Sound was muffled through the door, but from what she could gather; Garrett would be going home and was being discharged with some medication and strict orders for rest. When she heard the door to the room open and shut again, she stuck her head out slowly.

"Doctor and nurse are gone, you're safe you little law-breaker," he grinned.

His disposition was decidedly happier now that he was going to be released. He grabbed his clothes and went to the bathroom to change.

"Do you want me to call Jared to come get you?" she asked before he closed the door.

"Yes, let's blow this joint!"

It was blessedly quiet as Hannah lounged with her notebook propped on her knees. She glanced over to the side where Garrett slept. Instead of being on his tour bus, he had taken her offer of coming back to her hotel with her. He needed rest, and they agreed that he could probably get it better with her than he could on a bus full of men. Without a thought, she had re-arranged her schedule to allow both of them to stay at the hotel that night.

In sleep his face was relaxed, and he looked years younger. Faint freckles dotted his nose, and his eyelashes looked incredibly long against his cheeks. She couldn't believe that this was the person she called her boyfriend. The part of her brain that had been hurt when Ashton cheated on her screamed in this instance that she better enjoy it while it lasted because he wouldn't be around for long.

"Shut up," she told that voice in her head. It always seemed to come out in quiet moments, when she least expected it.

Beside her, her phone buzzed and she picked it up, her lip curling when she saw Ashton's name. He hadn't texted her in a year, and it figured he would pick the exact moment she was doubting herself to do it again.

Hope your 'boyfriend' is feeling better. What happened? Did you finally give it up to him, and he was as disappointed as I was? Made him sick to his stomach I'm sure.

Hannah wanted to throw her phone, and it took everything in her not to. Her personality wasn't given to outbursts of anger, but this was one of those times where she wished she could just beat up another person. It would feel so good to bury her fist in Ashton's cheek, maybe cut his lip on his teeth, mess up what he considered a perfect face.

"Hey, you okay?"

She hadn't even noticed that Garrett was awake. "Yeah." She did her best to smile for him, putting her phone on the bedside table.

"Are you sure? You looked like you were about to cry there for a minute."

It was stupid that he was the one sick and now he was worried about her because of something that Ashton had said to her. Story of her life. Pushing her hair behind her ear, she nodded. "Yeah, I'm fine. You feelin' better?"

"I am." He pushed himself up in the bed and held his arms open. "I could really use a hug though."

For some reason, she had the feeling that he knew she needed the hug more than he did. Sinking into his arms felt good. It was nice not to have to go through things alone. The strength with which he held her restored at least some of her equilibrium, some of her faith. Leaning her face against his chest, she listened to the beat of his heart and let it calm down her feelings. It was a steady rhythm that she knew instinctively wouldn't fail her. It was just so hard to let go of all the things that made her vulnerable.

"Thanks," he whispered, kissing her forehead as he buried his face in her hair. "I needed that hug."

"I did too," she told him, her voice thin even to her own ears.

To his credit, he didn't ask her a thing about it. Just got up from the bed and stretched. "I actually feel like I've joined the land of the living. I think it's all the fluids they pumped into me along with the medicine. I'm going to go take a shower if that's cool with you?"

"Sure, that's fine with me. Do you want me to order some room service for you? I have to leave in about an hour to go get ready. If you feel up to it, you could come see how my fans party," she shrugged her shoulder.

The way she said it, so unsure of herself, made him think again that something had happened. That while he was asleep she had started to question everything. Even though he was still feeling bad, he nodded. "I'd love to see your show, as long as you don't call *me* out to sing with you. I don't know that my reputation could take it. They might call me a pussy for singing country."

She frowned. "That's crass."

"That's me, and yes, I would love some room service," he grinned, running into the bathroom, away from her disapproving glare.

The room service had just been delivered when he emerged from the bathroom, steam billowing out behind him as he walked out. Hannah had been getting the food ready, and when she heard the door open, her head snapped up. Garrett stood in front of her wearing nothing but a towel, his tattoos, and a mischievous grin. Rivulets of water made tracks down his bare chest and arms. One in particular caught her attention as it ran from his hairline, down his neck, and onto his chest and abdomen until it disappeared into the towel he had wrapped around his waist.

"Hey, eyes up here," he teased, pointing at his face. "I'm not just some piece of meat you can stand there and ogle. At least let me eat some food and gather just a little bit of strength."

His teasing tone made her smile, but it also made her remember the text that was sitting on her phone from Ashton. When would she let him stop affecting her? Would she ever be able to say just 'f' it and go on with her life? If she was completely honest with herself, Hannah knew that she still couldn't answer that question, but she would give it a shot. The two of them had an extra night that they hadn't counted on, and it didn't matter to her that he had been sick. That text from Ashton showed her that she had something to prove to herself, and if she didn't do it tonight, then she wasn't sure she ever would.

Chapter Eighteen

Hannah was amazing on stage, Garrett decided as he stood in the wings. He had watched a transformation take place the closer they got to show time. Gone was the quiet and demure but fun woman—in her place was a woman who didn't recognize her sexuality as she strutted across the length of the stage. She smiled and flirted with the crowd, waving as she went from one end to the other, shaking her ass at certain times and then at others laying her soul bare. One thing he had never realized was how soulful her voice was. When she was really feeling it, there was a gritty tone, coated in what almost sounded like tears. It was the sexiest thing he had ever heard in his life. Pride flowed through his body as she held the crowd in the palm of her hand. He took pictures with his phone and looked down at them to make sure they weren't blurry, and he almost couldn't recognize the woman in front of him. It wasn't that he hadn't been able to understand why she made the "sexiest woman" lists, but he had always thought she was too "girl next door". Seeing her on stage, she was a fucking sex kitten, and he now knew exactly what other people had witnessed and wondered exactly what the hell Ashton Coleman had been doing wrong.

"She's amazing on stage, isn't she?"

He turned at the sound of Shell's voice. "She is. I hate to say it, but after some of the stuff she told me about herself, I'm surprised."

"Ashton did a number on her self-esteem." She folded her arms across her chest. "It was only recently that she told me exactly what happened. But let me tell you this, over the course of their time together, I watched her completely change. He was…controlling."

That pissed Garrett off. A woman like Hannah needed to be allowed to grow and spread her wings, not be squeezed into a mold and then locked away. "You can bet your ass that's not me," he told her, grinding his back teeth together.

"I know it's not, that's why I'm telling you this. Be patient with her, she's not the normal twenty-four-year-old who's looking to discover herself. She's scared of that."

He didn't need Shell to tell him that, but it was good to know that his initial thoughts weren't that far off the mark. "I want to help her through that. I want to show her that it's okay to be who you are. I'd be the luckiest bastard in the world if I could get her to open up to me."

The smile that broke across Shell's face was so genuine that he had to smile back. "I'm glad to hear that. She's my very best friend in the world, and I can't see her hurt like that again. I didn't think she would ever come out of it."

Garrett put his hand over his heart. "I'm not going to say I won't ever piss her off, because that's not me, but I can tell you that I won't intentionally hurt her."

"I'll hold you to that," Shell told him, putting her hand on his shoulder. "And if you don't live up to that, I'm not like Hannah, I'll cut off you're fucking balls."

He laughed, loudly, until he coughed slightly. "You say the 'f' word too, huh?" he grinned.

"She hates it, but sometimes freakin' doesn't seem to have the same oomph."

"That's the fuckin' truth."

They snickered, sharing in their own private joke.

Hannah stepped out of the shower at the hotel room and debated on what she should wear. For some reason, she felt different tonight. When she had gotten off stage, the look in Garrett's eyes wasn't one she'd seen before. It was almost as if he saw her for the first time.

"You looked beautiful out there," he had whispered in her ear as he grasped her around the waist and lifted her off the ground.

Her face warmed even now at the memory. She would remember the look on his face for the rest of her life. No one had ever looked at her that way before. It was a raw expression, and she thought that maybe it was filled with passion, but she had no experience with that. She didn't want to assume, but she also didn't want get on his nerves by acting so clingy that she pushed him away. It was a slippery slope that women like her navigated—wanting so badly to be different than what she was, but not knowing what being different truly entailed. Blowing out a frustrated breathe, she put on a pair of shorts and a tank top.

"One day," she told herself. "You're going to have to stop being such a fraidy cat."

When she walked out of the bathroom, she realized her mental debate had been for nothing. Probably completely worn out, Garrett was fast asleep. She couldn't help but giggle at the anguish she had caused herself before turning the bedside lamp off and crawling in beside him. Usually it took her hours to wind down, but because of getting up early to go see him, she was tired too. Within minutes, he rolled over and put his arms around her. In those strong arms she fell asleep, grasping his hand with hers. With everything she had, she wished she could fall asleep like this every night.

Hannah was roasting. Kicking the covers off with her legs, she squirmed against the mattress, wondering who in the world had turned the heat up. She fought to open her eyes, but she felt so lethargic.

"C'mon, Hannah," she heard Garrett's deep voice against her ear. "Wake up for me."

She wanted to ask him why, but in that moment, she felt his large hand run over her side, down past her ribs and over her stomach. Once there it moved up to cup her breast. Just like that, she was completely awake and she stiffened against him.

"Tell me to stop if you want to," he told her softly, his voice heavy with sleep. "I couldn't stop myself when I woke up with you plastered against me like this. You were amazing on stage, and now that I know what you're hiding in there, I want to bring it out."

What in the world was he talking about? She wondered what she should do. Should she just tell him to stop, or should she try to go on with this?

"Hannah, you have to tell me what you want," he told her, using the pad of his thumb to rake it across her nipple, kissing the side of her neck when it tightened.

"I don't know what I want," she admitted, swallowing hard against the lump in her throat.

"What are you scared of?" he asked, turning her over so that her back was against the mattress and he was looking down at her.

In her mind, he loomed over her, and it caused her to shrink back against the sheets, trying to make herself smaller. She knew he wouldn't hurt her, but she couldn't take another disappointment. "That I won't be what you want me to be."

"This isn't about what I want, Han, it's about bringing that part of you I see on stage out when you're off stage. I saw you out there tonight and you were amazing."

Tears glinted in her eyes. "I can only be amazing on stage."

"No, that's not what I'm saying. I'm saying it's there, you just have to push past it and get to it." He grasped her chin and tilted it so that she looked into his eyes. "It's there," he put his hand over her heart, "inside you. I get the feeling you've been told that you just aren't that kind of woman, but I'm telling you...what I saw tonight, you are way more than that kind of woman."

She heard what he was saying, but she didn't believe it. "I don't know what you mean," she shook her head. "All I'll do is disappoint you," she whimpered, the wetness falling from her eyes.

"There is absolutely no judgment here. If we don't like it, we keep going until we do. Not every relationship is the same—especially sexual relationships. You have to get to know your partner, you have to figure out what they like, what turns them on. Like with you, the way you bite your lip when you're unsure of something, it gets me hard every time."

Her face burned. No one had ever spoken like that to or about her before. "Please don't say things like that," she told him, shaking her head. She did the one thing that he had just mentioned, more than likely out of habit than anything else. When she did, he groaned and grabbed her hand, bringing it to the front of his shorts.

"Words lie, honey, but bodies do not. I want you." His breath was shaky as her small hand stayed there, even when he released it and moved his to her head, grasping her hair. "Let me show you how amazing it can be. Just give me one night. Forget everything you thought you knew and let me in. I promise you, you won't disappoint me, and you won't have to go to the bathroom and use a vibrator."

Her face really burned at that, and she couldn't help but giggle. "I can't believe you just said that."

He pulled a face. "Tell me you've never done that before." Something about her relationship with Ashton didn't ring right to him, and he knew that she had been just as unsatisfied as the other man.

"I can't," she admitted.

"Give me tonight, what few hours are left of it. Please, give them to me."

"I don't know that I'm ready," she told him, her voice tight as she pressed the words past the lump in her throat.

"I didn't say sex. I said let me show you how amazing being with someone who knows what the fuck they're doing can be."

Should she say yes? Should she give him the power to hurt her that much more? If she gave him this part of her, regardless of if they had sex or not, she would be laying herself bare. Women like her didn't do halfway on anything, and if she did this with him, she would want a commitment.

"I'm not the type of girl that you can do this with and then just not call tomorrow," she explained.

"What?" His eyes narrowed. "You don't think I know that? That's not what this is about. If I wanted to just get off, there's a shower in the other room. I want to get you off, not only tonight, but I'd be fine with every time we're together after this. Doing this isn't a joke for me. I don't take it lightly either."

"You never have?" She didn't quite believe him. It was too good to be true.

"I had a misguided youth, just like the rest of the band did. I'm over that now." He put his hands at her hips and pulled her to him. "I'm in this for however long it lasts, but you can bet your ass I won't be sharing my bed with any other random women. That's not who I am—not anymore. I've grown up. If I'm giving myself to you, it's going to only be to you, and I expect the same from you. You're not the only one who's had to deal with a cheating significant other."

What did she really have to lose? In reality she'd already lost everything. Her self-esteem, her sense of self-worth. "Okay," she grinned. "Show me what you got Reaper."

"Promise me," he demanded, holding her chin so that she looked into his eyes. "Promise me that it's just us."

"It's just us," she told him, throwing her body at his and pressing her lips to his. "Just us."

Chapter Nineteen

Garrett moved up the bed so that he rested with his back against the headboard. Using his strong hands and arms, he lifted her up and over his body, allowing her to straddle him.

"It's just us here," he told her again. "You do what you want to do."

That was the problem, what did she want to do? Never before had she been trusted with a man who did the types of things he did to her. Hell, looking at him now, he caused her stomach to flip and her hands to shake.

"I don't know what I want to do," she admitted. The words caused her face to redden with embarrassment. Who wouldn't know what to do with the man who lay in front of her?

He reached his hand up to the neckline of her tank top and pulled on it lightly. "I know what I want to do."

"Do it." She bit her bottom lip, wanting him to take the reins this time. Hannah didn't want to put a whole lot of thought into it this time. She just wanted him to direct her.

"You have to be okay with this."

"I am, I'm just nervous," she told him.

"No reason to be." His eyebrow quirked before he reached around her body and cupped her back with his hands. He brought her flush with him before moving one hand up to her shoulder and pushing her towards him. The other hand went back to the neckline of her tank top and this time pulled it down, baring one side to his eyes.

Would he like what he saw? He knew they weren't real. Would that make him feel weird about this whole thing? She watched with wide eyes as he dropped his head to her chest, his tongue snaking out to lick the hardened tip of her skin. She hissed, dipping her hips harder on him, grinding her body into his.

The smirk that covered his face showing his dimples was almost her undoing. "Glad to know you weren't one of those poor souls that lost feeling when they had surgery."

She couldn't help the giggle that came from deep within her throat. "I know, right? That would really suck because I like the sensation."

"Wow, you finally admitted something, color me surprised."

Any words to answer his comment were lost in her throat as his mouth returned to the spot he had just left. Digging her fingers into his hair, she held him there, not wanting this to ever end. Ashton had never done anything like this, had never done anything that she enjoyed.

Hannah arched her back, pushing against him as his tongue drew circles around the hard nub of her breast. She pulled lightly on his hair as he used his teeth to nip at the skin there.

"You like that?" he whispered as he pulled away.

Her eyes were clamped shut and she nodded, but that wasn't what he wanted. He wanted her to put voice to the things she needed from him. He wasn't the type to just read someone else's mind. If they were going to do any of this, he needed her to be involved.

"Tell me, Hannah. Tell me if you like it."

She bit her lip, throwing her head back as he kept at it, finding a rhythm to his movements that caused her to widen her legs and sink down further on him. "I do," she whispered.

"You do what?"

"Like what you're doing."

"That's good." She could hear the smile in his voice, could almost imagine the look on his face.

Suddenly she had to touch him; she had to feel his warm, hard skin. Opening her eyes, she ran her hands up against the muscles of his abdomen, pushing the shirt up. He took the hint and let go, reaching behind him to pull the shirt off his body. With her eyes adjusted to the dim light in the room, she could make out the tattoos that crisscrossed his arms and chest. They never failed to make her breath stick in her throat. Hannah didn't want to examine why, they had never turned her on with another man. She had never wanted a man she dated to have them, but everything about Garrett turned her on—including the tattoos. Running her hands up his stomach to this neck, she grasped him there and lifted her body off his slightly, readjusting herself.

He groaned as she adjusted so that his body lay cupped against hers. "You're playing with fire, Hannah. You are a hot piece of ass," he whispered, moving his lips to her neck before pulling the tank top off her body.

His hands were so large and she so small, his fingers almost fit together when they spanned her waist, pulling her closer to him. The fact that he was so much bigger than her made him feel like such a powerful man. It was a heady experience, and he wasn't prepared to give it up.

Moving his mouth back to her neck, he nibbled there, allowing one hand to trail down her stomach to her hips. He knew exactly what *he* wanted to do, but wasn't sure she would be along for the ride. Grabbing her chin, he forced her to look at him as he pulled back from her neck.

"Look at me," he demanded.

She tried to, she really did, but her eyes felt so heavy that they fell shut.

"Look at me, Hannah. Watch me. I want to see your reaction."

She desperately wanted to ask him what he meant by her reaction, but suddenly all the air from her lungs came out in a gasp as the hand that had trailed down her body went to her core and his fingers brushed her underwear to the side. There, he used his middle finger to dip into the wetness there.

"Oh, damn, Hannah," he breathed. "What part of you thinks you're not motherfucking passionate? Holy shit."

The words to answer him were on the tip of her tongue, but he surprised her by inserting that finger into her body, causing her to squirm and moan loudly. She couldn't handle the feelings that were rising up within her body. It had never been like this before, a sudden rush and a fast-paced race to the finish. It was almost scary, the way her body responded to his. Had he been right? Had Ashton just not taken the time to do the things she liked? Was she really not a cold fish?

"It's you," she told him, swallowing roughly.

"No," his tone brooked no argument. "No, it's *you*, Hannah. All I'm doing is playing with what you've given me. It's you. This is all you, baby." He leaned his forehead against hers, moaning as she ground her body against his hand.

His other hand came up to tangle in her hair, pulling slightly so that his lips could capture hers. His tongue coaxed her mouth open, moving in time with the finger at the core to her body.

"Garrett," she groaned, ripping her lips away from his.

"What do you need?" he asked, wanting this to be good for her, wanting her to realize that it wasn't always about the man in her life. "It's okay that you take what you want when you want it with me. Nothing excites me more," he assured her.

"Faster," she whimpered, moving her hips against him.

There it was, the wall she had built around her emotions was starting to come down. He could see it as she grasped his shoulders, throwing her head back again. His hand went to her neck and lifted it up so that he could look at her. She was beautiful. The look that had spread across her face, it was the hottest look he had ever seen in his life, and if he had been any less of a man he would have lost it there. But it would have been worth it for her.

"Open those eyes for me," he told her, his hand picking up speed. He could feel the tightening of her body. "Let me see it."

Her mouth opened, but a sound didn't escape as her fingers dug even deeper into his shoulders and he felt her body let go. Her limbs tightened one last time as she threw herself forward, leaning into his body, her forehead resting against the curve of his neck.

He laughed softly, "You okay?"

A throaty giggle escaped from her, and he felt her breath against his neck. "Oh my God," she whispered.

"That good, huh?" He moved his hand to cup the side of her face, to bring it back so he could see her.

Her face was red, and she couldn't bring herself to look at him. "You could say that." She bit her lip, not sure of what to say to him now, how to act.

"Don't get embarrassed on me now," he told her. "That was fucking hot, and I'm glad it happened with me. Do you believe me now?"

"That it wasn't me? It was Ashton?"

"Yeah. You can't fake that, babe. It either comes or it doesn't, and I'm pretty sure that was you coming."

Her face burned even hotter as she adjusted her hips and came into contact with the one thing that told her he hadn't been lying about any of this.

"Careful there," he laughed, reaching down to readjust himself under her.

She wanted to do something for him, but didn't know how to put it in words. As observant as he was, he saw the distress on her face.

"This wasn't about me, Hannah. This was about you, and I'm a big enough boy that I think I can deal with a hard-on. It'll be fine."

Even that made her heart rate speed up and her face burn even more. "I'm just so out of my element here," she stumbled, trying to get off his lap.

"It's how I talk, huh?"

"Kind of, but really it's the whole thing. I'll have to get used to it," she admitted.

"We have forever, it's going to be fine," he told her again.

He scooted himself back down in the bed, pulling her to him so that her head lay on his chest. The beat of his heart was fast as she snuggled against it, throwing her leg over his. This time, she wanted to be as close to him as she could.

"Thank you," she whispered after they had lain there for a few minutes.

"For what?" He let his lips graze her forehead.

"For being you and for giving me a piece of myself back that I didn't know I had lost."

"It's truly been my pleasure. Next time, it'll be our pleasure," he assured her, wrapping his arms around her. "Now get some sleep, because you have a plane to catch in a few hours, and I have to be on the road to catch up with my bus."

This time when they said their goodbyes it was more emotional for Hannah. Her bus had driven through the night to the next stop, so she was catching a plane to meet up with it. Garrett stood at the terminal with her, waiting for her flight to be called. He had his arms wrapped around her, and she didn't want to let him go.

"I've had a good time with you," she told him softly as they leaned against a wall, both watching as planes landed and took off again.

She was awarded with his dimples, although his eyes were hidden by the sunglasses he wore on his face. "I've had a good time with you too. I'm not sorry I got sick—that's for sure."

"So when will I see you again?" she asked. It was imperative that she know, she wanted to be able to keep this going, and in order to do that, they would have to make seeing each other a priority.

"In two weeks we'll be in California, I think you're around there too?"

"I'll be in Vegas, actually," she told him, mentally going through her itinerary.

"How about you fly over for an afternoon, or I can fly to you. Whatever. I just have to warn you, I'll be with my family."

Meeting the parents. That was something else she and Ashton had never done before, but she found it was something she really wanted to do with Garrett.

"Sounds good," she grinned. "We'll set it up sometime between now and then."

He opened his mouth to say something else to her, but her flight was called. "Well, I guess this is goodbye," he told her, frowning.

"For just a little while." She stood up on her tiptoes, giving him a lingering kiss.

When she pulled away, he put his arms around her, hugging her tight. "I'll FaceTime with you tonight," he promised.

She nodded. This wasn't the end of the world, but she hated this feeling. She didn't want to get on the plane, but she did, turning around when she got almost to the end of the walkway. Garrett still stood in place watching her. He waved and blew her a kiss. Knowing they had no other choice, she did the same before embarking and finding her seat. Sometimes long distance just plain sucked.

Chapter Twenty

"Today has been the absolute longest day of my life," Hannah complained as she lay in her bed on her bus.

Unlike the Black Friday bus, she actually got to have her own bedroom. It was one of the perks of being a solo artist. It made Skyping easier.

"Yeah, how so?" Garrett asked as he scratched his chest. He sat in front of her shirtless, and she thought that was just plain unfair. Since their night in the hotel room, she had become obsessed with his arms and chest, finding herself searching for images of him with no shirt on every time she was bored or online.

She sighed. "Just one of those days, ya know? I had a lot of stuff to do today with not a lot of downtime, but it still felt like it took forever. And I got my first haters."

"Haters? What do you mean?" he asked, his eyebrows scrunching together. "Who could hate you? I happen to think you're pretty awesome."

"Your fans," she told him, pursing her lips. "I got some notifications today from somebody named BlackFriday-

FanGirl on Instagram. Apparently, I'm not good enough for you."

He laughed, rolling his eyes. "I figured I'd get haters from your fans."

"I consider myself lucky that it's not happened before now. And you, buddy, you just wait. I'm sure they're coming."

"That's so true, some fans are batshit crazy." He took a drink of water from a bottle next to him, and she couldn't help but watch his Adam's apple as it moved up and down.

She was officially going crazy. She couldn't stop looking at him, and she could tell by the cocky expression on his face that he had indeed noticed.

"Are you okay?" he asked, amusement lacing his voice.

"Yes. I'm fine," she shook her head. "Anyway, how are you?"

He yawned widely and gazed at her, a lopsided grin showing on his face. "I'm tired, but I really miss you."

She tilted her head to the side and grinned back at him. It had been over a week since they had seen one another. A few more days and they would be seeing each other again. She would definitely be meeting the parents. "Aww, I miss you too. It won't be long until we can see each other again though. Are you sure it's gonna be okay for me to visit while you're visiting family? I hate to mess up their time with you."

"No, Mom is super excited, to be honest with you. You know I told you I brought one other woman on tour with me?"

She nodded, but she hated to hear about that woman. It made her just a tiny bit jealous, and she wasn't too proud to admit it. "Yeah, I remember you talking about her."

"Well, nobody has ever met my mom or dad. So we're moving into uncharted territory here."

She blinked, surprise showing on her face. "You've never introduced a date to your parents?"

"Nope." He let that sink in for just a second. "You're the first."

"Now, I'm nervous," she laughed, moving her hair out of her face.

"No reason to be. It's just my mom and dad."

"Garrett, seriously? Let me just fly my mom and dad out...that way we can all meet them together. How's that?" she deadpanned.

"Fine with me," he shrugged. "It's bound to happen. In a relationship like ours, things just move at different paces."

"Oh my God, you are really okay with this."

He frowned. "Why wouldn't I be? I like you, you like me, we have fun together, we don't bullshit each other, I'm more honest with you than I've ever been with any other woman, you let me see you the way you've never allowed another man to see you. Obviously, whether we want it to be or not, we're venturing into serious territory here. Sometimes that just happens."

"But so quick?" She shook her head, putting her thumb to her mouth and biting on the nail there.

"If you haven't noticed, our lives are pretty fast-paced."

"You are such a smart—"

He cut her off. "Please call me a smartass." The smile on his face was completely genuine, and his eyes twinkled with mischief.

"I was going to say smart aleck," she sniffed.

"One day, I will make that mouth get dirty, you mark my words," his voice growled, low in his throat.

Hannah didn't know what to say to that. For some reason she didn't think that all he meant were curse words. She brushed her hair back from her face. "I'd like to see you try." Had those words just come out of her mouth? That truly wasn't what she had meant to say.

"Oh, I haven't tried yet, baby doll, but give me time. You won't be able to say no when I do try. I promise you that."

He was being serious and she knew it. "I just don't even know what to say to that," she admitted, laughing nervously.

Garrett didn't want to scare her off, so he deliberately steered the conversation to another topic. "So what are your plans tomorrow?"

"I have a concert tomorrow night, and then we're flying into Vegas directly after it."

His eyebrows popped up. "So you're gonna be in Vegas a day earlier than you had originally thought?"

"Yeah, I just found out today. I forgot to tell you that."

"What do you know? We're on our way home right now."

She began to get excited. "Really? You should come out early then. Bring your family."

"Are you sure?" He didn't want to impose; maybe she wanted a day for just herself.

"Very, I can't wait to see you again. Did I mention that I think Shell is asking Jared to come out too?"

"Jared mentioned something the other day. I hope she knows what she's doing with him. Sometimes him and

Vegas don't get along, but whatever will be, will be, I guess."

That worried Hannah, but like he said, Jared and Shell were grown. They, above anyone else, knew what they wanted. "So we have two extra rooms booked, that should be enough for your family right?"

"Oh yeah, and you don't have to do that at all. It's just my mom and dad. I can get them a room."

"I invited you."

"Actually, I invited myself," he laughed. "I'm good at that, but if that's what you want to do, then I appreciate it."

"It is what I want to do," she told him, pulling her leg up against her chest and resting her chin on it.

He cocked his head to the side, and a lazy grin spread across his face. "Are you wearing pants?" He could see bare thigh and that was it.

She looked down at herself. "Shorts, why?"

"Just wondering."

"Are you trying to come on to me over Skype?" she blushed, giggling.

"Maybe," he grinned back at her, ducking his head.

"Are you actually blushing too? Oh my God, Garrett Thompson is blushing!"

His teeth showed white against the dark stubble on his face, his grin was so wide. "I don't even know why, but you got me, I am."

"I feel all powerful and womanly now, I got you to blush."

He opened his mouth to say something when she heard noises in the background. Jared and Brad appeared, waving at her. "Hey Hannah."

"Hey guys, what's going on?"

Jared punched Garrett in the arm before facing the computer. "We're hanging out and watching dude flicks, but this dude," he pointed at Garrett, "is late, so we came to get him from his love session with you."

She snorted. "Love session? Right."

"Considering I heard him ask if you were wearing pants, I'm thinking we made it here just in time," Brad said from behind Garrett.

"Okay, this is over, I'll see you in a day or so," he told her, waving the guys away with his hands.

They were making crude comments, and Brad was thrusting his hips at Garrett's back. She couldn't help but laugh at the spectacle they made. "Yeah, see ya," she got out before he slammed the laptop down. Sometimes she wondered what it would be like to travel with that many close friends, and other times, she was glad that she didn't. Grabbing her remote, she threw herself back on the bed and turned on her Netflix. With any luck she would be able to sleep until they made it to the next venue, and then it was on the way to Vegas.

"Are you as excited as I am?"

Hannah glanced over to her left where Shell sat beside her. Because they had been so excited, they had booked a 2 A.M. flight to Vegas. They were going to get there before everyone else, sleep, and then be awake for when the boys showed up.

"I really am. Vegas usually doesn't do much for me as far as cities go, but I have a feeling that I'm going to experience it much more fully with Garrett. Speaking of, wonder if he's awake?"

"Jared's not, he stopped texting me about an hour ago," Shell pouted.

"So what's the deal with the two of you?" Her friend had not been very forthcoming about what was going on with her and the lead guitarist for Black Friday. To say that she was interested was an understatement.

"He asked me to coffee that one day, I said yes. Ever since then we've been like talk, text, and computer buddies," she shrugged.

"What do you mean talk, text, and computer buddies?"

Shell rolled her eyes. "You remember when we were younger and AOL was the shit and it was the thing to IM people a/s/l, and then sometimes you would luck up and find somebody interesting?"

"That crap never worked for me, ever," Hannah groaned, "but please continue."

"Well, Jared's pretty interesting in that kind of way. He knows a gazillion things that I don't know. He's been a million places that I've never been to, and he's experienced things I've never even thought of. I get the feeling he needs a friend."

"Has he told you about himself?" Hannah asked carefully.

"That he's a drug addict? Yes." She made a face. "But I'm trying not to let it cloud my opinion of him. I know by talking to him that he wants to be in a better place, I'm just not sure he knows how to get there. And he mentioned that Vegas is a test for him, so to tell you that I'm worried is putting it lightly. I just wanna see him though—after talking to him for these past few weeks I feel like I've known him my whole life. That's what I mean by that AOL remark. You know how you thought that person was going to be 'it' for you until the day they stopped logging onto AIM, or you finally met them in person and you realized all they wanted was sex and your whole world ended? That's kinda what I'm expecting from this meeting with Jared. I need to know if he's anything like what I think he is or if I've built him up in my mind."

"All I'm asking is that you go into it with two eyes wide open. It's never easy dealing with someone who doesn't want help," Hannah whispered.

"Just like you didn't?"

"My addiction wasn't drugs," she argued.

"It wasn't, but bulimia could have killed you just as easily if you hadn't gotten help when you did. I helped you, I can help him."

Hannah closed her eyes and wondered if she should say her next words or not. In the end, her conscience won over, and she knew she had to. She had to be honest with this person she considered family because; after all, friends are family. "Please remember that sometimes people don't want to be saved, and if that's the case with Jared, it's not your fault."

"I know that," Shell nodded her head affirmatively.

But in her heart, Hannah knew that Shell cared about everyone way too much to just let things go, and in the end that would be the one thing that could hurt her. Caring so much, when maybe Jared really wouldn't care at all. Shaking the melancholy off, Hannah did her best to smile for her friend before taking a picture of the two of them and uploading it onto Instagram with the caption *Vegas or Bust!*

Chapter Twenty-One

"Do you think the guys are here yet?" Hannah rolled her head to the side and opened her eyes. The two of them had rented a cabana at the hotel and were currently sitting poolside. Even though it was early April, it was a hot 90 degrees in Vegas, and they were going to enjoy it. Shielding her eyes with her hand, she held her phone up. "Garrett texted me about fifteen minutes ago and said they just got to the hotel. I told him where we were and where he could get the keys for his parents. So he's going to come down here when they get settled. He's bringing his mom and dad with him."

"Are you nervous?" Shell took a drink of beer, turning over so that her back faced the sun.

"I'd be lyin' if I said I wasn't," she admitted, taking a sip of her own mixed drink. "I mean, I've talked to his mom on the phone, and we do the social media thing back and forth, but that's different than meeting someone in person. I hope they like me."

"I'm sure they will. You're a great person, and I'm not just saying that because you're my bestie. I'm saying it because you are a good person. They'd be crazy not to like you, but I can see where you're nervous. Hell, I'm nervous about meeting Jared, so I can kind of get where you're coming from."

"Is Jared coming down here with the rest of them?" Hannah asked, excited about the possibility that maybe other people would be meeting each other at the same time.

"He actually just texted me and asked me to meet him at the bar, so I think I'm going to do that. Ya know, give you some time alone with his family. It's important that you make the first impression," she said as she got up and put her cover-up on. "I have every faith that you'll be the amazing woman that you always are."

Hannah wanted to ask Shell to stay, but knew that this was something she had to do on her own. "Oh alright, have fun without me."

"We're meeting up later, and you know it." Shell smacked her in the arm as she got up to leave. "But look alive 'cause here they come, and your boyfriend is attracting a lot of female attention. You need to lock that down." Shell gave her a thumbs up.

"Shut up," Hannah hissed.

"Where are you going?" Garrett asked Shell as they passed each other.

"Meeting Jared at the bar," she admitted. "Figured he might need somebody there with him."

"That's probably about right, but before you go, Shell, these are my parents Marie and Kevin Thompson. Mom and Dad, this is Shell. She's Hannah's best friend and personal assistant, also the girl Jared's been talking about," he grinned, shooting his eyebrows up and down.

"Nice to meet you two," Shell reached out her hand, shaking theirs. "And you, shut it about me and Jared. I don't tease you." She slapped at his arm.

"Yeah, yeah. Are we seeing you for sushi later?" he asked.

"Definitely. Just have Hannah text me what time. My room wasn't ready when we got here, so my stuff is in her room anyway. See y'all later."

Hannah watched the meeting between them wringing her hands together, hoping that this would go well. She desperately needed this to go well. It was at that moment that Garrett turned so that he faced her and saw her for the first time. A grin broke across his face, and he hurried over to where she stood, scooping her up in his arms and twirling her around. She squealed, clasping him around the neck, before he stopped and brought his lips to her ear.

"You look hot in a bikini. I'm glad I get to see it."

"Garrett," she laughed, reaching down with her feet, but he was so much taller than her that she couldn't make them touch the ground. "Put me down."

He did as she asked and stood with his arm around her waist, facing his parents. "Mom and Dad, this is Hannah Stewart. Hannah, this is Marie and Kevin Thompson, even though you and my mom are like Instagram buddies now." He rolled his eyes, pulling a face with his dad.

"It's so good to meet you," Marie said as she opened her arms for Hannah. "Even though I already feel like I know you because we talk a few times a day."

Hannah laughed. "I know. It's nice to put a face with a name though, right?"

"So true, and you are more beautiful in person than you even are in your pictures."

Garrett loved the way Hannah's face turned red. It was nice to hear someone else give her compliments. His mom could hopefully help in convincing her that she really was beautiful.

"Thank you so much." She pulled away from Marie and turned to face Garrett. "She's so sweet. I see where you get it from."

"He does get it from me. He gets his temper from Kevin over here."

Marie pulled Kevin to stand beside them. "She's beautiful, isn't she?"

"She is." He hugged her to him and then looked up at his son. "You didn't tell us how polite she was either."

"One thing you need to know about her." Garrett's large hand cupped around her hip, and he couldn't help the mischievous grin that came to his face. "She hates the word fuck. So be sure and say it as much as possible."

Hannah's mouth twisted in a frown. "You know I absolutely hate that word. Between you and Shell, I'm beginning to think you guys are saying it just to make me mad."

"Nooooo." He put his hand up to his chest. "Never...I mean, would I do that?"

"I think you would," Marie told him, slapping him in the stomach.

"Damn Mom, last time you were cockblocking me, and now you're beating me up."

"She's good at that," Kevin laughed. "Beating up someone, I mean. Not the cockblocking."

Hannah couldn't believe what she was hearing. They were so comfortable with each other. Her family wasn't like this at all, but at the same time, it intrigued her.

"If you don't mind, I'm gonna take your mom out of here to get a drink. Us old folk have never been to Vegas, we'll catch up with you in a few."

The younger couple watched as the older couple waded into the pool and made their way up to the water bar before placing their orders.

"They're cute," she told Garrett, looking at him as he watched his parents.

"They are," he nodded. "Married thirty-five years and counting. A few times I thought that maybe I'd stressed them enough to break up, but I never did. When I get married I want it to be like that."

"Me too," she echoed. That was definitely what she planned on. One and done, she didn't want to be one of these performers who married three to four times before they got it right. She would do it once and that would be it.

He wrapped his strong arms around her again. "God, I missed you." He led her over to the cabana and out of the eyesight of most of the people at the pool. They had a seat so that they could relax.

"I missed you too. I'm so glad that you're here. And we have three days together. Can you believe that?"

Her excitement made him excited about everything that was to come in the next few days. He had never been this ready to spend time with a woman. "I can and I wanted to make sure, I'm staying with you in your room, right? Or are you and Shell bunking together?"

"You're staying with me. It's just us for a few days. How does that sound?"

He turned in his seat and spread his legs, bringing her to stand in front of him. "That sounds pretty damn good," he whispered, tilting his head up as he put his hands in her hair and pushed her lips down to his. "But before we talk about anything else, I gotta get me a taste of those sweet lips."

Those words warmed a place inside her that she didn't know was cold without him. It was like she'd lost a little bit of spark in the weeks since she had last seen him, but she hadn't realized it until she saw him again. This was quickly moving into dangerous territory, but strangely it didn't scare her. It felt like a natural progression. Maybe what he said about them moving along at a different pace because of their lifestyles had some truth to it. She let herself sink into his arms, her mouth melt against his, allowed his tongue to coax hers into his mouth and moaned when he nipped softly at her bottom lip.

"I needed that too," she admitted as she reached up to his face and took his sunglasses off.

"Sometimes I like to see those eyes." They were impossibly green against the backdrop of his face. He had gotten a little bit of sun since the last time she had seen him, and his freckles were much more prominent, causing his eyes to pop. She could just imagine how he would look after three days in this paradise.

"All you gotta do is ask," he told her, his hands caressing her lower back. "I'll give you pretty much anything you ask for, all you gotta do is say the word."

That was power, a lot more power than she had ever had before. The feelings weren't scary, but the power was. Power could hurt, and she hoped with everything that she had, they wouldn't hurt each other.

"So we're having sushi later?" she asked, putting her hands on his shoulders.

"We are." He placed a kiss on her chin. "You need to text Shell and let her know that we're meeting at six. Mom and Dad can't party like they used to." He kissed her nose. "Which is a good thing because I have such plans for partying with you later." He kissed the side of her neck, using his tongue to lick a trail to the juncture where her neck and shoulder met.

She gripped his shoulders. "You do, do you?"

"I do, I can't wait to get you alone. I mean, it's cool and all that you can meet my parents and all our friends can come, but I need some Garrett/Hannah time."

She needed that too. It had happened so quickly, the fact that she ached to have time with him, that she hadn't even noticed it. But he was right; they did need some time alone. There were still things that they hadn't learned about each other that would take time, and that time would need to be between the two of them. They didn't need an audience to move their relationship forward. They needed peace, quiet, and possibly a few mixed drinks.

"I do too," she bit her lip. "After sushi we hit the hotel room with some drinks?"

"Sounds like a plan to me. We can always go out to-morrow night. And I can always tell my parents I have jet lag."

"Do you think they're going to believe you?" She nod-ded her head to where they sat in the water, drinking from plastic cups.

"Probably not, but to be with you, I don't care."

That was one of the things she liked most about him. He didn't mind expressing his feelings to her, and that was something that she needed. Ashton had been such a closed book when it came to how he felt. With Garrett, if his sunglasses were off she could look in his eyes and see what his feelings were. Looking there now, she saw an honesty that hadn't been there before.

"Then I don't care either. After sushi, it's me and you, Garrett Thompson. You better bring your 'A' game," she grinned.

"Babe, my game is always A+...you better bring yours."

Chapter Twenty-Two

Garrett sat on the bed of the hotel room he was sharing with Hannah and watched her put on her makeup. This was different for him out of all the other relationships that he had been in. Even with Vanessa, who had traveled with him, it hadn't been this intimate. He theorized that maybe this time it was because he was older and he could appreciate the little things about being with a woman that he hadn't before.

"Why are you staring at me?" Hannah asked, turning from the mirror where she was sweeping blush across the apples of her cheeks.

"Can I not just look at you?" He grinned.

"I guess so, but it's sort of unnerving." She turned back to face the mirror, using a mascara wand this time to put color on her lashes.

"It's nice, ya know?"

Hannah looked back at him. "What's nice?"

"The fact that you're standing in front of me in just a bra and underwear. I'm enjoying the view."

Flipping the mascara wand up on its end, she put her arms across her stomach. "I'm working on not being embarrassed to be myself in front of you."

"Good," he smiled. "I'm really glad to hear that."

"You're making me feel like a piece of meat, though," she laughed. "Sitting there staring at me like that."

He didn't say anything when she turned back around to finish applying her mascara and then moved to her lip gloss.

"You're pretty patient to be sitting there, watching me do all this."

He watched as she plugged in what he assumed was a curling iron, but it looked a little bit like a wand. "I'm enjoying myself, to be honest with you."

Grabbing up a section of her hair, she turned to face him, hitching her hip out. "Why don't you get ready? Because as soon as I'm done with my hair, all I have to do is put my dress and a jacket on."

"I guess I could," he sighed as he got up off the bed. "Why are we hanging out with the rest of them and not just ourselves tonight again?"

She laughed. "You're crazy. But they are your family, and we do have friends here too."

"I know, it's just…" He couldn't exactly put into words what he wanted to say, but he crowded against her in the bathroom, needing to be near her.

"We just don't get to spend much time together?" she supplied for him.

"Yeah, but I get what you mean. I don't get to spend much time with my family either. I'm just kind of selfish when it comes to you."

"I'm good with that." She leaned up to give him a kiss on the cheek.

He turned his head at the last second and captured her mouth with his lips. "Please tell me this dinner is going to be quick," he whispered against her lips.

"It's sushi." She turned back towards the mirror, meeting his eyes as she lifted her arms over her head to curl one more strand of hair. "Sushi is never quick."

"I know." He rubbed his hands over his face. "You're right, I need to enjoy the time I have with my parents."

She grabbed her perfume and sprayed it on her neck and wrist before turning back around to face him. "It's true. My parents hardly ever get to come out with me, and I'm sure yours miss you. Are you an only child?"

He couldn't believe that they had never talked about that, but it just proved that they did indeed need more time together. "I have a sister, she's younger than me." Even though Hannah was a fan, she wouldn't know that. He purposely kept her name out of the press. Just because he was famous, didn't mean she had to have her life intruded upon.

"Where is she?" Hannah asked as she walked into the bedroom and went to the closet. They had been lucky to get a suite with a living area. And of course, they were going to be there for a few extra days.

"She's in college right now. Stacey's in her senior year. I invited her, but she was worried about getting behind. Graduation is in May, so I can understand it."

"It's weird that we've been talking for such a long time and we haven't gotten into stuff like that. I'm an only child." She wrinkled her nose. "I think that's why Shell and I are so close. She's the sister I never had."

"There are perks to that, trust me. She drove me insane when we were younger. Now I'm pretty proud of her. One of the best things I've been able to do is put her through college. My parents wouldn't have been able to afford it on their own. It's not like I take care of them, they don't really let me because they say I'm the child, they're the parents and they should be the ones taking care of me," he grinned. "But they let me take care of her."

"What do your parents do?" she pulled her dress out of the closet and slipped it over head. It was very spring-like, and she loved the blue and white color of it.

"Mom works for the city and dad works in a factory. They've had the same jobs for about the same amount of time they've been married. I keep bugging them to retire. They could take early retirement next year, but neither one of them really pay any attention to what I tell them they should do."

As he talked, he was also changing, and she frowned when he put on a button down shirt. "Is something on it?" he asked, looking down the front.

"No, I just don't like that it covered up your arms," she admitted.

"This obsession you seem to have with my arms is cute, I like it. Unfortunately, my mom isn't a huge fan of my tattoos. Plus the place we're going is nice, so I'm trying to look nice too. I don't want to look like a piece of shit next to a hot woman, now do I?"

She eyed him up and down. "You look like a lot of things, Garrett Thompson, but a piece of shit ain't one of them."

He grabbed his chest and fell back onto the bed. "You cussed, oh my God."

"I do every once in a while. I just have to really feel strongly about something."

Garrett sat back up and looked her in the eyes, his twinkling. "But you'll never say fuck, right?"

She pursed her lips at him and scrunched her nose together. "It would have to be something very bad to make me say that."

Something about his mood tonight made him test her. He wasn't sure why, but he felt the need to. Sliding his hand up her leg, he cupped her thigh under the hem of her dress. "Or maybe something very good?"

Her mouth went dry, and she used her tongue to lick her lips. As she started to talk, there was a knock at the door.

"Saved by the bell." He stood up and went to answer it, winking at her before he opened the door.

"Y'all ready to go?" Jared asked, standing there with Shell.

"Yeah, but where are my parents?" he asked, grabbing his sunglasses.

"You really think you're gonna need those?" Shell asked. "You do realize it's dark out, right?"

"I'm a rock star, we always need sunglasses."

Hannah laughed from where she stood beside him. It was weird, knowing something about someone that others didn't know. He kept her guessing, but she figured he had contacts in because he'd been able to watch her getting dressed. He apparently liked to keep everybody on their toes.

Jared shared a look with her. Obviously he was in on Garrett's little secret too. "Anyway, your mom and dad are already in the car. Let's get going. I want some sushi, and I'm starving."

"You lead, we'll follow," Garrett told him as he put on his sunglasses and grabbed Hannah's hand.

"Have you guys been here a lot before?" Shell asked as they sat in a round booth at a local sushi bar.

Jared and Garrett looked at each other, both grinning. "Fuck yeah, we love this place. It's a must see when we come to Vegas. We're the only ones who like sushi though," Jared shrugged. "I'm glad you two like it. Now we can actually have other people to talk to."

"It took me a while." Hannah took a sip of the drink sitting in front of her. "But I finally found a few things I liked, and then I ventured out and found I liked other things too. Now, I know how to use chopsticks, and I can properly eat my sushi. I like to think I'm legit," she grinned.

Garrett laughed. "Look how proud she is." He ran his hand along her thigh under the table, and she shifted, sitting closer to him.

"She is," Shell affirmed. "It took her a good year to learn to use chopsticks, and even then it was touch and go. She used children's for a long time."

Hannah threw her napkin at Shell. "Stop telling them all my secrets!"

"Is there going to be a chick fight?" Jared asked, looking between the two of them. "Because I can so get behind that."

Kevin raised his napkin as he took a drink of his beer. "I could also get behind that. I'm not too old to admit it."

Hannah cleared her throat. "Southern women *never* have a chick fight. We settle things a little bit differently."

"Oh yeah, how's that?" Jared asked.

Garrett grinned. "They say 'bless your heart,' which I've learned is Southern debutante for fuck you."

Shell cracked up. "Oh my God, you really *do* catch on quick!"

"Hey, I'm a smart guy."

Just then their food came to the table, and Hannah pulled her phone out of her purse. "Can you take a picture of all of us?" she asked the waiter.

"Oh, that's a good idea," Marie beamed.

The waiter kept motioning for them to get closer together, until every girl sat in the lap of the guy they had accompanied to be able to fit together. Once the picture was taken, Hannah uploaded it to her account and tagged everyone in it.

Having a great sushi dinner with @ReaperBF @ReapersMom @NightTrainBF @SeaShell here in Vegas! Hope to see everybody at the show tomorrow night!

"So do we get to go?" Marie asked from across the table.

"Go where?" Hannah asked, wiping her mouth with a napkin.

"To your concert tomorrow night. Kevin told me to keep my mouth shut about it, but I would like to see you perform."

"Of course!" Hannah answered. "I didn't realize you wanted to come. You can watch from backstage if you want, or you can watch out in the audience. We will find room for you."

"You're going, right Garrett?" Marie asked her son.

"I had planned on it."

"I'm gonna make him come sing with me." Hannah pinched his side.

"That would be amazing. I saw the video of the two of you at his concert on YouTube. I would love to see that in person."

"Well hell, Mom, kick a beat and we'll sing you something right here. I don't have to go out in front of a bunch of people to do that."

"Are you worried?" Hannah couldn't believe that he would ever be worried about anything like that.

"It's not my crowd," he shrugged.

"Yours wasn't mine and it turned out all right," she pointed out. "If you're worried, I won't make you do it, but I might shame you into it."

"Shame me? I can't believe you."

She leaned into his side and put her mouth up to his ear. "If I work hard at it, I usually get what I want."

His eyes darkened to a much deeper green, and he leaned in towards her. "Are you flirting with me?"

"Maybe." Her answer was a bit flippant and her perfume hit him as she moved.

"Then I say, you tell me what you want, and I'll let you know what my terms are."

Biting her lip, she leaned back towards him. "I really do want you to sing a song with me tomorrow night. I wasn't joking about that. I love singing with you."

"Then you do what I tell you to tonight," he whispered in her ear, keeping the smile on his face so that nobody at the table realized what they were saying to each other.

She eyed him. What did he have planned? What was he going to ask her to do? Did she trust him enough just go blindly into this? Swallowing roughly, she nodded. "Okay, I do what you want, you do what I want."

He stuck his pinky out to her. "Deal?"

"We're gonna pinky swear on it?"

"In my experience there's nothing that Southern girls consider more sacred than a pinky swear."

She laughed, throwing her head back. "Then I'll pinky swear, but you have to realize what I'm trusting you with here."

"I think I know exactly what you're trusting me with, and I know exactly what to do with it."

Those words caused her to shiver, but she wasn't sure if it was from fear or excitement.

Chapter Twenty-Three

"So why don't you want to sing with me?"

Garrett's eyes cut over to Hannah. She sat on the couch in the living area of their suite, a glass of Crown and Coke in her hand, her feet and legs in his lap. He too had his own drink, but his was straight Crown. For an hour they'd been here, just talking. Hannah had yet to ask what he would consider a probing question, and she had just come up with a doozy.

"It's not that I don't want to sing with you." He ran his hand through his hair and set it on her leg, rubbing softly. "I just don't want anyone to think differently about you because of me."

She was confused. What did that have to do with anything? "I don't understand what you're saying, Garrett, and it may be because I've had three of these," she shook the glass, "in the last hour, but you're gonna have to explain this to me."

He hadn't realized she'd had so many, but now he did notice that her face was red and she'd shed her jacket. "You may wanna slow down on those," he grinned. "Anyway, your fans and country radio are just so conservative. That's not me at all. What if they decide to not like you because of me? What if radio decides you aren't a good role model anymore because of me? You had that damn magazine bothering you on all the social media outlets. That's because of who I am."

"Wait, wait, wait." She set her drink down and moved her legs back, coming up on her knees, kneeling next to him on the couch. "Don't even think that. If fans are fans, then they're going to be fans no matter what I do. I think I've gotten more fans because of you, if you want me to be completely honest with you. I think 'our' fans, meaning mine and yours, are happy that we're together and that we are happy, period. There's going to be people that hate us, no matter what we do, but I'm not letting them rule my life. If people in the business can't be happy for us, then that's on them, not on us."

He put his hand in her hair, cupping the back of her head. "I just don't want you to have to change for me, and I don't want to have to change for you," he admitted.

This was a new side of him, something he'd never shown to her before. He was nervous about this. He was scared that being with him would hurt her career. "I'm not scared, Garrett," she smiled at him. "I love this journey you're taking me on. Why are you being so self-conscious about this now?"

"You got your first hater and that was one of my fans." He gripped her head in his hand. "I just don't want the batshit crazy ones to ruin something for either of us."

She put her hands on his shoulders and widened her knees so that she had a little bit more leverage. "I'm going to be completely honest with you right now. Are you okay with that?"

"Of course." He turned on the couch, bringing her closer to him. He leaned his back against the arm and pulled her over onto his lap. He wanted to be able to see everything that passed through her eyes and on her face as she talked.

"I let people tell me what to do for the first couple of years of my career and for almost the duration of my relationship with Ashton. When I broke free of Ashton, I broke free of my old management. One thing you don't know about Shell is that not only is she my personal assistant, but she's my manager too. We keep that quiet, people assume I'm under some management company's thumb and I'm not. We have an LLC name for it, and it's only under the worst of circumstances that we even tell people. They assume that they can walk all over me because some company is telling me what to do. I do what I want to do when I want to do it. If I need to be put in my place, Shell does it. Every once in a while, I do have to bow down to what my record company tells me, but I employ a damn good lawyer and I really do make my own decisions. My career and my life are completely mine. That's not to say Shell and I are in this alone, we do have someone that we talk to when we aren't sure if we should do something or not. He's kind of a silent partner in our LLC. If we need a male figurehead, he goes out there for us. What I'm getting at is, I don't let people tell me what to do anymore. So if you think that I'm going to let my fans tell me who to be with, you and they have another thing coming. I've spent too long being unhappy and being alone to let anyone tell me what to do anymore."

He put his hands on her thighs, holding her there. So much honesty and fire came from her eyes that he couldn't help but to lean forward and capture her lips with his. "You're amazing," he whispered as he claimed them again in a slow press to the smooth skin there.

"I'm not," she told him, pulling away and shaking her head. "I let them make me get implants. I stayed in a crappy relationship for way too long, trying to make it work, only to have it backfire in my face. I got sick of it, and I learned to stick up for myself the only way they allow me to. Shell is my rock; she is the only one that gives a crap about me when it comes down to it. Why wouldn't I give her the power? She knows me better than anyone, and trust me, she is paid well for what she does, but looking at the two of us—you would have no idea how much power the two of us really hold in our hands."

"That's pretty fuckin' hot." He ran his hands to her back and pulled her so that the cradle of her thighs cupped his.

Running her hands down his chest, she worked to get the buttons undone. "So now, are you going to come sing with me or not?"

He glanced down to where her small fingers were working the buttons on his shirt, laughing when she got frustrated on the fourth one. "Would you like me to do that for you?"

"My fingers don't want to cooperate with what my brain wants them to do," she admitted, huffing.

With soft hands, he pushed her back away from him slightly before unbuttoning the final buttons on the shirt and pulling it off. "That better?"

She nodded, using the tips of her fingers to trace the tattoos along his arms and chest. He watched as her fingertips traced a demon in a hood riding a horse on his right bicep that dissolved into a scene of smoke and a dragon on his forearm, down to a date on his wrist before clasping their hands together. "It is," she told him. "What does that date mean? July 16th, 1999."

"I graduated high school in 1999—don't make fun of how old I am compared to you—we made a pact as a band that we would do our first tour the summer we graduated. That date is the first show we ever made money on. Granted, it was all of five bucks that we had to split about fifteen different ways because of all the friends we had helping us load our gear and stuff, but we made money."

"So you had a dream and you never looked back?"

"Never did." He tightened the grip of his fingers on hers. "I wanted to, more times than I can count, but I never did. I didn't want to go back home and tell my parents that they were right. So we just kept going."

Her fingers went to his other arm and made the same kind of path there; tracing patterns, stopping when she came to one that was interesting to her. "What did you get this one for?"

He glanced down to where she had stopped, and there mixed in with a fantasy scene was a heart with a sword through the top of it. It was brightly colored, standing out against the black and grays he had along the other parts of his tattoos. "I got that one when Vanessa and I broke up. I was feeling sorry for myself, so I went out and got stupid ass drunk, then I got a tattoo. Really not that smartest thing in the world to do, if I'm being completely honest."

"You cared about her that much? To get a tattoo?"

She felt him flex his arm underneath her hand as he looked at the ink there. "Not really. I made everybody think I did, but I didn't care about her that much. I know that's bad to say, but the only reason I got the tattoo was because I wanted to have a pity party. We were never good together, and the next day I could breathe so much easier, but it seemed like that was the part I should play."

"I'm not following."

"We were together for two years. It would stand to reason that I would be broken up about it, but I wasn't. That was my way of hiding my true feelings. I was relieved. She was something I needed to let go of, but I was too much of a pussy to do it myself. I ended up making her hate me, and that's why it ended badly. We should have been adults about it and let it end the way it should have, but instead we played games with each other."

Hannah wanted to ask him what he meant by all of that, but she got the feeling that he didn't really want to talk about. "What about this one?" she asked, her eyes twinkling. Her fingers were lingering next to his belt buckle, on his lower stomach he had gothic script that read Black Friday.

"I don't think you can see that one, I think you should definitely get rid of my pants so you can see the whole thing."

"Whatever you say," she told him, standing up as he unbuckled his pants and lifted his hips off the couch, leaving him in only a pair of boxer briefs.

"You remember well that I told you at sushi, you do what I want you to, I'll do what you want me to."

"I do remember that," she nodded. He watched as her white teeth sank into her bottom lip, and she waited to see what he told her.

"Did you think I forgot about that?"

Her curls bounced as she shook her head. "No, I didn't think you had forgotten about it at all."

"Good, Hannah, that's real good. What I want for you to do is take off your dress. Can you do that for me?" His voice was impossibly deep; it lulled her into a sense of security, no matter what he was asking her to do.

"Right here?"

"Right here," he confirmed.

Her stomach firmly in her throat, she reached behind her to loosen the zipper on the dress, closing her eyes as it fell to floor. There was no going back now.

Chapter Twenty-Four

Hannah's heart was going to come out of her chest, of that she was sure. Just because she was working on being more comfortable around Garrett, didn't mean that she actually was. With her eyes closed, it was easier to regulate her breathing, to believe he didn't see all the imperfections of body.

"Open your eyes, babe, look at me," he said it softly, not wanting to spook her.

She shook her head, not wanting to see herself in the harsh light of the room. Before dinner when she had been in the bathroom getting dressed, there had been no expectations. Here, in this moment, there were a ton of expectations, and she didn't want to ruin any of them. Never in her life had she wanted something to go so right.

Her hands shaking, she raised her head and opened her eyes. The brown of hers met the green of his, and her breath hitched at the heat she saw there. "Come here." He motioned for her with his finger.

Hannah shuffled her feet, and his deep voice sounded again. "That wasn't a request."

The demanding tone of his voice made her want to listen to him, made her want to do what he told her to. This was a first for her, usually demands made her shrink away and shut down. Instead of wanting to shut down, she wanted to perform for him. Putting one foot in front of the other, she walked over to him.

He pushed up off the arm of the couch and swung his legs over the edge, opening his knees as she came to a stop in front of him. Using his hands, he cupped her around the thighs, smoothing his fingers up so that they caught in the strings of the hipster underwear she wore. When he pulled, she put her hands on his shoulders to brace herself.

"If I take these off, are you going to get shy on me?" He was toying with her, trying to push her, to see how far she would go.

Shaking her head, she let her hair fall in her face, obscuring one side from him. "No, I'm not going to get shy on you," the tremble in her voice belied her words, but he would have to trust her on this.

He flexed his wrists, catching the cloth, and pulled it down her legs. Clasping her thighs shut, she rubbed them together as she watched him. The feel of his rough fingers against her smooth legs caused goose pimples to rise across her skin. Running his hands up to her waist, he pulled her against him. As she stumbled, her legs spread to keep her balance, and he pulled her so that she straddled his waist. His arms went around her body, and she could feel his hands at her back, unhooking her bra. The band tightened and then released, the straps falling to her elbows.

She didn't want to straighten her arms, when they had done this before, it had been dark. Here she was now in the harsh light of a hotel room. What kind of imperfections would he find now? Would she be enough for him? Would the small scars that she did have from the surgery sicken him? They sickened her, and in her mind, she always thought that others saw her the same way she saw herself.

Slowly, he grabbed the cups and pulled them down, revealing the skin underneath. Hannah wanted so badly to take her arm and hold it over herself, she made a move to do just that, but his strong fingers clamped on her wrist.

"Don't. You're beautiful. There's nothing about you that I don't think is beautiful. When are you going to get that?"

She wanted to tell him that she already had it, but at the same time, she realized just how insecure being in the business and being with Ashton had ended up making her. "I'm working on it," she whispered.

"I'll tell you as often as you need, but at some point it has to come through on your end."

Hannah nodded. "I know, and I'm not fishing for compliments, it does give me anxiety."

"I know. You've completely tensed up. There's no reason to. Just take a deep breath and just relax, babe. It's just us here, remember."

She did what he asked. Taking a deep breath, she released it slowly, letting it flow through her. When it did, she opened her eyes, and there she saw his. There was no judgment there, no pity, nothing that made her feel like she was lacking in any kind of way. She realized in that moment that she trusted him. What he told her, she could believe because he had never lied to her, never made her feel like she wasn't everything that he wanted. He was right, she had to trust in him, and she had to take the risk. There was nothing in life without risk, and the only thing holding her back was her own mind.

"I trust you," she told him as she leaned forward and kissed him. For the first time, she really kissed him.

She threw herself into it, not holding back, not worried about him saying it wasn't what he wanted. She put all the feelings into it that she had wanted to since the beginning. Her fingers went to his thick, black hair and twisted, holding his mouth to hers when she would have broken the kiss before. She stumbled as her head swam; his large hands gripped her hips and pulled her against him. He stood with his hands still clamped on her hips, and she squealed as he lifted her, putting her legs around his waist. Ashton hadn't been strong enough to manhandle her, and she realized that she liked it as her body heated up.

"Hang on tight," he told her as he ripped his mouth from hers and buried his lips into her neck, sucking at the skin exposed there.

She did as he instructed as he walked them into the bedroom, almost dropping her when he had to turn to get through the hallway. She giggled, tightening her arms around his neck. He answered her laugh with a deep one of his own. When he made it into the room, he set her down on the bed and stood in front of her. "Lay down."

Scooting back against the covers, Hannah did as he said. The heat in his gaze made her swallow roughly. "What are you gonna do to me?" she asked, her chest rising and falling rapidly with the tension of not knowing exactly what that would be.

"I haven't quite decided yet." He turned off the overhead light before going to the bedside lamp and flicking it on. A soft glow ensconced the room, allowing her to breathe easier. His eyes traveled up and down her body, making passes as he stood in front of her.

"Are you going to get naked?" she asked, licking her lips. The drinks she had consumed over the course of the day making her mouth dry.

"I don't think you're ready for that just yet, but I will." He grabbed her foot and pulled her closer to him. "Right now, I want to get my fill of you."

Immediately, she was grateful for the pedicure she had made time for earlier in the week. That thought caused her to giggle. Did other women think of this kind of stuff when a man like Garrett Thompson stood in front of her, getting ready to devour her body?

"What's so funny?" he asked, running his hand up her leg to her thigh.

"Nothing, it's just me." She really didn't want to tell him what went through her head.

"If you're laughing, then I must not be making this serious enough for you," he whispered darkly.

Before she could even open her mouth again, he stretched himself out along her body. There, she could feel just how serious he was taking this, and it caused all thought to flee her mind, all words to die in her throat. His eyes captured hers for a split second before he leaned down and swirled his tongue around her bare nipple. Moaning deep in her throat, she arched into him while at the same time scrambling with the heels of her feet to move further up the bed. His hands clamped on her hips, holding her there for him, allowing him to manipulate her to his satisfaction.

Hannah opened her eyes, looking down to where he toyed with her. Her fingers dug into his hair again, holding him tightly there. When he used his teeth to nip at the sensitive flesh, all she could do was throw her head back and let him do what he wanted.

Running his hand down her side, he stopped at the indention of her waist and then trailed down to her thigh. There he gripped her flesh and pulled her leg behind his back, opening her body up to him. That same hand went around cupping her ass, pulling her even more tightly against him.

"God, Garrett," she hissed between clenched teeth. This man, somehow, knew every button to push. Where it had taken her what felt like hours to warm up with Ashton, all Garrett had to do was look at her and she was ready to go. The wetness between her thighs was evidence of that.

"I know," he moaned, moving up her body, kissing the side of her neck. "I can't seem to ease into anything with you. One look and I'm gone," he admitted, breathing heavily against the flesh his mouth devoured.

It was nice to hear that she affected him the same way he affected her. This was the first time she'd heard the need in his voice, the control slip. It made her feel good, made her feel powerful, made her want to completely blow his mind. Slipping her hands down his back, she pushed them underneath the cloth still covering him, easing it off his body. He was obviously on board, because he kicked at the offending clothing with his feet, getting them off as quickly as possible.

"I want this, just do it," she begged him, her breath coming in gasps. This had gone from slow and easy to out of control in the space of seconds, but when she made up her mind to do something, she wanted to do it. Right now, she wanted him to make her his in every way possible.

Garrett pulled away from her, letting his heart rate slow down, letting his body slow down. He didn't want to ruin this for either of them. "Hey, we'll be good," he whispered, running his hand down her face.

"Don't treat me like that," she told him, her bottom lip jutting out.

"Like what?"

"Like I won't be able to handle this. I have had sex before." Her body was on fire, and he wasn't quenching it. It was beginning to piss her off.

"I know, but you have to understand, Hannah. Sex with me isn't like sex with Ashton. We do this and I'm not going to be able to let you go. You've wormed your way into every part of my life. This seals the deal." His eyes were impossibly green as she looked up into them.

"Then do it," she pushed at him with her hands. "I want to seal the deal with you. I want to be the woman that you need me to be, but I'll never be able to unless you tell me how you want me."

That was the thing, he wanted everything with her, and he was so afraid of scaring her off that he couldn't be completely honest with her about it. Instead, he cupped her chin and made her look at him. He pushed deeply into her body. The bite of her nails into his shoulders and the tightening of her legs around his waist told him just how good it felt for her. Allowing himself a moment, he committed the look on her face to memory—the way her eyes lowered, the way her mouth opened before digging her teeth into her lip, the way her head tilted back against the sheets. He'd remember that look for the rest of his life. It was only when he knew he had a snapshot in his mind that he allowed himself to bury himself—mind, body, and soul—in her.

Chapter Twenty-Five

Sunlight streamed into the room, bathing it in a soft glow. Glancing to this left, Garrett saw that it was just after seven in the morning. The events of the night before had left him tired, but in a good way. Twice more he had awoken her, and she had answered him each time. It amazed him how perfectly she fit him, how he didn't have the fears with her that he had with other women. Usually after sex, he worried that they would become too clingy, they would expect a commitment that he wasn't ready to give, they would expect to meet his parents and travel with him. With Hannah, it was different, he had already done these things, and there was such contentment in his heart and soul right now. He didn't want to let it go, he didn't want to let her go.

Slowly, he ran his hand up and down Hannah's arm, smiling when she snuggled closer to him. It was humbling how completely she trusted him, especially after what she had endured before him.

"Han," he whispered, running his finger along her nose, before leaning down and kissing her there. "Wake up, babe."

She moved slightly, putting her leg over his and scooting even closer into the warmth of him. "Don't wanna," she mumbled, burying her head into his shoulder.

"C'mon, we only have two more days together," he said near her ear, his morning stubble scratching against her skin.

"But someone kept me up really late last night, and I have to perform tonight," she argued.

"Tough tits, lady. Get that fine ass up," he lightly smacked her on the leg.

He was rewarded as one eye opened. "I'm not the best of morning people," she warned him.

"Really? I would have guessed you were sunshine and rainbows at all hours of the day," he commented dryly, a smile tugging at the corner of his lips.

"It takes me a frappe, and then I'm ready to go. If you call Shell, she'll tell you what kind I like, and you can go get it for me while I take a shower. Then I'll be prepared for the world as a whole," she told him, stumbling to the bathroom.

He thought twice about calling Shell. She was probably still asleep, and what if Jared was with her. Going with his gut, he texted.

I've been informed that Princess isn't fit for public without a frappe and I'm not sure what kind of frappe that is??

He threw the phone down on the bed as he went to grab some clothes. The bathroom door was closed and he didn't hear the shower running, so he took his toothbrush and toothpaste to the kitchen and quickly took care of business. If there was one thing he couldn't stand, it was not brushing his teeth. When he went back to the bedroom, he noticed the bathroom door was now open and he had a message on his phone.

LMAO! She's a tiger in the morning before coffee. Good luck buddy! It's a grande (venti if she's really bad) light caffe vanilla WITH the whipped cream. You might get an extra shot in it too. It just depends on how she is.

With the order on his phone, he walked to the bathroom. "Hey, I'm gonna go get your coffee. Do you want anything else?"

"Some breakfast if you get some. I don't care what, but I'm starving," she shouted over the sound of the water.

Her voice already sounded much more awake. "All right, I'll grab something then. I'll see you in a few minutes."

"Garrett," he heard as he turned out of the bathroom. He turned back around and saw her sticking her head out of the shower, her hair plastered against her head. She looked like a drowned rat, and he couldn't help but laugh.

"Yeah?"

"C'mere." She moved her index finger in a come hither motion.

He stopped in front of her and tilted his head to the side, giving her a grin. "Whatcha want, grouchy?"

She rolled her eyes and leaned in, giving him a quick kiss. "Thank you for my coffee."

"You're welcome, Princess," he laughed.

"Princess?" She wrinkled her nose. "What the crap?"

"You act like a princess in the morning. It's okay though. We all have our little quirks," he told her as he backed away.

She flicked water at his back, causing him to run when it splashed against his arms. "You better run."

As she got out of the shower, Hannah grabbed her phone to see that she had a few texts from Shell and one from Marie. As she read Shell's, her face burned.

> *So please tell me that you're getting some tonight?? Jared is being a gentleman and I think that at least one of us should be having a good time!*

The next one came about thirty minutes after that.

> *No response, I'm assuming there's some bow chicka bow wow goin' on since it's still early and your phone is surgically attached to you.*

A few hours later, there was another.

> *Must have been good if you haven't picked the phone back up yet.*

Hannah snorted, pushing her face into her hands. She loved Shell, but sometimes it was scary how well the other woman knew her. Scrolling through her texts, she came to the one from Marie.

> *If you want, Kevin and I are hitting the pool around 9 this morning. We'd love to spend some time with you guys.*

Maybe we could play tourist until you have to go get ready for your show tonight? Just let me know!

She figured Garrett wouldn't mind if she answered for the both of them. Hitching her towel around her chest, she typed out a reply.

Sounds great! Garrett went to go get coffee and breakfast. We'll be done in just a few. Just let us know where you are and I would love to play tourist! Mind if I invite Shell and Jared??

Throwing her phone on the bed, she went over to her suitcase and grabbed a bikini along with a pair of shorts and the shirt that read Reaper's Girl. She laughed, getting a kick out of it herself. If the soreness between her thighs was any indication, she definitely was his girl. As she put on her bikini, the door to the suite opened, and she heard Garrett throw his stuff on the counter.

"I'm back," he yelled, glancing up as he saw her walking into the living area. "If you could just live in one of those, my life would be made," he grinned, grabbing her around the waist and kissing her cheek.

She blushed. "You'd probably like it better if I was just naked, but your mom texted that she and your dad are at the pool and asked if we wanted to join," she told him as she grabbed her coffee and took a large drink off of it. "That's the good stuff," she sighed.

"You just drank that like an addict getting a hit from a pipe," he told her, raising his eyebrows. "Why weren't you like this before?"

"I'm only like this if I don't get enough sleep, and given the number of times you woke me up last night," she threw him a look, "I really didn't get a whole lot."

A small smile played across his lips as he set out a bowl of fruit for her along with some bagels and cream cheese. He hadn't been exactly sure what she wanted, but he'd seen her eat fruit on several occasions. "You didn't seem to mind it too much, Princess."

She opened the bowl and popped a strawberry in her mouth, chewing thoughtfully. "Didn't say that I minded it, just said I didn't get much sleep. I'm much more awake now though. I just gotta do something with my hair, and then we can head down as long as you're ready."

He nodded, taking a huge bite of the bagel he had spread cream cheese on, chewing slowly, and then he held up a finger. After he swallowed and took a drink from a bottle of orange juice, he answered. "Just gotta change into some swim trunks."

"You probably wanna grab an extra shirt, your mom wants to play tourist before I have to get ready for the show tonight," she told him as she took her bowl of fruit with her to the bedroom and set it on the dresser.

He watched as she took a brush to her hair and pulled it all to the side, then used her fingers to plait it. It was interesting to watch her, he had no idea how women did these types of things. "My hair would be in such a knot," he told her as she secured the end with a hair tie.

"What's funny is if I don't do this, my hair will probably be in a knot."

"I need you to do something for me," he told her as he turned his back to her.

"Okay." She stood there, unsure of what he wanted her to do.

"Be honest, do I have scratches on my back? I don't want my mom to see that. We're open, but seriously, I wanna keep that between us. It's kinda private." He turned his head around so that she could see him. His cheeks were a little pink as he pulled the shirt over his head.

"You're gonna have to bend down, I can't see," she stood on her tip toes as he bent down towards her. "You do, but it's not too bad. I'm so sorry." She bit her thumbnail. "I didn't mean to do that."

"No," he told her. "I'm glad you did. You had a good time, I had a good time, I just don't know that I want my parents to know how much of a good time we had. You get what I'm sayin'?"

"I do and I understand, but won't people question why you're keeping your shirt on?"

"Nah, I'm self-conscious too, ya know?"

"That is the biggest line of bull I have ever heard, but I'll cover for you if you need me too," she laughed, as she put her shirt and shorts on.

She went over to where her bag was and put another pair of shoes in it, along with a brush, some makeup, her wallet, sunscreen, and another shirt just in case. "I'm ready when you are," she told him as she put the bag on her shoulder.

"You mind putting my wallet in there?" he asked as they walked to the living area.

She disposed of her empty bowl of fruit, and he held out his last bite of his bagel to her. Looking at it, she shrugged and then let him shove it in her mouth. "Sure," she told him as she took his wallet and put it in her bag.

"Shell and I still have that cabana rented." She held up the key that would allow them to get into it. "So our stuff should be fine."

"Sounds good, don't forget your coffee." He pointed to her still frosty cup.

"Not on your life, buddy. This venti will get me through the day."

He opened the door for her, holding it open with his back. "And here I thought that I got you through the day."

"Ha! You're thinking way too highly of yourself right now, Garrett Thompson," she teased, pulling her phone out of her bag. It was buzzing at her. She scrolled through her message. "Jared and Shell are downstairs too, and they're hanging out with us today."

"Awesome," he nodded. "Wonder if they had a good time last night."

"Not as good a time as Shell wanted to have apparently," Hannah mumbled under her breath.

"What?" he asked, grabbing her hand. "I didn't quite hear that."

"Apparently Shell was all for a little getting to know you time, and Jared was too busy trying to be a gentleman."

Garrett threw his head back with a laugh. "Oh my God, you just wait until I get him alone. The way I'm going to bust his balls is going to be epic."

"You be nice. Maybe he was trying to impress her and be good."

He leveled his gaze on her, a mocking grin on his face. "Jared Winston is a lot of things, and good has never been one of them. This is going to be great!"

He was still laughing as they hopped the elevator that would take them down to the pool.

Chapter Twenty-Six

"About time y'all made it down here," Shell yelled from her place on a lounge chair in the cabana. Obviously, she too had remembered they still had it.

"We had to eat," Hannah told her as she set their bag on one of the tables and then went over to greet Marie and Kevin.

"Yeah," Garrett grinned down at Jared, speaking a little more softly to him. "Some of us worked up appetites last night."

Shell laughed from where she lay on the lounge chair, shooting Garrett a thumbs-up. "You, sir, are a good man."

Jared hit Garrett on the back. "Asshole," he mumbled, throwing his hands up as Garrett moaned.

"Are you two beating each other up?" Marie asked as she stuck her head around Hannah.

"Mama Thompson, you think I'm gonna beat your baby boy up in front of you?" Jared pulled a face. "Noooo, never."

"You two behave over there." She pointed at the two of them.

"We will," Garrett told her, flipping Jared off before he turned to face his parents.

"Pussy," Jared mumbled under his breath.

Shell laughed at the two of them as she sat up and looked at Hannah. "Come out into the pool with me. There's a lazy river on the other side."

"Anybody wanna come with us?" Hannah asked politely. When they all declined, she shed her clothes and quickly put her sunscreen on before she grabbed her sunglasses. "We'll be back," she told them.

The group waved at them as they made their way out into the general public area of the pool.

"So, how was your night?" Shell asked as they walked towards the entrance of the lazy river.

"I should have known you didn't just want to have a conversation, you were wanting to be nosey."

"Like you wouldn't be if it was me," Shell smirked.

Two people vacated their tubes and handed them to Hannah and Shell. Within minutes, they were floating along on the river. "My night was great," Hannah finally admitted.

"I won't embarrass you by asking for details. Obviously, you're going to remain pretty close lipped about it, but just tell me this. Was it better than with Ashton?"

Hannah snickered. "Ashton who?"

Shell held her hand up for a high five. "That's what I'm talking about. I'm so excited for you. Now you'll understand what other women are talking about when they rave about their sexual experiences. I always felt sorry for you about that."

"I felt a little sorry for myself," Hannah admitted as she took a drink of the coffee she had brought with her.

Turning herself around in her tube, Shell faced Hannah. "I'm just gonna come right out and say how excited and happy I am for you. I really hope this works out for you. You deserve the best, and I've seen a change in you— for the better. You don't look so tense; you seem to be a little more comfortable in your skin. It looks good on you."

"It hasn't taken long has it?" she asked, realizing she and Garrett had only been involved for a little over a month.

"It never does when it only takes one person to bring it out of you. I was just waiting on that person to meet you. I've been hoping for it for a while."

"What the world are you talking about, Shell?" Hannah asked, confusion apparent on her face.

"Ashton took a lot more from you than I think even you realize. You haven't been the same. I love you because you're my best friend, you're the sister I never had, but you got scared. You were no longer that girl who decided to jump before you asked how high. You didn't take those risks anymore that left us laughing and asking how we didn't get arrested. There was no more of that," Shell explained.

"I'm sorry," Hannah started to apologize.

"No, please don't apologize. That's not at all why I'm saying this to you; I'm not trying to make you feel bad at all. All I'm trying to do is to tell you how excited I am to see you coming back. To see that you're still in there and Ashton didn't snuff out the fire that makes you Hannah."

Hannah was quiet for a full minute, and Shell got a sinking feeling in her stomach. Maybe she shouldn't have opened her mouth. It was then that Hannah rubbed her eyes.

"Are you crying? Please don't cry."

Hannah shook her head "I'm crying, but not in the way you think. I'm crying because you are so right. I did lose a piece of myself, and I finally feel like I can breathe again. But right when I feel like I can breathe, I still can't let go of Ashton."

"What the fuck does that mean, Hannah? And you better be honest with me."

"He texted me the other day."

"Erase it. Erase it and block his damn number, do you hear me? He can see that you're happy—hell; anyone looking at you can see that you're happy. He wants to ruin that because he's not happy and because he's not involved with it. I'm telling you, just let him be his normal self and you keep being who you are with Garrett.

"I'll admit, I was worried about Garrett when you first told me about him. I mean, it was cute that you liked him and he liked you. But seeing the two of you together and meeting his family—you've got a keeper, and you've got someone who really likes you for you. Don't let that go. He's the type of man you've been searching for—whether you knew it or not. I'll be damned if I let that sleazy little rat ruin this for you."

"I'll delete it," she told Shell. "I promise."

"Did you tell Garrett?"

"No, I was worried to. Garrett hates Ashton, with a passion. I didn't want to make it any tenser than it already was."

Shell started to say something, but they had floated back around to the beginning, and the rest of their party stood there waiting on them.

"Hey y'all," Shell called out.

"The 'rents want to go walking on the strip, is that good for you two?" Garrett asked as he stepped into the water and helped Hannah put her tube up.

"Sounds good," she smiled up at him.

Something about the tone of her voice didn't sit well with him. "Hey, you okay?" he asked, pushing his sunglasses up so that she could see his eyes.

"I'm great." She reached up and hugged him around the neck.

"You sure?"

"I'm good," she told him again as she grabbed his hand. "We got to catch up with the rest of them."

"Garrett, that looks like you when you were little," Marie pointed to a child running on the opposite side of the road wearing a Pantera t-shirt. It was too big for him, and he was holding it up to keep from getting his legs tripped up.

Garrett laughed, a thoughtful grin covering his face. "Jared too. We were all the time trying to find something that would freak you out more. Remember when we wore the eye liner and black fingernail polish? We were hard-core."

"That was the absolute worst." Marie rolled her eyes, looking at the two women. "Black nail polish is okay for women, I see you're wearing some today." She pointed at both Shell and Hannah. "But when you're son comes home wearing it, along with black eyeliner, you wonder just where in the world you went wrong."

"What did you think, dad?" Garrett asked, letting go of Hannah's hand and slinging his arm around his father's shoulders.

"I was just wondering if I was going to have to bail you out of jail."

The boys all shared a look. "There have been a couple times," Jared smirked.

"What about your parents?" Hannah asked Jared. "Did they ever have to bail you out?"

Jared ducked his head. "My parents weren't exactly...how should I put this...supportive of anything we did. Luckily, these two took me under their wing, and they've been my surrogate parents ever since."

"Look at this face." Marie cupped his chin and kissed Jared on the cheek. "How can you not love him?"

Hannah and Shell exchanged a look. It was obvious there was more to it than what they had said, but neither wanted to press the issue since they were having a great time together.

"Resistance is futile, it's true, you can't help but love him." Garrett cuffed him on the back of the head.

"When did you two start playing music together?" Shell asked. It was a question she had been wondering for a while, but it never seemed to be a good time to bring it up when she and Jared were alone.

"We've known each other since second grade," Garrett told them. "But in eighth grade, I started my first band, and I asked him to play lead guitar for me. You know what this bastard said to me?"

They all waited, knowing it would be good the way the two men smiled at each other. "I told him that I was too good for his damn band. We could be friends, but I didn't think I could lower myself to play with him."

"Ouch," Shell laughed. "That's pretty harsh, even for an eighth grader."

"Yeah, talk about screwing with somebody's self-esteem," Garrett said. "But I'm persistent, and I kept at it until he agreed to play. Best decision this fucker's ever made."

"Is that true?" Hannah asked, side eyeing Jared.

"I guess so," he sighed. "I mean I don't know that I could be touring the world and making hundreds of thousands of dollars with anyone else. So I guess if I have to do it with someone—it might as well be with him and the rest of the group."

"Gee thanks, man."

"Somebody's gotta keep your big-ass head under control."

Hannah interjected. "How did you two put up with these two?" she asked Kevin and Marie.

Kevin slipped his finger into his ear and pulled out a piece of something. "Ear plugs. I wear them a lot when they're all together. I've gotten pretty good at reading lips. So I know when I really need to discreetly take it out and listen."

There was a moment of silence throughout the group before they all busted out laughing.

"Dad, man, what the fuck? How long have you been doing that?"

Kevin grinned. "Long enough."

"I never had any idea, at all. You are one slick badass, I hope I can be like you when I grow up." Jared clapped his hand on Kevin's back. "You need to teach me that trick, it gets annoying listening to Garrett and Hannah on FaceTime at night on the bus."

"Whatever, dude. You just wish you had somebody to FaceTime with." Garrett slung his arm around Hannah's shoulder, hitching his chin up in acknowledgement of Jared's words.

"He does now," Shell piped up.

"Well there ya go then. Now I'm gonna need a pair of those earplugs too."

"Reaper, Harmony!!"

The group stopped and turned to face the person yelling.

"Oh hell," Garrett mumbled as he saw a group of girls running towards them. Some of them wore Harmony Stewart t-shirts, some wore Black Friday t-shirts.

"Hey," Hannah waved at the group. "How are you ladies doin'?" she asked, as they came to a stop, all heaving.

"Good," they answered.

"Where did you all run from?" Garrett asked as they each tried to get their breath.

"From way up there." One of them pointed almost a mile down the road. In the distance, he could see two parents trying to make their way through the crowded streets.

"Are those your parents?" he asked, squinting in the bright sun, even with his sunglasses on.

"Yeah, Mom is gonna kick our asses, but we really wanted to get a picture with the two of you. We like both of you," one of the girls said.

"Don't you ever run away from us like that again," the lady, who they assumed was the mother, screamed as she and the man finally caught up with the girls.

"Sorry, Mom, but do you see who this is?"

The girl wore a Harmony shirt, so Hannah smiled warmly, putting her hand out. "I'm Harmony. I am so sorry they scared you like that. It's not the smartest thing to take off running in Vegas, but I would have done the same thing if my favorite artist was walking down the street, so I can understand."

The woman shook Hannah's hand and then took a good look at Garrett. "I can see why they did," she said on a low breath. "Would you mind if they got pictures with you?"

"Not a problem," Garrett grinned, putting his arms around the two girls with Black Friday shirts on.

Hannah smirked as the girls smiled so wide she thought their cheeks were going to break. He seemed to have that effect on any woman, young or old.

Fifteen minutes later, the girls had autographs, pictures, and a story to tell their friends when they got home. They had even been introduced to Kevin and Marie. Garrett saw the time on his phone and turned to Hannah.

"It's going on three, do you need to go?"

"I should. There's a few things I need to do, and I need to be at the Hard Rock for sound check at five. The show starts at eight, so make sure you're all there on time. I have no opening act."

"We'll be there with bells on, honey," Marie assured her.

Shell and Hannah broke off from the group and went back to the hotel while the rest of them continued on their tourist adventure.

Chapter Twenty-Seven

"**S**he's amazing on stage, isn't she?"

Garrett smiled, not turning away from where he watched Hannah to answer his mom. "She is. I wish we could be the way she is on stage. Her crowd isn't as angry as ours, if that makes sense. I know that has to do with the kind of music that we do, but it would be nice every once in a while if it wasn't so hardcore."

"I can see where you're coming from, but that is who you are. You're passionate and you aren't soft. Your voice is strong and your sound is loud and aggressive. It really wouldn't be you," Marie told him.

"You're so damn smart." Garrett put his arm around her shoulder and hugged her to him. "You wanna take a picture, Momma?"

"I would love to," she beamed at him.

He pulled his phone from his pocket and stuck his arm out, turning them around so that Hannah was in the background. He quickly took the picture, kissing his mom on the cheek, allowing her to hug him just a little bit longer than he normally did. "Love you, Mom."

"Love you too, and I am so glad that you invited me here. I really have missed you," she said with uncharacteristic tears in her eyes. Marie Thompson was a strong woman, and she hardly let anything ever get her down, but the water he saw swimming there hit him in the gut.

"I missed you too, but you've got me for one more day."

"I know, but that doesn't mean that it's enough. I hope you slow down, we're all missing you," she told him wiping at her cheeks.

"I'm planning on it very soon."

She nodded and went over to stand with his dad as they watched Hannah put on her show. Quickly he uploaded his picture to Instagram, tagging his mom and Hannah.

Me and my beautiful mother @ReapersMom watching the equally beautiful @HarmonyStewart kill it tonight here in Vegas.

"Hey, Shell," he yelled as he realized what song Hannah was on.

"Yeah?"

"Did you get that shirt I asked you to?"

She grinned. "I did, let me go grab it for you. She's going to call you out on stage during the next song."

He waited patiently for Shell to come back, and when she did, he shed his shirt and placed the one she had handed him over his body. It fit very tightly. "Does this make me look fat?" he joked, trying to stretch the sleeves so that they didn't cut into his arm muscles.

"That's the biggest we have, and you know all those are feminine cut. You look ridiculous," she giggled. Jared sat next to her, tears streaming down his face as he laughed.

"Do I look that bad?"

"Damn, son. What the hell are you wearing?" Kevin asked as he and Marie got a good look at what was going on.

"It's a Harmony Stewart shirt, but they aren't made for 6'3", 245 pound men," he said as he stretched the bottom of the shirt, hoping that it covered his stomach. A flash in the corner caught his eye. "Oh, tell me you didn't just take a picture of me," Garrett pointed at Shell.

"It's not like all those people out there aren't going to do it once you walk on stage," she reasoned. "Just let me have my fun."

"Y'all want to see my boyfriend Reaper come out here?" they heard Hannah ask the crowd from on stage. When there was an overwhelming scream of affirmation, he plastered a smile on his face, made sure his sunglasses were in place, as well as the hat he normally wore on stage, before making his way out.

"Tell me," Jared said, putting his arm around Shell's neck and pulling her against his side. "Did you purposely get him a smaller shirt? You can be honest."

She bit her lip, shaking with the effort it was taking to hold in her laugh. "I did. It's a large; I can't believe he even got it over his head."

"That was great. He's going to be so pissed when he looks at that tag."

"No he won't," she shook her head. "I removed it."

"You're kinda evil, and I kinda like that," he told her, his mouth close to her ear.

"Thanks," she smiled. "It takes one to know one."

He kissed her temple, and they both turned their attention to what was happening on stage.

"So y'all may have heard or read, or seen in some magazine or online, that I'm dating this guy right here. Who is looking hilarious in a Harmony Stewart shirt," she laughed, bending over at the waist.

"Hey, it takes a real man to wear a Harmony Stewart t-shirt," he said deeply into his mic. "I'm a real man when it comes to this woman," he told the crowd.

They roared in approval. "It sounds like you've won them over." She pointed out to the crowd. "So do you want to sing with me or not?"

"Why you gotta put me on the spot like that?" he teased her.

"I dunno, I seem to remember a bet that was made between the two of us. Your part of that bet was that you have to sing with me." She walked up to him and tilted her head back to look at him.

"I guess you're right. You did do your part, so now I guess it's time for me to do mine. What do you want me to sing?" he asked her, putting an arm around her waist.

"We seem to sing one song pretty well, and my band learned it just for you. Do you think we could do it again?"

"Does this crowd know it?" he asked out to the crowd. It was his song, he wasn't sure that they would know it. They screamed that they did. "Well if you know it, why don't you start it off?" He held his mic out to the crowd, and a large grin broke over his face as they sang the opening line and the band started.

"I think they do know it," Hannah grinned right along with him.

For the first time, he thought that maybe he would fit into her life. Maybe together they would help and not hinder one another.

"I about died when you came out on stage wearing that shirt," Hannah laughed. They sat at the table in their suite, eating room service.

"Tell me the truth. Was that shirt really an extra-large?" Garrett asked as he looked at Shell. "That damn thing about cut the circulation off on my arms."

"They told me it was," she answered vaguely.

"For some reason I don't believe you, but I'll let it go for now." He pointed at her, a mock scowl on his face.

"Did you two like it?" Hannah asked his parents. They were sitting at the table with them, also eating, but the older couple looked tired.

"I don't know how you have so much energy. Just watching you, I feel like I need to go have a nap," Marie told her, taking a bite of her burger.

"I am kind of tired tonight, but it's like when you get on stage, you just feed off the crowd. Heaven forbid your crowd sucks, because then it can be like pulling teeth." She wrinkled her nose. "Those nights aren't fun."

"I can't imagine that you ever have a crowd that's not excited to see you."

Shell and Hannah both laughed, loudly. "You weren't around for her early years. There were many nights that she played to around five people. On more than one occasion, those five people were pervy old men who wanted to know if she would be willing to give them a blow job for a little bit of extra money, and I was only her makeup artist back then. I wasn't even around for everything."

"Are you serious?" Kevin asked. "You were very young."

"She is absolutely telling the truth," Hannah confirmed. "I was nineteen or twenty. It was definitely something that I wasn't used to. It was crazy, because these men could see that we were hungry, that we were riding around in a van. My mom came with me sometimes, but she and my dad own their own business and she was needed at home. I told her that since I was technically an adult, she could let me go on my own. Sometimes that wasn't the best idea, but we made it through."

"It's made you appreciate this a lot more hasn't it?" Garrett asked.

"Oh yeah, I remember when I had to share a hotel room with my band. Now I have my own suite. I'm not gonna forget where I came from. That's for sure."

Garrett's phone buzzed, and he looked at it before laughing loudly. "Stacey's sad," he told them.

"Who's Stacey?" Shell asked.

"My sister," Garrett told her, showing the picture to everybody. She was sitting on what looked like her bed with the picture of Garrett and Marie behind her on her laptop, her bottom lip sticking out in a mock pout.

He connected to FaceTime with the push of a button. "You were invited, you brat." He didn't even start the call with a 'hello', and Hannah had to shake her head.

"Some of us have class," she told him, and Hannah had to do a double take. Their accents were so similar. "Some of us also have overbearing older brothers who bitch if we don't bring home a certain GPA average."

"Hey, if you're gonna do something, you gotta give it all you got, balls to wall and alla that."

"If you haven't noticed, bro, I don't have balls."

"As if you couldn't tell, she gets her mouth from him," Marie put her face in her hands. "He had absolutely way too much influence on her as a child."

"Is that mom?" she asked.

"It is," he turned so that she could see the rest of them. "And we also have Hannah, and her friend Shell, you know Jared, and then there's mom and dad."

"Nice to meet the two of you," she waved. "I so should have come," she sighed.

"We'll come again. You graduate next month," he told her.

"Finals are the first week of May, my last final is Wednesday. If you want to be an absolutely kick-ass brother, you could fly me out Wednesday night."

He arched an eyebrow. "Jared, what we got going on?"

"Our last concert is that Tuesday night. It's the final add-on at the back end of the tour," he told them as he scrolled through his phone.

"Then we'll all come out, how's that?" he asked her.

"Will Hannah be there too?"

Hannah didn't want to speak up because she wasn't sure if that's what Stacey wanted. Maybe she wanted to spend time alone with her older brother.

"Do you want her to be? You have to speak up, sis. Can't read your fuckin' mind."

"I would love to meet her. I definitely want her to come along. Can she?"

"I don't know. Can you, babe?" he asked, turning to look at Hannah.

"The first week?" she confirmed to make sure she had heard the conversation correctly.

"That Tuesday night through Friday, would that be too long? Stace, we'll stay until Sunday if you want, but that's a long time to ask her to stay, especially if she's still touring."

"Sounds good," Stacey answered.

Both Hannah and Shell were looking through agendas on their phone. "Well what the fuck do you know?" Shell grinned, looking up at Hannah.

"Did you really have to say that?"

"I did, her last concert on this leg is that Monday. Then she's off for a full six weeks. How awesome is that?"

"All right, Stace. We're partying big in Vegas in two weeks. Go big or go home. Better get your liver prepared," he grinned, his dimples deepening in his cheeks.

"Shut up, Garrett."

"You better be nice to me or you won't be coming out here at all," he told her.

"Garrett," Marie chastised him from the other side of the table. "She's working hard and she deserves it."

"Thank you, Mom," she heard from the phone.

"Okay, okay, so I'll send you the info that you need. We'll see ya. Love you, Stace."

"Love you too! It was nice to see everybody," she said as he turned his phone and she waved at the group.

After he hung up, he turned to the group, a big smile on his face. "Vegas twice in two months, oh fuck yeah!"

Chapter Twenty-Eight

"**D**o we have to leave here today?" Hannah asked as she lay in bed, her head on Garrett's chest. His hand rubbed against her back, much like it had the morning before.

"Unfortunately. And you have to be gone way earlier than we do. At least I get to spend a little bit of extra time with my parents, but I would love to spend some more time with you," he admitted, kissing her forehead.

"I know, but you heard what Shell said last night. In a mere fourteen days we will have a whole six weeks free. Obviously, I don't think we'll spend that whole six weeks together, but maybe we can spend some of it together. I would love for you to meet my parents, and I would love to see your house in California. Just, you know, do regular couple things."

He sat up in the bed, bringing her with him. "I think we do normal couple things now. I mean, it would be nice to spend the day in bed with you, no clothes on, no place to go. I think that's gonna be the first thing I do with you when we see each other over the long break. Keep your cute ass in bed for one full day. Do everything I've always wanted to do to you," his grin was salacious and it warmed her—to know that he wanted her this much.

"If that's what you want to do, who am I to stop you?"

"Exactly, who are you to stop me?"

"Nobody," she squealed as he tickled her sides so that she moved up his body, trying to get away.

He hauled her over his body and pulled her face so that it nestled in the crook of his neck. He ran his hands over her hair, smoothing it back from her neck and cheeks. Surprised, he felt wetness on his neck. "Hey." He cupped her cheeks and pulled her back from him. "What's wrong?"

"It's stupid," she laughed, scrubbing at her face with her hands.

"No, it's not," he told her, pushing her back so that he could completely see her. "What's got you upset? Please talk to me."

Letting the wall around her emotions slip was the hardest thing she ever did, but something told her she should allow him to see this side of her. "I don't want to leave you," she admitted, her lower lip trembling.

"Oh, babe, I don't wanna leave you either." He hugged her tightly to him.

She gripped his shirt in her hands, and she held on for dear life as she sniffled. "It's stupid, I know the life we lead, and I know this is going to be the way our lives are. I don't know why it's getting to me today," she whispered.

"Because, for me anyway, I feel like these past few days have given us a taste of how our lives could be. How they will be at one point, when we get everything straightened out."

"Exactly," the tremble in her voice was killing him. "I don't want to lose that. Because I feel like if I leave here today, I'm going to lose it, and we won't get it back."

He knew without her having to say the words that this was leftover bullshit from Ashton, and he knew that he would have to deal with it. There were no words that he could say that would make her forget about it. The only thing that would make her forget out about it would be him showing her that this was going to be different.

"Look at me." He pushed her head up with his hands, forcing her eyes to look at him. "We aren't going to lose this. What we're going to do is build on it. Just because we've had a great few days doesn't mean that's all this is going to be. We know we're going to see each other in a few weeks. We can make it, remember, you were just telling me. It's only going to be fourteen days. But you've got to stop crying, you're tearing me apart," he told her, allowing his own walls to come down and moisture to pool in his eyes.

"You're right," she sighed. "You're right. I just gotta get my head around it."

"We'll just keep doing what we've been doing. No relationship with either one of us is going to be easy, and it may be a little bit more difficult because we're both entertainers, but we will make this work. We're the only ones who can make it work. We're also the only ones who can put doubt there about our situation." He kissed her softly on the lips. "I'm in this with you, are you in this with me?"

"I am," her mouth tilted at the corner. "And I know you're right. Together, we can make this work."

"Damn straight."

"Thank you for inviting us out to spend time with all of you," Kevin told them as they stood in front of Hannah's bus.

"You are so welcome, and it was such a pleasure to meet and hang out with the two of you. I can see where Garrett gets all his quirks and amazing qualities from," she told them as she hugged each of them. "Will the two of you be here when we come back?"

"I think Vegas once in six months is enough for us," Marie confessed. "We're getting just a little too old for this."

"Then I will definitely see you when I come to California in a few weeks, and you two will have to come see me in Nashville. It's not Vegas, but it's got its own small town/big city feel. I think the two of you would like it."

"We will, we'll plan something soon." Marie hugged her again. "Thank you for caring about my son, I see it in your eyes. He seems much more settled, even in the short time the two of you have been together."

"You are very welcome, and I think he cares for me too, at least I hope it's not one-sided," she teased.

"It's not, at all. Trust me on that one, pretty girl. It's not one-sided at all."

Hannah laughed and hugged the older woman one more time. Kevin also offered her another hug. She waved at Jared, knowing that she would see him again very soon. The next person on her list was Garrett.

"I'm not gonna cry this time," she did her best to grin.

"I'm going to hold you to that. I can't stand to see that right now," he told her, putting his arms around her and lifting her against him.

"So I'm not saying goodbye, I'm just saying see you when I see you." She reached up, clasping her arms around his neck and burying her hands in his hair.

"Is that how we're going to do it?"

She nodded. "That's how we're going to do it."

"Then I will be seeing you when I see you," he told her, leaning down to give her one last kiss.

He held her in his arms for what felt like hours. But after a while, Shell came off the bus. "We gotta be leaving to stay on schedule, Hannah. Let's go." She touched Hannah's arm lightly and directed her onto the bus.

"See you," she blew a kiss at Garrett.

He waved, a smile on his face, but there were no dimples, which meant the smile wasn't genuine. He was hurting as much as she was, and there was some comfort in that thought as she boarded the bus.

"Sucks, doesn't it?" Shell asked, putting her arms around her friend and putting their heads together.

"It really does, but we'll FaceTime later, and it will be just like it was last week. I just hate that I got used to him, you know?"

"I know, but it'll make those times that you are together that much better," Shell assured her. "You know what they say, absence makes the heart grow fonder."

Hannah nodded, but she didn't want to hear this right now. "I know. I'm tired; it's been a long couple days. I'm going to go lay down for a little while."

"All right, but if you need me, I'm up here."

All Hannah wanted to do was be alone, and she hurried to the back, closing her door. It was quiet back here, and she needed that. She needed to just be alone with her thoughts, alone to absorb all the feelings that had transpired. Taking off her pants and her shirt, she put on a comfortable pair of sweat pants and a t-shirt that she had taken from Garrett's bag without him realizing it. It smelled like him, and she put it up to her nose, inhaling the scent. Slowly, she felt better, felt calmer.

You okay?

The text was just what she needed.

Sad, but I'll be okay. Just want you to know, if you look for your Black Friday shirt you packed, I stole it.
Are you wearing it right now? I didn't wash that thing before I put it in my bag; I meant to wash it at the suite.

She smiled, that's what she loved about it.

I am and I love that it smells just like you. I'm not washing it, jsyk!

Just like that, her mood lifted, and she grabbed her notebook. It was time to journal about her time with Garrett. Her journal was the most important thing in her room on the bus. Journal entries usually turned into songs. She felt like she had so much to say, but when she opened the book and poised her pen to write, she didn't know what she wanted to say at all. After a long time, she just started to write thoughts that came to her head.

There's this guy I met, he challenges everything I've always believed about relationships. He wants me to be myself, but I don't really know what that is. I'm learning it with him, though. I'm learning to be myself. I'm learning that I don't have to change so that others like me. I'm learning that I have a voice and that my voice matters.

I'm learning what it's like care about someone more than you care about yourself. Is this how people know that they're in love? Is this how my parents felt when they first met? Do I love Garrett? I think I do, but I'm so scared, and I don't know what to do about it. I don't want to talk to anyone about it either—it sounds so juvenile. I'm a grown woman. I should know my feelings, I should know how I feel about someone, and I shouldn't question myself. But thanks to Ashton, I think I always might have to think twice about everything. I wish I wasn't like this, I wish I was so much more confident. Maybe I can fake it until I make it????

She set her journal down as she heard her phone buzz. A bright smile on her face, she checked it, only to have her smile fall. Instead of Garrett answering her, it was something from someone she didn't want to hear from.

So now that you and lover boy have parted ways—how can you be so sure he's not having someone else warm his bed? I did…don't forget that.

Hannah wanted to scream as she threw her phone on the bed. There was no doubt in her mind that she would ever forget that. Taking a few deep breaths, she promised herself that she would do her absolute best not to let Ashton take away her happiness, but he was doing an excellent job of making her question everything—like he always did. In the back of her head, she heard Shell telling her to let Garrett know. She would, but not this night. This night, she just wanted to remember all the good times they'd had and try to decide if her feelings really were what she thought they were. In the morning, she could wake up, and tomorrow would be a new day. Granted, it would be a new day without Garrett at her side, but it would mean she was a day closer to being back with him.

Chapter Twenty-Nine

"**D**id you see this?" Shell swirled her laptop around so that Hannah could see what she was talking about.

"What is it?" she asked, putting a chip in her mouth as they sat at the kitchen table on the bus.

"Looks like Ashton is still sticking his nose where it doesn't belong."

Ashton Coleman Breaks His Silence:

How he's moving on from the heartache of his breakup with Harmony Stewart.

"Are you kidding me?" Hannah clicked on the article and began to read. Shell watched as her face got redder the further into it she got.

"Are you gonna be okay?" Shell was beginning to not only wonder but get worried. It took a lot for Hannah to get mad, and it looked like she was working on a good one.

Hannah held up her hand as she finished the article and slammed the lid on the laptop.

"Hey, don't hurt my laptop because it told you what an asshole Ashton is. That's something you should have already known."

"Shut up right now, Shell. I'm furious. Livid." She cut her eyes at her friend, her hands shaking as she gripped the edge of the table.

"I didn't read the article. What did it say?"

She blew out a breath and ran her hand through her hair. "It said I was the one that cheated on him, and it's taken him this long to move on from it, to be able to trust others again. I basically ripped his heart out and stepped on it." She slammed her notebook on the table. "I am so mad that I could spit," she told Shell, getting up.

"We know the truth," Shell tried to console her.

"But he's so full of…he's so full of shit. I'm sick of him. He hasn't bothered me in almost two years. Why is he doing it now?"

Shell's eyes widened. It was very rare to see Hannah this riled up. She usually kept a tight lid on her emotions, especially anger. Something else appeared to be going on here.

"Be honest with me, what's up?"

Hannah sat down, putting her head in her hands. "It's just everything with him is coming to a head. He's texted a few more times, all of them might be small things to other people, but they're huge things to me. Him saying that he's seen pictures of Garrett with other women, when they're obviously pictures he's just taken with fans. I don't understand why I matter. Why now?"

"Because you're happy. He was a controlling dickhead when the two of you were together. He hasn't had to worry about you being with another man since the two of you broke up. You haven't been with anyone else. Not seriously. Unless I'm completely reading all of this wrong, you and Garrett are pretty damn serious. He's feeling threatened."

"But what does he have to be threatened about, that's what I'm confused about. I should mean nothing to him; he means nothing to me."

Shell slowly took a breath. "Please don't get mad at me for saying this, but I have to."

Hannah chewed on her bottom lip, not sure if she wanted to hear the words that were about to come out of Shell's mouth.

"You're naïve when it comes to Ashton. For you, he was just somebody you hung around with—your first real boyfriend—who ended up being an ass. But I'm telling you, for him, you were something. You were a possession. Until you show him that you are no longer a possession, he's going to play with your head."

"It's not like I want to be with him again," Hannah argued. "I want absolutely nothing to do with him."

"I know, but you can't tell me he doesn't probably have a fake Instagram account, Twitter account, and any other account that he can use to follow you. You're very open with your life. It's not too hard for him to keep up with what's going on with you and Garrett."

"I don't want to close my life off to everyone because of him. I enjoy being accessible. I don't want to change because he makes me feel uncomfortable."

"Then don't," Shell was terse with her answer. "But don't expect him to go away either, because he's not going to. I say show Garrett just what exactly Ashton's been sending you and let Garrett fuck shit up, because he will. He will tear Ashton apart. You know this, right?"

"I don't want Garrett getting in trouble because of someone that doesn't matter. Why can't you understand that?"

"Listen to me, Hannah. He does matter. He matters because he's making you question Garrett, when Garrett doesn't deserve it. You need to grow a pair and do something about it. If not, I don't feel sorry for you when this all backfires."

Hannah didn't want to be in the same room as Shell anymore. She hated when they fought and when she couldn't seem to articulate how she was feeling, but she also couldn't stand it when Shell felt like she knew what was best for her. "I'm gonna go back to my room before I say something I regret, but I want you to stop telling me what to do. I'm a grown woman."

"Fine, I'll stop, and I'll be here when this goes south, but stop being blind to how Ashton's manipulating you."

Her feet picked up the pace as she went to her room and slammed the door. It felt good as it rattled the bus, but at the same time she had to wonder. Was Shell right?

If you text me again, I'm going to seek harassment charges on you. Don't text me, call me, or mention my name in the press again. I'm serious.

She fired off the text message to Ashton, feeling better than she had earlier in the day. It made her feel like she was taking charge of something in her life.

This isn't Hannah. Its Shell, isn't it?

Why would he think she couldn't stand up for herself and tell him to leave her alone? Without a second thought, she pressed the FaceTime button. Immediately, he picked up.

"No, it's really me. I'm asking you to leave me alone. Stop texting me."

He smirked, his mouth twisting. "You know that you don't want me to leave you alone. It was good between us."

"I don't know why you're even saying that. The only thing you liked about me was the fact I bowed down to whatever you told me. I did everything you told me to do. You had me under your thumb, and I'm not there anymore. I'm asking you to leave me alone."

"Or what? You're gonna sick *Reaper* on me?"

She hated the way Ashton said Garrett's stage name. He added a shiver for effect and then laughed.

"I'm not scared of him."

"Maybe you should be," she told him, wishing Garrett was with her right now. That he could rip the phone out of her hand and tell Ashton something that would make him shut up.

"You haven't even told him about this have you?"

Her face reddened. "I've told him enough."

He smiled. "You never were a good liar, sweetheart."

"Don't call me that," she frowned.

"Maybe I should tell him myself," Ashton threatened.

"What? You're going to tell him that you're harassing me? Yeah, that's a great plan." She rolled her eyes.

"C'mon Hannah, I'm a lot smarter than that. Give me some damn credit. If I tell him about this, he's gonna think we have something else going on too."

"He won't believe you."

"Oh really? Just like I don't put doubts in your head?"

She was furious again, nothing new where Ashton was concerned. "I'm going to tell you one more time, leave me alone."

"And I'm going to tell you one more time. I haven't even started."

The rage finally overtook her, and she hung up on him, screaming loudly as she threw her phone on the bed.

For just a moment, she allowed herself to let the tears fall. For everything she had lost, for all the anger, for all the fear, for all the sorrow that he had placed on her. More than anything right at this moment, she wanted Garrett here, to tell her that everything would be okay. To tell her that she wasn't crazy, that sometimes things like this happened and you couldn't change them, you could only learn from them. She was sick of giving herself the lessons that other people learned in relationships. Looking at the calendar, she tried to console herself that it would only be seven days until she would be in his arms again.

She needed that more right now than she needed her next breath, but it wasn't meant to be. The lives they led would never make their time together a priority, and for the first time, that made her question whether she wanted to continue her career or not. The thought alone scared her, but it was a legitimate concern.

Grabbing her journal out of its hiding place, she began to write. They had no concert this night, so she figured she would just write herself to sleep. Tonight was one night she felt that she couldn't face Garrett—for the first time ever.

Hannah was having the absolute best dream. It was warm where she was, and she could hear the beating of another heart. The chest felt like Garrett's, and she snuggled closer to it, wanting to stay there forever, needing it after she had written in her journal until her hand hurt, pouring out everything that lay so heavily in her chest.

"Hannah, babe, wake up." That voice sounded so real, so deep.

This was definitely a dream that she didn't want to wake up from. She fought opening her eyes, wanting to stay in this space where it felt as if she floated.

"I'm here, open those eyes and look at me," he whispered.

Did she dare? What if she couldn't get this back? But then again, what if it was real? What if she was missing out on being with him? Taking a chance, she slowly opened one eye.

"Hey." His dimples greeted her when she opened the other eye.

"You're really here?" She put her hands out, feeling of his chest, his hair, sinking her fingers in the warmth of his body.

"I am," he laughed, pulling her to him, holding her tightly against his body. "Surprise."

"This is the best surprise ever. How did you do this?" she asked, kissing his cheek before tangling her legs with his.

"Your stop tomorrow is only an hour and a half away from mine if I take a flight. I needed to see you, especially after I read the article about how Ashton's 'getting over' you."

That was the perfect time for her to tell him about everything that was happening, but she was so excited to see him and to feel his arms around her that she didn't want to ruin it. Hannah knew she should tell him, she did, but she couldn't bring herself to do it.

"I'm glad you're here."

"Do you wanna talk about it?" He cupped her cheek with his hand, his eyes looking deeply into hers.

"I don't know about you, but the last thing I want to do is talk," she whispered, rolling him over so that he lay flat on his back. His eyes widened when she straddled his waist and rocked her body against his. A part of her realized she was doing this for the wrong reasons, but she couldn't face the truth, and she needed to feel close to him. In her mind, there was absolutely nothing in the world that made her feel closer to him than giving her body to him—even if her heart told her she was wrong.

Chapter Thirty

"**I**'m so glad that you came to see me," Hannah smiled as she looked up into Garrett's eyes.

"I'm glad I was able to. We're just going to have to make time whenever we can. This is just me showing you that I'm willing to do that."

She grinned, pushing her cheek against his chest. "Makes me feel pretty special," she admitted.

"You should." He buried his hands in her hair and combed his fingers through the brown length. "There's not a lot of people I would do this for, and I'm not just trying to impress you. When I'm not on tour, I can be a jackass, but there's something about you that makes me want to live on three hours sleep and surprise you for a few hours. Even if it is only for a few hours."

Hannah wanted so badly to tell him about Ashton and what was going on, but at the same time, she didn't want to ruin this. What if Ashton was right and he didn't believe her?

He tilted his head to the side. "What's going on in that head of yours?"

"Nothing," she shook her head.

"If you say so, but I had another reason for surprising you. I was worried about that article that popped up about Ashton. I know that had to hurt your feelings."

He just kept opening the door, allowing her time to tell him everything that was going on. "It did, especially since I know that he's the one who cheated on me and not the other way around."

That pensive look was on her face again, and he couldn't place it, but he got a feeling that she wasn't being completely honest with him. It took him back to a time and place he didn't like to revisit. "If you have something to tell me, please do it. Don't hide things from me or play games. The look you have on your face tells me that something else is going on. Just tell me."

She got up from the bed and put on the shirt that she had stolen from him, hugging her arms around her middle. From her charger, she grabbed her cell phone and put in the lock code. "Here." She handed it to him. "It's all there."

He sat up, a scowl on his face as he saw Ashton's name and the fact that there were texts as well as a FaceTime session that had ended hours before. "What the hell?"

The silence in the tiny room killed her as she started to pace. He was obviously reading and taking in everything that had been said between the two of them in the past couple of weeks. "I'm sorry," she whispered. "I thought I could handle this on my own, but I'm worried about what he may do next."

"Goddamn it, Hannah," he glared at her, his voice hard. "You're not supposed to try and deal with this shit on your own. You're supposed to tell me and let me handle it."

"No, I don't need you to fight my battles for me. I just need you to let me know that you're here."

"Where the fuck else would I be? Where the fuck else have I been?"

"Please don't yell at me." She ran her fingers over her forehead. His anger frightened her, even if it was directed more at her actions than her. "That's not what I need right now."

"What you need is a fucking reality check. This man is harassing you. You even said it yourself…"

"I know what I said," she yelled back at him. "I know what I said, and I know what he's doing, but he's just trying to spook me."

"Which he's obviously done. He's just trying to steal your happiness because he's not a part of it."

"Now you sound like Shell."

"That's because she has a brain in her damn head."

"So what? Now I'm stupid?" she fumed, turning her back to him.

"No, you're not, which is why I don't understand why you don't see this asshole for what he is." He got up and put his pants on, so that he could come face her.

"What am I supposed to be seeing that I'm missing? Why do you think you know him so well? You didn't even know who he was before me."

He ran his hands through his hair, pushing it back from his face and tried to tell himself to calm down with her. She wasn't used to his explosive temper; she wasn't used to the words that sometimes came out before he could control them. She had mentioned that Ashton was a dick physically; he had his own thoughts about what that entailed, so he tried valiantly to keep his temper from flying off the handle. "I don't have to know him. All I have to know is that he's a man. Because let me tell you this, if you left me, my world would be over, and I would walk through fire and over glass to figure out how to get you back. Don't you understand that? You are the type of woman who gets under a man's skin so deep that he can't breathe without knowing that you're going to be there. He felt safe when you had no one because he figured that you were still healing, he figured you didn't have enough self-esteem to try it with someone else. Now that you do, and now that we're together, he's feeling threatened. So he wants to threaten this." He gestured between the two of them.

"But he's not going to," she argued.

"Fuck!" he screamed, pulling at his hair. "He already is. Don't you see that? You were questioning my intentions, what I'm doing when you're not around, if you're enough for me. You weren't doing that before he started sending you these messages."

"That's my own baggage," she screamed, not able to keep the tears out of her voice this time. "That's mine, no one else's."

"But baby," he lowered his voice, his chest heaving. "It's your baggage because of him."

Inside her head, she could see where Garrett was coming from, but that meant that Ashton had once again played her for a fool, and she wasn't ready to admit that to herself again. She turned from him, not wanting to look him in the eyes, not wanting to see his face.

"You could be doing things," she lamely threw out there.

He laughed, but it wasn't heartfelt, it was hollow. "I could be. You have no idea what I could be doing. And I think that's what pisses me the fuck off more than anything. Before you, I could go out, find some bitch in the audience who was gorgeous. Oh my God, would she be gorgeous. She would suck my dick right after coming off stage, stinkin' and sweaty. God as my witness, she'd drop to her knees right there in front of the rest of the band if I asked her to. Any of them would. Then I'd pick another and we could go back to the hotel. I had so much free pussy, I was handing it off to road crew."

"Stop," she whimpered, putting her hands over her ears.

With rough movements, he pulled her hands away, before dropping her wrists when her eyes widened. "But that's the thing. It did nothing for me, here." He pointed to his chest. "It was a hollow pleasure that I didn't even like, but I felt like I had to live up to it. You can ask Jared, the night I met you, the night we took a picture together on the red carpet, that all changed, and I don't know why, but there was something about you that got to me. I haven't even looked at another woman since that night. Do I see them? Fuck yeah, they throw themselves at me every day. Do I take them up on it? Not on your life, because I don't want to lose you. I don't want to lose what I've managed to build here. So the next time you wanna listen to that little pencil-dick motherfucker, think about all that free pussy that you *think* I'm getting and know I gave it up for you."

She felt raw; the things he said to her were hurtful and truthful all at the same time. Pulling herself away from him, she walked until her back hit the wall and then she slid down it, putting her head on her knees. "I don't know what went wrong here," she cried.

"You don't trust me, Hannah, and that's pretty much the end of it."

"No, I do." She threw her hands up in the air.

"No you don't, not where it counts. If you did, then the things that Ashton said to you wouldn't have stayed on your phone, and you would have told me the first time he contacted you."

She knew that he was right. That Shell had told her all along that she needed to include Garrett in all of this, but she had stupidly wanted to take care of things by herself. Asking him for help had, in a backwards way, felt like Ashton making her do something she hadn't wanted to do. He still exerted control, because she really had done what he wanted her to do. She'd hidden things from Garrett and let those things start to come between them. She had played right into his hands.

He started angrily stuffing his clothes into a backpack, not looking at her when he finished. She watched as he put a shirt on and then sat down on the bed to put his shoes on.

"Where are you going?" her voice sounded so small in that room. It was a reminder of how she had sounded her whole relationship with Ashton, and it upset her.

Taking a deep breath, he ran his hands over his jeans. "I need to leave here before I say something I don't mean. My mouth gets me into trouble, and I don't want to be that with you. I don't want to say something just because I'm pissed and then have you hate me for it later. I've done enough of that in my life."

"Where are you going to go?"

He smiled, but it was empty. His dimples didn't even show, not once. "We're on an interstate; there are exits all over the place. I'll have the driver drop me off at one, and I'll make my way to where I need to be tomorrow."

"Is that safe?"

"You don't know how I started out in this business. Trust me, I can take care of myself."

That was the truth; he really could take care of himself. It was another bitter pill for her to swallow. Without Shell she would probably be completely lost.

"Please don't leave here mad at me," she begged. She still sat on the floor, but she couldn't make herself move. She couldn't make her body get up and go to him and apologize.

"I'm not mad at you, Hannah. Truly I'm not," he sighed. "What I am is pissed off at this situation and more than a little bit disappointed. Until you can get over him, you can't be with me."

"I am over him," she insisted. "I am."

"But you're not over the things he said and did. You have to come to grips with that. There's only so much I can help you." He came over and kneeled down next to her. "I'll be here when you figure it out. I'm not going anywhere. I swear on that. Call me tomorrow and we'll talk about this, but I can't talk to you about it anymore tonight. I might ruin everything that we've worked so hard to have."

He opened the door to the bedroom and quietly shut it as tears streamed down her face. A part of her wanted to run to him and beg him to stay, the other part knew that he was at least telling a partial truth. She did need to let Ashton Coleman go in more ways than one. When the bus stopped, she ran to the window and looked through the blinds. They were in the parking lot of a motel, and she saw

Garrett get off the bus, with a hug from Shell. He stood and watched the bus roll away, probably not seeing as Hannah blew him a kiss from the dark back room. As the wheels rolled, her mind rolled too, trying to figure out just how in the world all this had turned around in the span of hours and what she could do to correct it.

Chapter Thirty-One

Hannah gazed at her phone. It was now 6AM, and she had watched the hours tick by since Garrett left. She had seen all of them, and she wondered just what she would have to do to make her eyes close without remembering the look on Garrett's face before he walked out the door. Many times she had open and shut her journal, not able to write about the riotous feelings coursing through her—it was unusual that she couldn't, but not unheard of. Just the fact that she couldn't put her thoughts onto paper told her exactly how much this was affecting her and just how right Garrett had been. Her bottom lip jutted out, and she allowed tears to pool in her eyes once again. Hannah knew what she had to do.

With a super human effort, she got up from where she still sat on the floor and went to the bedroom door. She locked it in case Shell decided that she wanted to come in and talk. What she needed to do at this point, she needed to do alone. Walking over to the closet, she stood on her tiptoes and pulled down a box from the top shelf. She took a deep breath as she pulled her metal trash can over, grabbed a candle and lit it, then sat back down on the floor. Still, she couldn't open that box.

You can't be with me until you let him go.

Those words turned over again and again in her head, like a record skipping on a player. Squaring her shoulders, she opened the box and took a deep breath. Inside this box was her entire relationship with Ashton. As many women do with first loves, she had saved everything—from emails, to birthday cards, to ticket stubs from movies they had gone to see together. Her whole life with him was in this large box. Two years that had gone from one of the happiest times in her life to one of the absolute worst. It was in chronological order; she remembered putting it that way one long night when she was still torn over the break up, but she hadn't read any of this stuff in years.

Lifting a piece of paper out of the box, she noticed the date. The day after they had started calling each other girlfriend and boyfriend. She threw her hair out of her face and began to read.

I'm on the road and you're in the studio. I miss you and wish you were here with me. Just wanted to tell you what a happy man you've made me. Can't wait to see you again!

Those words made her stomach hurt. In the beginning he had been such a nice guy, trying to impress her and letting her know exactly how much she meant to him. They had been the quintessential young entertainment couple. Now, she knew that it wouldn't last—it was never meant to—she realized that. All signs of her heart and mind were telling her that God had put Ashton in her life to make her appreciate Garrett, to get her ready for how her relationship would evolve with Garrett.

Closing her eyes, she picked up the candle and lit the edge of the paper on fire. She threw it in the metal trashcan, and watched as it burned. She had texted Garrett a few times, and he hadn't responded, but she wanted him to know what she was doing. Taking a picture of the burning piece of paper, she posted it on Instagram with a caption.

Purging some old memories so that I can move on with my life and make new ones.

And so it went for the next hour. She saw the disintegration of the love that she had once felt for the other man, the rude, cold, messages that he had sent before their breakup. Tears slid down her face at different intervals until she came to the last piece of paper in the box. This was the one that would hurt and she knew it. An email between the two of them, it started out with her words to him.

Ashton,

I miss you. I'm off the next few days, let's go to someplace warm so that we can sit on the beach and drink those drinks with little umbrellas in them. I feel that there's been a disconnect with us lately, and I need that to change. I don't want to lose what we have. I love you and I'm willing to do whatever it takes to make this work. You let me know where you want to go and I'll make that happen!

Love you!
Hannah

Her mind took her back to that time. She could almost remember what she was wearing. Just before she got his response, she had gotten the text messages and video that proved he was cheating on her. When the email icon had dinged, letting her know she had a new one and she noticed it was from Ashton, she had come very close to deleting it, but something stopped her. She had to read it. Always she was a glutton for punishment.

Hannah,

We can't go someplace to the beach. We can't do anything together anymore. You're too clingy—to the point that I'm embarrassed to be seen with you. There is a disconnect, and it's because I don't feel the same way about you as I used to. Nothing about you turns me on; nothing about you makes me want to make time to see you. I don't really see how we can be together anymore—unless you make some major changes. Which, if you want to be with me, you will make those changes. If you're not willing to be the woman I want you to be, then don't bother responding.

Ashton

The email was so cold, everything that Ashton had ended up being. Try as she might, she couldn't ever imagine Garrett doing something like that to her. If ever there came a time he didn't love her anymore—and she prayed that would never happen—she knew that he was man enough to tell her. He wouldn't string her along for months, letting her believe that things were fine while he was screwing other women and laughing at her behind her back. What happened with Ashton was unfortunate and humiliating, but she finally realized that the man who wrote these emails was a different kind of asshole. Garrett could also be one, but he cared about her, really cared about her. There was no doubt in her mind that he would do whatever it took to make things work. He would never make her feel like a second-class human being because his feelings had changed. Garrett Thompson was a real man, and real men didn't lie about their feelings.

Her throat closed, and she sobbed so loudly that she was afraid Shell could hear. Bringing that last email to the candle, she watched the flames lick the paper, flaring brightly as it caught on fire. When that final flame burned and then puttered out, she tilted her head to the ceiling and tried to breathe. It was easier, so much easier than it had been for years. This box of mementos had been weighing her down in a way she hadn't even realized. The tears dried up and her stomach stopped cramping. The tightness in her chest eased, and she stood on shaky legs.

Hannah went over to the mirror and looked at her face. It was drawn and tight from the lack of sleep and the emotional turmoil that had gone on for the last few hours, but at the same time she saw a relief there, a calmness she hadn't felt in years.

"You no longer have control over me, Ashton Coleman," she spoke out loud. "I will not let you ruin what I have with the most amazing man I've ever met. I'm going to fight for what I want, not to spite you, but because of you."

As she said the words, she believed them. She felt stronger, and she knew what she had to do. Grabbing up her phone, she made phone calls that would ensure the right path for the rest of her life.

Garrett groaned as he saw his mom's name flash across his phone. Usually he would ignore it, but he needed to hear her voice right now.

"Hey," he answered.

"Is everything okay with Hannah?" she asked immediately.

Was she psychic? He had made it back to the bus early in the morning, having not been able to sleep by himself in that hotel room. The guys had been giving him a very wide berth. He hadn't spoken a word to them, but they knew that him not being with Hannah was not good news.

"What do you mean?"

"She posted a weird picture on her Instagram. I tried to call her, but couldn't get her. It's got me worried about the two of you," she gently pried.

He sighed. "We had a fight last night that got way out of hand. Went way farther than it should ever have gone. I'm not sure where we're going to go from here. I said a lot of things I shouldn't have said, and I'm not sure that she'll forgive me. I'm not sure that I can forgive her. It's just complicated."

"That's love, Garrett."

It really was, but he didn't want to put a label on it. "I don't even want to get into it, Mom."

"You do, otherwise you wouldn't have answered my phone call."

She had him there, but he didn't know where to go from here. "I just, I just don't know what to do," he admitted. "I need some guidance right now, Mom. I'm lost."

The pure desperation in his voice tore at her. She wanted to come through the phone and put her arms around him, hold him as tightly as she could, and take away all the pain she heard there. "Give it some time...the two of you will work it out. Sometimes you say things that you don't mean, but that's what a relationship is about. You forgive each other and you work it out."

"I told her I would be here if she wanted to call, but she hasn't done it yet. I'm scared that she isn't going to. I let my temper get the best of me."

"She will. If you didn't get a temper with her, then that means you don't care."

"Then I care a damn lot because I got downright rude. I can't believe the shit that came out of my mouth," he whispered.

"It'll be okay, just believe that. I wish I could make it all better for you. I would if I could, you know that, right?"

"I do," he smiled softly. "Love you, Momma."

"Love you too. It's probably not as bad as you think. If you need me, call me."

"I will."

They hung up, and he put his phone to the side, lying back against the bunk mattress. Closing his eyes, he hoped that things would work out. If they didn't, he wasn't sure what he would do. All he knew was that he would go to a dark place he'd only been to a few times before. The only difference was this time, he wasn't sure he'd be able to come back from it.

For hours he lay there, wondering what was going through Hannah's head, wondering how things could have been different, wishing he could change the way things had gone down. It hadn't been pretty, and he would regret that for a long time, but he couldn't go back and change it now.

His phone finally buzzed at his side, and he picked it up quickly, praying that it was from Hannah. Disappointment and fear caused his stomach to drop as he read the message from Shell.

We can't find Hannah; do you have any idea where she is? Has she tried to contact you?

Chapter Thirty-Two

Hannah was still missing. Those were the only thoughts that seemed to occupy Garrett's mind, had occupied his mind since he'd received the text message from Shell. They were going on hours, and none of them had heard a word from Hannah. Even her parents were worried. She had performed an afternoon concert and then told Shell they needed to stop the bus to grab a snack. She hadn't returned to that bus, and nobody knew where the hell she was. They had even contacted a lawyer to see what they needed to do to file a missing persons report and keep it out of the media, but they had been instructed to let it go at least twenty-four hours.

"You hanging in there?"

Garrett looked up at Jared, who was the only one to even attempt a conversation with him. The rest of the guys had already verbally gotten the shit kicked out of them by their frontman and were leaving him be. "Do I look like I'm hanging in here?"

"I know you're worried."

"I'm going outta my fucking mind," he interrupted Jared. "It's my fault that she's missing. I should have reigned in my mouth before it got too out of control."

Jared had a seat and faced Garrett head on. "Look, I've known you a really long time. I know how you get, but she doesn't. I think maybe she just needs time to process things. This is all new for her. We're new for her. She's never known people like us, Garrett. The two of us—we're passionate motherfuckers about everything, and we expect everybody else to be too. We shoot off when we think we're right, but there's one thing about the both of us. We never intentionally hurt the people we care about."

"But that it's, man, I did. While I was saying all that shit, I knew it was hurtin' her. I could see it in her face. I could see it in her eyes, but I couldn't stop the words from coming out of my mouth. I wanted a reaction. I told Shell I would never intentionally hurt Hannah, and I did it last night. What kind of bastard does that make me?"

Reaching over, Jared clapped him on the shoulder. "One who cares enough to stand up for what he thinks is right."

"When did being right involve making a woman cry? She's never going to want to see me again. I'm totally sure of that." Garrett shook his head, burying his head in his arms.

"I think you're selling Hannah short. I think she needs some time to get her head on straight. Let her do that, and I think you'll be surprised."

"I hope like hell I am, but I'm not holding my breath."

After coming off stage, the first thing Garrett did was check his phone to see if Hannah had been found. The only thing there was another text from Shell that said they were still looking for her. Picking up his phone, he dialed Hannah's number, cursing loudly when it went straight to voicemail.

"Babe, I'm worried. Forget all that shit I said last night, I'm sorry. Call me. For the love of God, please call me, I'm going out of my mind right now. If you can't call me, call somebody else. We're scared to death."

Sitting alone in one of the backstage rooms, he allowed his head to fall back against the couch. The weight was too much for his neck; he felt like it would snap off if he didn't relieve some of the pressure. He knew they had to leave soon, but he didn't want to get any further away from where Hannah had last been seen if he could help it. Just being within a night's distance made him feel closer to her. What he wanted to do was to tell the promoters to fuck themselves, and they would all as a whole just take a loss on the concerts, but he knew that wasn't fair to the fans. If Hannah wasn't found before the next morning, he knew without a doubt though that's what he would do. Sighing didn't seem to help anything, but it also didn't stop him from doing it. A knock sounded on the door, and he wanted to tell the person on the other side to go to hell and leave him alone. But, he reasoned, it might be part of the clean-up crew, and they didn't deserve his anger. When he swung the door open, the person on the other side was the last person he'd expected to find.

"Oh my God, Hannah," he breathed, reaching out and folding her up in his arms. "I've been worried sick about you."

"I know," she nodded, holding her phone up. "I got your messages."

"Where in the fuck have you been?" It was out before he could stop it, but he had been so worried all day, he couldn't help it.

"I know, I worried all of you, but I've just texted Shell and my mom. They know I'm fine. I saw the guys and told them that we would be driving to the next venue on our own. I have a car, so we can get there," she explained.

"What are you doing here?" he asked, once he came to grips that she was standing in front of him. She was okay, something horrible hadn't happened.

"I need to talk to you. I don't know if you want to do it here or some other place. I'm not sure how much time we have here. I do have a hotel room if you want to go back there and have our talk in private. That's where I've been a good portion of the day after I left my bus."

Her mood was different than he had ever seen. She seemed so pensive and so…unsure of the situation. Garrett knew that he was to blame for all of that. "Let's go talk this out someplace private, just in case you decide to scream at me again." He hoped his joke broke the tension and it did. Not enough to make him happy, but enough to satisfy him to a small degree that this just might be okay.

Hannah's palms were sweaty as she let them into the hotel room she had secured for the night. After their previous experience, she was downright scared of what they could do to hurt one another. At the same time, she knew this had to be done. She had to prove to him that she could move on with her life. She had to explain to him and then see if he could move on with her. Hannah wanted that, so badly.

They entered the room, standing there in complete silence. Even on the first night they had spoken with each other, it hadn't been this awkward. She absolutely hated this.

"I need you to listen to me, if you can," she started, her voice small, but strong.

He had a seat on the bed and looked up at her. "I'll listen to you all damn night if that's what you need me to do."

The smile that came to her lips was the first genuine emotion he had seen from her. It gave him hope. "This may take me a while, you have to be patient and hear me out, that's all I'm asking from you. If you decide when I'm done that you don't want to do this relationship anymore, then I'll respect your wishes. It'll hurt like you wouldn't believe, but I'll do what you want."

His mouth wouldn't open to respond. That was the last thing he wanted, but he had promised to hear her out. So hear her out he would.

It took her a long time to start; his eyes followed her as she wandered around the room. Finally she came to a stop in front of the window and opened the curtain, gazing out. When she began to speak, it almost startled him.

"You were right when you accused me of hanging onto Ashton," she admitted, her voice strong and clear. "But I was hanging on in a much different way than what you assumed."

That was it, he wanted to beat something. She still had feelings for this guy, and she was going to give him the kiss off. This was going to hurt like a motherfucker.

"I'm not hung up on Ashton because I still love him. As I realized over my night and long day of no sleep, I'm long over that part of our relationship. I'm not even sure now that I ever really did love him. I feel much more for you than I ever felt for him, but we've not said those words to each other—but right now, that's neither here nor there. What I was hung up on was the hurt."

She turned from the window and walked over to the dresser. Turning to face him, she leaned against it, crossing her arms over her stomach. "That hurt I held in front of me like a shield. It was a coat of armor I could put in place every time another person did something that I didn't like. It was convenient. Someone hurt my feelings? I could blame it on Ashton and the way he left me, the way he hurt me. I've been hiding behind that fear, that hurt, for so long that I didn't even realize it. I didn't realize that even though I've given myself to you, I always expected him to come back. That's why his number was still in my phone, that's why I still had a box of old letters and ticket stubs from our relationship, that's why I constantly think that nobody ever likes me for me. It's been easy to let myself wallow in this pool of self-pity. If you expect to be hurt, then when it happens, it's just something else that someone has done to you that makes you feel like a second-class citizen. You were right in every damn word you said to me, Garrett."

He breathed heavily. He may have been right, and while that did feel good, he had to wonder at what price. What was this affirmation going to cost him in the long run? He didn't want to ask. She had told him to listen, and that was what he intended to do.

"When you left, I took a good, hard look at myself and realized that I am different now. I'm not that same girl that I was a few years ago. I don't need that protection because I know without a shadow of a doubt you aren't going to hurt me. You told me—even though I kind of wish you hadn't—exactly what you've given up to be with me."

He blushed at that. "I really wish that I could keep my mouth shut sometimes."

"Even though it wasn't the most pleasant thing in the world to hear, I needed to hear it. I'm glad you shared it with me. I get so caught up in my own crap that I forget about other people, and that's not the way I need to live my life. I need to live it happy, not worried about what other people are going to say about the things I do. That's something I got from him. His presence is a skin that I need to shed. I started that this morning. I burned everything he ever gave me. I allowed myself to cry over it and have a pity party for what I once thought was the most important decision of my life. Then I called my cell phone carrier and blocked his number. I also spoke with my lawyer about getting harassment papers drawn up just in case. There are still a few things he could do to hurt me, but if he does, I'll be ready."

This woman standing in front of him was amazing. "If he does anything else, I can't guarantee you that I won't kick his ass," he warned.

"At this point, I'm thinking he deserves it. But what I'm trying to tell you is that I am ready. I can be with you. I want to be with you. I hope you haven't given up on me," she swallowed roughly, for the first time emotion clogging her throat.

He stood up and walked over to her, putting one arm around her waist and pulling her to him. The other arm went around her neck. "God, no. I thought my mouth and my temper had lost you. I'm sorry for the things I said. I never meant for all that to happen, but if it brought us here, then I'm glad it did."

"I'm glad it did too." She threw her arms around him then, holding on for dear life.

They stayed that way for long moments, him breathing in the scent that he had learned to associate with her. Her fingers dug into his shirt, clinging roughly. Finally she pulled her head back. "Can you do something for me?"

"I'll do any damn thing you want me to, you just have to ask."

"After you go take a shower, because you stink, can we go to sleep? I'm so tired. I haven't slept in almost a full twenty-four hours."

He chuckled. "Yeah, that can be arranged. Right now, I need to sleep too, but it's not going to happen without you in my arms."

That was exactly where she wanted to be.

Chapter Thirty-Three

Garrett awoke to Hannah loudly whispering on her phone.

"Shell, I understand that you're upset." He watched as she held the phone away from her ear and he could hear Shell's voice from the other end.

"I was worried out of my fucking mind. You got off the bus to get a snack, a damn snack, and then we couldn't find you. Do you realize every scenario that played through my head? You're famous and people want you. I thought someone had abducted you!"

Hannah breathed slowly. "I needed to get away, Shell," she said patiently.

"Take your needing to get away and shove it up your ass. I'm furious right now, and I've never known you to be this selfish—ever. Don't call me—I'll see you tonight. I have a huge mess to clean up!"

Hannah looked at the phone as the call disconnected.

"She's pissed I take it?" Garrett asked, sitting up in the bed.

"I think that would be an understatement. Apparently everyone is. My mom is furious, and you of course just heard Shell. I have to figure out how I'm going to fix this."

"She's right you know," he gently told her as he came over and had a seat next to her.

"You think so?" she was honestly asking him.

He got the feeling that she had never done anything like this before. She had never really been selfish with her time and her feelings. Good girl Hannah had always done what was expected of her and what she was told. "Yeah, I do. You have no idea how freaked out we all were. I'm right there with her. I thought maybe someone had abducted you too there for a while. After that picture you put on Instagram, I worried that maybe you were going to hurt yourself. You do have a lot of work to do to clean this up. What are you going to do? You need to make it right. I think your Mom will understand if you just explain it to her."

"I needed some time to myself." She ran her hand through her hair.

"And while I understand that because I live this life, I've needed the same thing. Not everybody does, not everybody has. As the person who brings in the money, you have to take care of the people that take care of you. Don't disappoint me here, babe. Make this right."

"I don't even know where to start. I've never had to apologize for anything before. I've always done what people asked of me."

He laughed and pulled her over in his lap. "Lucky for you, I have a shit-ton of experience when it comes to groveling. On the drive, we'll figure something out." A thought hit him. "By the way, how are you getting to your own show?"

"I'm going to have you just drop me off at the airport. I have a ticket that should get me there a few hours before."

He kissed her on the neck and squeezed her tightly around the waist. "Things are going to be fine; you just gotta work it all out. Instead of letting Shell do everything this time, you're going to have to do it for her."

Hannah knew that he was right. It was time to grow up and be an adult and to take control of the consequences of her actions. Everybody made mistakes; it was how they came back from those mistakes that truly mattered.

Shell felt like she was going to kill someone. Her phone was ringing off the hook, and she kept pushing everyone to voice mail. She was tired, so tired. Worrying about her best friend had taken a toll on her, and then the anger that had rushed through her body as she realized that Hannah was indeed okay had given way to a bone-deep fatigue. Sighing as her phone rang again, she saw Jared's name. This one she accepted.

"How are you holding up?" he asked.

"I'm so tired, and I'm so upset with her. How could she do this to everybody?"

He was quiet for a beat, and she wondered if he was still on the line with her. She was about to ask when his voice sounded again over the line. "I'm not saying that what she did was right. Lord knows I'm not the type of person who should throw stones, but I'm going to tell you where I come from. I think maybe she was coming from the same place. Sometimes in this life, people—meaning fans and even your best friends—they look at you and they think you have this amazing life. That you have it all completely together and there's nothing that you could want for."

She gave him the respect of really listening to him and trying to put herself in his shoes. She wanted to understand this. The absolute last thing she wanted to do was be mad at Hannah. In all the years they had been friends, they had never let anger separate them. Never. As women that was saying something.

"I'm here to tell you that's not the case," he told her. "With the life we lead, you don't get any time by yourself."

"She's in hotel rooms by herself all the time," Shell argued.

"That's not what I mean," he interrupted her. "When you are on the road, you're 'on' all the time. You're that person that the fans expect you to be. You're the person the people you work with expect you to be. Sometimes that's not you, and you become a caricature of yourself. You lose yourself in everything you're supposed to be, and you have to take time to recalibrate your life. Sometimes you need to be away from yourself."

"Is that why you do what you do? The drugs?" she asked quietly.

"When you're as creative as we are, that place within yourself can sometimes be very dark. I'm not expecting you to understand it, but I'm asking you to give her a break. She didn't do this to hurt you; I can assure you of that. She did this because she needed it for her. If she's not selfish for herself, no one else is going to be."

"That doesn't make it right," she argued.

"I'm not saying that it does, but I'm just trying to give a different perspective from someone who's been there. If she needs a day to herself to figure her shit the fuck out, give it to her. Don't let her get so messed up that she does the things I do."

Shell swallowed roughly against the lump in her throat. That was the last thing she wanted. "But I need her to tell me when she needs that."

"Then explain that to her," Jared told her. "Nobody said that to me until it was too late, and I still can't shake my demons."

That was a problem and she knew it, but she could only deal with one at a time. "Okay, I will try to cut her some slack and be polite about this, but I have to warn you, I'm pissed as fuck."

"You wouldn't be her best friend if you weren't."

They hung up a while later, and Shell sat there, still stewing when she saw an email alert on her phone. She opened it and her mouth hung open. Hannah had purchased a three-night vacation stay in Cozumel for Shell and a guest, to be used over their break. Along with it was a note.

I'm a brat, thanks for loving me! If I feel like I need a vacation, then I know you most definitely do. Have fun and I love you!

Shell couldn't help but smile. Hannah was trying to do the right thing.

"On a scale of one to ten, how mad are you at me?" Shell heard her before she saw her. Shell was sitting in the backstage area of their venue for the night, waiting for Hannah to show up. She was relieved to realize Hannah had made it there with plenty of time to spare.

"Yesterday afternoon and last night a fucking twenty, but since talking to Jared, I'm at a firm seven."

"That's better than I thought it would be."

Hannah walked in carefully, not sure of what Shell would say to her, and had a seat across from her. "I'm sorry that I worried you. I want you to know that."

"I appreciate that, and I'm sorry that you felt like you had to leave here without telling anyone. For that I will take responsibility. I would have talked you out of it and probably have made you feel worse. As hard as it is for me to admit this, I sometimes think more as your manager than your friend in situations like that. It's good, but it's bad at the same time. I'll take responsibility for the fact that we should communicate better."

"And I'll take responsibility for the fact that I shouldn't have done it without letting someone know beforehand. I was selfish, and I can't be that way anymore. I have too many people counting on me." She bit her lip and pressed on. "I just felt so stifled, and it was such a strong feeling, I had to get away. I had to be able to breathe, and I just felt suffocated."

"Next time you feel that way, you let me know. It's my job to make sure your mental health is as good as your physical health, and you can thank Jared for reminding me of that. It would kill me if you did the things he does, because it's preventable."

"It is, and I don't ever want to be like that. To be honest with you, I was in a very dark place. I don't ever want to be there again. I'm going to work on my own self-esteem issues and make myself into the person that I should be, not the person that I let Ashton make me think I was."

It had never occurred to Shell before this moment that Hannah was exhibiting signs of abuse. Not only the physical kind that showed on her arms in the form of bruises, but the mental kind that made her question every rational thought she had. It never should have gone that far, and she would make sure that from now on, they were all taken care of. Shell threw her arms around her friend, so glad that she was back and that she appeared to be no worse for wear. That had been one of her major fears when she had discovered Hannah missing. In their business, in their world, it could mean bad things. Someone could have hurt her, she could have had a mental break, and suicide had even flashed through her mind. It hadn't been pretty as she had sat up all night with every scenario running through her head.

"You, my friend, are gorgeous, and you're a great person. You may make some bad decisions, and you may have made them in the past. But like you said, don't let those dictate your future."

Hannah breathed a huge sigh of relief. "I just hope the fans come out for the free show as my apology."

"I'm sure they will. It's going to be a busy couple of days. That free day we had no longer exists, but if we can make it through the next four days then we've all got six weeks."

"Speaking of," Shell grinned. "Thank you for the vacation."

"Take Jared and have a good time. You deserve it. I'm putting a bit of extra money in everyone's bonus that we're handing out today for the trouble too."

"That's good." They had been just as worried as Shell, but she didn't want to bring that up again. Looking at Hannah, she could tell this had all taken a toll.

"Do you think the fans truly believe what Ashton said," Hannah asked softly.

She shrugged. "You never know with fans. There are those that will believe anything that is written in any magazine. All we have to do is what's best for you and what you think is best for them. I think the free show will go a long way in offering some goodwill to them. You kill it tonight and you do that. Next week they will have forgotten it."

"You're right. I'm learning," she frowned.

"You are, and it's not easy, but we'll all come through everything on the other side together. I'm not going to lie and tell you that I'm not still just a little bit pissed, but I accept your apology, and I do understand why you did it."

Hannah hugged her friend tightly. "I'm really thankful to have people like you in my life. I'm truly sorry that I caused so much worry."

"I know, now just go out there and kick some ass and let's get these four days over with so that we can have some time off. I don't know about you, but I'm ready for Vegas, and then I'm ready to put my toes in the water, ass in the sand for a few days."

Hannah laughed as she went over to hair and makeup. Everything would be just fine, no matter what happened or came up, things would be okay. If there was an important lesson to be learned from all of this, that was it.

Chapter Thirty-Four

"You excited?"

Hannah smiled widely. She was FaceTiming with Garrett, and they had mere hours to go before they saw one another.

"I am, but I'm also really, really tired. We had an unplanned radio show. I'm definitely sleeping on the way to Vegas."

He scratched his cheek. "I didn't know you had a radio show."

"Yeah, it was tacked on at the very last minute. I was so happy to be getting to the end of everything that I just told Shell to say yes, and we just did it," she yawned as she leaned back against her pillows.

"I miss you," he told her, his eyes shining. He, the band, and his sister had arrived in Vegas the day before.

"I'll be seeing you tomorrow afternoon," she assured him. "I wish I could have come up today, but we have to close out everything with the tour. Since Shell and I are the management team, it requires both of us. Besides, I'm sure you're having fun with your sister."

"I am," he nodded, but then his smile turned sexy and he winked. "But I could be having *so* much more fun with you."

He adjusted himself on the bed, and for the first time, his face wasn't in the shadows. "What is that on your face?" she asked, trying to get a good look.

"It's called a beard." He ran his hand over the hair that had grown along his jaw line.

"Hmmm."

"You don't like it?"

She tilted her head to the side, trying to see it better. It gave him an older, more distinguished look. It wasn't that she didn't like it, it was just different. "It's different. I'll hold off on official word until I can see it in person."

"I don't normally do it, but I've been incredibly lazy the past few days."

"Your hair grows that fast?" As weird as this conversation was, it really did interest her. She never had this ease with Ashton; she could never ask him questions that came to her mind without him making her feel stupid.

"Yeah, I usually shave every day. It's the one thing I kinda do for my mom. She hates the tattoos, she hates the piercings in my ears, but she likes me clean-shaven."

"You're so cute," she giggled. "As much as you try to be hard, you are so sweet when it comes to your mom."

"I don't have to *try* to be hard where you're concerned." His eyes darkened and his voice dropped.

"That's not what I was talking about, and you know it."

"Can't help it, Han. One-way street with you."

She liked that, she really did, the fact that he wanted her so much, but it was intimidating at the same time. "I'll be there soon."

"Do I need to pick you up at the airport tomorrow?"

"I hadn't planned on asking you to, but if you want to that would be great. Shell's taking a later flight because she has a few other things she needs to do, so I would be by myself."

He nodded. "Then that's what we'll do. I'll pick you up tomorrow afternoon, and we'll spend some time together before I introduce you to my sister."

"I'm nervous about that," she admitted.

"About meeting Stace?"

"Yeah. She's your sister, she's obviously very important to you."

"You're important to me."

She rolled her eyes. "You can stop trying to impress me, I'm a sure thing."

He laughed loudly. "Good to know, but I'm not ever going to stop trying to impress you. That's kind of my job. When I stop trying to impress you, that means this is over."

"You are kind of right. It's one thing to be comfortable with each other, it's another to not care at all."

"Exactly." He watched her yawn again. "I'm gonna let you off here. You're tired."

"I am," she nodded.

"Sleep good, and I'll see you tomorrow." He blew her a kiss into the phone.

"You too! I can't wait!" She blew him one in return and then disconnected.

Rolling over onto her side in the bed, she did her best to turn her mind off and close her eyes. It was difficult, but she knew that when she woke up in the morning, she would be that much closer to vacation and Garrett.

Garrett was nervous and he wasn't sure why. Maybe the fact that this kind of sealed the deal with the two of them? It felt official, and he wasn't even sure what made it that way. As far as he was concerned, it had been official since their time at the diner in Nashville. But he was nervous this time, meeting her at the airport. He'd even stopped to get her flowers—which he now held in shaking hands.

Pulling his phone out of his pocket, he checked the time and realized he was going to make it with just enough time to spare. Quickly, he found the gate for her flight and sat back against the wall. He didn't want to cause a scene if he could help it. His phone vibrated and he flipped it over, seeing his mom's picture there.

"Hey," he answered.

"Hey, I was just checking on you and Stacey. How are things going?" she asked. He could hear her doing something in the background.

"We're doing good. What the hell are you doing?"

"Making cookies. Your dad's having poker night," she explained as he heard a timer go off.

"He always does that when I'm not around, it's not fair," Garrett complained.

She laughed. "He's afraid you'll beat him, but you'll be home for a while…make him have one while you're here."

"Good idea."

"Can I talk to Stacey? She wasn't answering her phone earlier, and I have a question to ask her."

"She's not with me."

"What do you mean she's not with you? She's your little sister, and the two of you are in Vegas. Please tell me you know where she is."

"Mom, I'm not a dumbass. I'm picking Hannah up at the airport right now, and I left Stace back at the hotel with Brad."

Marie didn't say anything for a few seconds. "Brad, huh?"

He scrunched his nose up. "Why did you say his name like *that*?"

"No reason," she said much too quickly.

"Ohhh, there's a reason, but I don't have time to get it out of you right now. Hannah's plane is starting to de-board."

"Okay, well when you see your sister again, have her call me."

"Will do, right after I ask her about Bradley."

"Garrett, leave it alone," his mom warned. "Seriously, I don't know anything. I was just making a statement."

He, of all people, knew that his mother never made a statement she didn't mean, but he would leave it alone. For nothing else than to keep the peace. He wasn't really sure he wanted to know what the hell was going on anyway. "Alright, will do. Love you, Mom."

"Love you too, and tell Hannah I said 'hi'."

They hung up, and he watched as passengers trickled off the plane, glad, for not the first time, of his height. Because Hannah was so short, her head couldn't be seen over the other passengers. He was about to give up when he noticed her, wearing a hoodie with a Black Friday hat.

"Hannah," he called out. Most people never called her by her real name, so he didn't think they would be in too much danger of others knowing who exactly she was. For his part, he was actually wearing his real prescription glasses and a long sleeve shirt.

"Look at you," she said as she walked over to him and put her arms around his neck. "I love the glasses."

"I figured the sunglasses would totally give me away, even with a long sleeve shirt on."

"You're probably right," she told him, dropping a light kiss on his neck.

"For you," he told her, handing the flowers.

Her face beamed. "Thank you! If I wasn't worried about an audience, I would kiss you right here," she told him.

"Then let's go to the car."

They walked down to the baggage claim and grabbed her bags before walking out, hand in hand.

"You have a lot of stuff." He eyed her suitcases.

"I know, sorry about that, but since it's the end of the tour, they were taking the busses to get cleaned. I'm either going straight home or straight to your house after Vegas, so I needed all my stuff. I'm not even going to tell you how much I had to pay for being over the weight limit. These airlines should be ashamed." She shook her head, taking it out of the hat she wore.

When they were in the safety of his car, he turned to face her. "So what do you think?" he turned his jaw to the left and right.

"It's sexy," she winked. "You look like you just rolled out of bed, put on some clothes, and came to pick me up."

He reached forward and grabbed her behind the neck, allowing himself a moment to explore her mouth with his tongue. "That's pretty much what happened," he whispered as he pulled back.

She giggled. "At least you're having a good time on vacation."

"You have no idea, baby, but I am so glad you're here with me now. You ready?" he asked as he put the car in gear and went to check his blind spot.

"Sure am. Can we stop and get some coffee though? I'm a little tired."

After the last time in Vegas, he realized that she wasn't playing when she said those words. "I passed a coffee shop right up here; let's hit the drive-thru."

She couldn't help but laugh at how quickly he was in the turning lane and hitting the coffee shop.

"I'm not going through that again. I like you every way you are, but I can only handle Princess for so long."

"I'm so glad that we're now being completely honest with each other," she laughed.

"Hey, if we're in this for the long haul, there are just things we have to get out in the open. So I'll start, I'm not a fan of Princess."

She was giggling over in the passenger seat as he handed her the frappe he had ordered without even asking what she wanted. "Fine, if we're going to go there, I'm not a huge fan of scared-of-country-music-fans Garrett."

"That's fair." He nodded as he leaned over and took a drink from her straw. "Now that that's out of the way and we're getting some caffeine in you, let's party."

Chapter Thirty-Five

Day two in Vegas was turning out to be one of Hannah's favorite days ever, she realized. Shell had arrived two hours ago and had been introduced to Stacey, and then the three of them had commandeered Garrett's rented SUV for a shopping excursion.

"I'm so excited to have women to hang out with." Stacey clapped her hands as Shell maneuvered them through traffic. "Don't get me wrong, I love hanging out with my brother and the guys, but there's only so many fart jokes, noises, and smells you can take."

"They've had girlfriends before though, right?" Hannah asked. She knew that Vanessa had toured with the guys.

Stacey snorted. "Yeah, you could say that. None of them were ever as nice as the two of you, I can promise you that."

Hannah wanted badly to ask about Vanessa. Garrett didn't like to talk about his ex-girlfriend, and Hannah didn't like to pry, but she did want to know. "Vanessa wasn't nice to you?" She could have bitten her own tongue off when those words came out of her mouth.

"Vanessa was all about doing whatever Garrett wanted her to and servicing to his needs. If you get my drift."

"Really?" Hannah had never taken him for the kind of man who would demand that.

"Oh don't get me wrong, it's not because he wanted her to, that's just how she was. She wanted that diamond ring, car in the driveway, and her name on the deed to Garrett's house. Luckily, he saw right through it. I'll admit, he strung her along for a lot longer than he should have, but she deserved it."

"Did she cheat on him?" Hannah blurted out.

"Towards the end, yeah. I'd venture to say they cheated on each other. Garrett did try to do right by her, but it wasn't there between the two of them. Like," she licked her lips and looked at Hannah, "I can see the two of you together, and I know that my brother would do anything for you. You can see it in the way he looks at you and the way he treats you. He almost treated Vanessa like a groupie towards the end."

The word groupie made Hannah flash back to the argument the two of them had, but she slammed the door on that conversation. "So there's absolutely no shit that Vanessa can just show back up and Garrett will go running to her?"

"Are you for real?"

"She is," Shell piped up from behind the wheel. "It's a sickness with her, to be honest with you. She is the only person within a thousand mile radius of that man who thinks he's going to find someone better."

"Hey, I'm still here you know?"

"I do, and I'm just telling you like I've been telling you the whole damn time. You have nothing to worry about."

"She's telling the truth," Stacey agreed. "Garrett's not going anywhere. In fact, he told me he's going to invite you to stay at the house, but he's not sure if you'll say yes because you haven't been home in a while."

That made Hannah very happy. "We'll see," she shrugged.

"You are so full of shit." Shell threw a piece of paper at her. "Stop playing hard to get and just let the man get you. He's hot, you're hot, go have a houseful of hot kids."

"Oh my God, don't say that around my mother." Stacey held up her hands. "She has grandchild fever. She's extremely excited that Garrett has a nice, normal-looking girlfriend. I heard her talking to her friends about it the other day."

They had arrived at the mall, and Hannah hopped out of the backseat. "Can we please go shop and stop taking about babies? Don't think I'm ready for that yet."

Garrett and Jared lay poolside, watching the rest of the guys swim. It was probably going to be another long night on the strip, so the two of them were trying to catch up on some sleep while the women went shopping. Garrett had drifted off, and Jared was trying to follow behind, but Garrett's phone was blowing up.

"Man, you might need to check your phone." Jared poked his friend. "It's been going off consistently for the last fifteen minutes."

"Even though I know this phone is my lifeline, it sometimes pisses me off," Garrett yawned, clearing his throat as he picked it up and started scrolling through the messages.

"That motherfucker."

The way he said the words caused the hair to rise on Jared's arms. "You okay?"

"Not in the very fucking least. I'm gonna kill that asshole with my bare hands. Swear to God," he was mumbling as he punched in numbers on his phone.

"What are you talking about?" Jared was thoroughly confused, and the only one who could answer a question at the moment was completely pissed off.

"Ashton Coleman."

"I thought you and Hannah were over that little piece of shit."

"Me too, but obviously, he isn't over her." He flashed his phone at Jared who opened his mouth, then shut it, opened it again, then shut it again. "Am I gonna need to bail you out of jail?"

"I don't know, keep your phone by you." Garrett was gone in two seconds flat. Jared wasn't sure where he was going, but he didn't like the look in his friend's eyes, and he hoped against everything he held dear that Ashton Coleman was not in Las Vegas.

Hannah let herself into the hotel room that she and Garrett were sharing, hoping that he was already there. She held a new dress in her hands to go with the new shoes she'd gotten on her shopping trip with the girls. They were pink and sparkly, something that had become a bit of a trademark for her. Excited didn't even begin to describe how she was feeling. They were going out tonight, and she wanted to look good for him. It made her happy to look good for him and to make him see her as a woman. Not to mention, one night with him hadn't been enough. She needed many more. Her soul needed to be around his to breathe, and it had been too long since she'd let out a good, long breath.

"Babe?" she called as she put her stuff down in the hallway. He had surprised her yesterday by booking a large suite for the two of them. She enjoyed the space and hoped that maybe they'd get to christen most of it before the next few days were up. Her face burned as those thoughts crossed her mind. They were out of character for her, but Vegas held great memories for the two of them. She had missed him in the few hours she had been gone.

"In here." His voice was deep, and her stomach did a somersault. That's how excited she was to see him. Kicking off her shoes, she took off at a run for the living area.

He sat on the couch, looking out over the strip, the glass wall that made up the suite allowing him to do so. She ran over, throwing herself into his lap and holding on with both arms around his neck.

"I missed you so much!"

It took a moment for it to sink in, but it did when she realized he hadn't put his arms around her in return. He had barely even acknowledged that she had launched herself at him. Even more oddly, he sat with his sunglasses on, she couldn't see his eyes.

"Is something wrong?" she questioned, backing up off of him and standing so that she could look down at him.

He cleared his throat and grabbed the iPad that sat next to him. Her stomach continued to flip as he turned it on and then tapped it a few times. Within minutes, he turned it to face her, and what she saw there made her stomach drop like she was on a roller coaster.

"You want to explain this?" he asked, his voice different than she had ever heard it before. He was obviously pissed, but she couldn't tell if it was at her or not.

Reaching down, she grabbed the iPad and scrolled through the website. It was a gossip site, famous for busting all celebs for anything that they might have done. It seemed that this time, they'd busted her. Pictures that she had taken and sent to Ashton towards the end of their relationship, all in her underwear, thank God, were up for the world at large to see.

"I think I'm going to be sick," she told him, throwing down the iPad. "Why would he do this to me?"

"Why wouldn't he? He's an ass; I don't know how many times I have to tell you that."

Garrett's voice was hard and lacked emotion. She had never heard him like this before, and it left a cold spot where she was normally warm around him.

"Those were for his eyes only…"

"You're about three more words from really pissing me the fuck off," Garrett fumed, getting up to pace around the room.

"I'm sorry," she started, running her hands through her hair.

"Goddamn it, Hannah. Why are you sorry? You didn't leak these pictures to the press. That fuckin' piece of dog shit did."

He was aware that his voice was getting louder the more he talked, but he couldn't help it. The woman in front of him was his; he didn't want others to see her the way he did. Just the fact that she had done this for Ashton, of all people, pissed him off. He wanted to rip off the kid's dick and shove it down his throat.

She turned around to face him, tears in her eyes. "This is so embarrassing. I never meant for others to see those."

"I'm sure you didn't," the tone of his voice was so smart, she couldn't help but let the tears fall.

"You could be a little bit nicer about this. It's not like I'm the only one you've ever slept with. Do you want me to tell you about these?" she asked, her voice becoming shrill. "Do you really want me to tell you what these represent?"

Pushing his hands out to the side, he turned his palms upwards towards the sky. "Please enlighten me baby, because this doesn't seem like your shtick."

That hurt, but she refused to let him see it. "This was the end of our relationship. We hadn't seen each other in a few weeks, and to be honest with you, it had more than a month since he had kissed me, since he'd made any kind of advance towards me. I wanted him to want me. I wanted to feel pretty and sexy and loved. You know, all of those feelings that women want. It started out as a joke." She walked over to the glass window and looked out at the strip. "I had gotten a new bikini, and I wanted to see what I looked like in it, so I asked Shell to take my picture. When she did, she told me I looked hot and I should send a naughty picture to Ashton."

She could hear him breathe deeply behind her, but she wasn't going to stop this now. He wanted to judge her; he could know everything about what had transpired.

"Stupid me, I went back to my hotel room that night and did just that. Only, those pictures of me wearing a bra and panties was as naughty as I got. I sent those to him."

She turned around to face him, pointing at the iPad. "And do you know what he said?"

Garrett refused to answer. He just hitched his chin up further and glared at her. She assumed he glared because he still wore the sunglasses, not allowing her to see his expression.

Her chin trembled. She hated to admit this to anyone, much less to this man who had her heart and could make her day better by just smiling. "He said maybe if I lost a few pounds, they'd be enough to get him going."

She crumbled into herself then, tears flowing, sobs gushing out of her body.

His heart was breaking as he watched her, but Garrett couldn't make himself turn off the fury he felt, and it wasn't even at her—it was at Ashton. At the same time, he wanted to shake her and make her see what a horrible piece of shit Ashton was, but she continued to make excuses for him. She refused to see the bad in people. Shaking his head, he fisted his hands over his chest, tucking into himself.

"Never mind that at that time I was puking up everything I ate and working out three hours a day," she continued, tears rolling now. "I still wasn't good enough. I'm never going to be good enough."

She used present tense, and that got him back in the game. "Stop Hannah, no one said you aren't good enough."

"Don't tell me what to do. That's like him."

He saw red. "Do not ever compare me to that shit for brains, ever. Do you understand me?"

She didn't answer, and he advanced on her. For a split second she was scared. "I said, do you understand me? He liked you a certain way, I don't. I like you just the way you are. He didn't like to have something to grab onto when he's fucking you, I do. Don't change who you are because of his narrow-minded ideas of how women should look."

"I hate when you talk like that," she whispered, a tear dripped down her cheek, over her lip. "We aren't like that—it's not crude like that."

"Sometimes it is what it is, Hannah. It's not always fucking rainbows and unicorns. Sometimes real life gets in the way."

His words caused her to shrink back, almost like he had hit her with the back of his hand. "Why are you being so mean?"

Finally, he ripped off his sunglasses and she could see the green of his eyes. There was anger, pain, compassion, but there was also something here that she couldn't place. "You think I'm being mean? How the fuck do you think I got the Reaper nickname? It wasn't just something that people made up, Hannah. I'm an asshole sometimes, and I'm sorry that you're getting the pissy end of it this time, but it is who I am. I am not always a nice guy."

"I know, it's just…what do you want me to do?"

"Nail his ass to the wall. Get out in the press and tell them what a lying sack of shit he is. Don't let him walk all over you again."

"Is that what you think I did last week? Let him walk all over me?"

"You should have made as big a fool outta him as he made out of you. It would have taught him a goddamn lesson is what it would have done."

She shook her head. "I'm not like you; I don't have to get even. I know in my own heart what I'm okay with and what I'm not. Don't let him ruin our time together…please?" she begged.

He couldn't do it. He stayed completely silent as she pleaded with him.

"I'm going to go into the bathroom and change into the amazing dress and shoes I just bought. When I come out, I want us to go out with our friends and have a good time," she told him. "Can you please just do that?"

Garrett shook his head. "I can't. I can't let that little prick get away with talking about the woman I love that way. It's not in my makeup. So you do what you want to do, but I can't promise you I won't be a fuckface tonight, and you can take that to the fuckin' bank."

He turned on his heel and stormed out of the room, leaving her there in his wake.

"Great way to tell me you love me," she yelled back at him, completely sure he didn't hear her. And just for good measure she added. "And you know I hate the 'f' word too!"

No matter what happened, she was determined that this would remain a good day.

Chapter Thirty-Six

Garrett knew that he'd had too much to drink. He was very well aware of that, considering he was having a hard time keeping his eyes open. The words he and Hannah had exchanged with each other before they came out with the rest of the group had been so far from nice and polite that he felt like he needed to go to church. They had been rough, and he was still feeling raw. Things couldn't always be happy, he knew that, but he hated fighting with her. He really hated fighting with her. They didn't get to spend much time together, and he didn't want to spend it arguing. She had been upset with him the whole night and even more so when he had all but demanded she go to the bar and get him another shot. At one point, he recalled, he told her he could be a bastard, and she was getting it in full effect tonight.

"Hey, isn't that her ex-boyfriend?" Bradley pointed to where Hannah stood at the bar.

Swinging his gaze over to where she stood, he spotted the man that pissed him off beyond belief. Sure enough, it was Ashton Coleman. Just knowing that he was in the same breathing space as Hannah made Garrett want to beat the shit out of him. The things he had said in the media, the pictures, and the fact that they had argued about all of it caused Garrett's blood to boil.

"He touches her, I'm gonna go apeshit," he warned the guys at the table as he took another drink from the bottle sitting in front of him. It wasn't like he needed another drink, it was just a distraction—he really was afraid he'd kill the guy.

His green eyes flashed with barely leashed anger as he trained his gaze on his woman and the asshole standing next to her at the bar.

"Ashton, now isn't the time for you to be doing this. Do you understand?" Hannah sighed, grabbing the tray of drinks she had ordered for the guys at the table. Out of the corner of her eye, she could see Garrett watching them, and she wasn't sure how long he would just let them stand there and shoot the breeze. His eyes were murderous, and she wanted to avoid a confrontation between the two of them—no matter what it took.

"When is a good time? I know I hurt you, and I'm sorry that I ruined what we had."

She couldn't understand his reasoning. "So you think leaking pictures of me to the media in various stages of undress and telling them that I cheated on you is going to make me take you back?" she hissed angrily. "It embarrassed me, not to mention you've really ticked off Reaper."

"I'm not scared of him." Ashton ran a hand through his hair. "I'm sorry that it embarrassed you, but what we had was good. I wanted you to remember that."

"You're crazy. You cheated on me because you said I was a cold fish and I couldn't sexually satisfy you. Now you're telling people that it was me who cheated on you, and then you released pictures of me that I never intended for other people to see. Again, I ask, are you crazy?"

"Jesus, Hannah, it's not like you were naked in any of them."

"It doesn't matter," she screamed at him. "Those pictures were private. I sent them to you because you were my boyfriend and because I was trying to put a spark in our relationship, trying to hold onto something that I never had. If I would've known you were screwing other women behind my back, you can bet your ass that I never would have sent them to you to begin with."

"What a mouth on you? Did he teach you how to cuss?" Ashton's gaze sharpened. "What else has he taught you how to do?"

His tone was ugly and what he was suggesting sounded dirty. Nothing that she and Garrett did was ugly. He had taught her the beautiful part of sharing your body with someone else. There was nothing cheap or dirty about it, and it really made Hannah mad to hear Ashton try to belittle it.

"That's none of your business. Please, get out of my way," she told him.

Instead of doing what she asked, he grabbed her arm and turned her to face him. He moved his hand down her body and lightly cupped her breast. "You know you miss it."

She didn't have a chance to respond. He was a blur as Garrett tackled him to the ground.

All he saw was a black and red haze as he threw his fists at the man under him. He could hear Hannah in the background, from what sounded like a million miles away, telling him to stop. But he couldn't. The crack of this asshole's bones against his felt so good.

He grabbed Ashton's hair and pulled his ear up to his mouth. "You are a piece of shit who doesn't deserve to touch any woman, much less mine. You don't get to decide if other people get to see that luscious body that I get to see. That's my decision. You see that." He shoved Ashton's face around so that he could look at Hannah. "You had that, and you lost it because you're a dumbass. That's mine now. You don't touch what's mine. We clear on that?" He grabbed Ashton by the throat and hauled him up, pushing him against the top of the bar.

Ashton coughed, nodding.

"I asked you a question motherfucker…are we clear on that?" Garrett asked, shoving his arm up against Ashton's throat.

It was then he felt small hands against his biceps, soft hands. Those were the hands of the woman he loved, and he fought against the anger and rage in his body, in his mind.

"He can't answer unless you let go of him. You're choking him," Hannah said slowly, so that he could understand, as she pulled at his arms.

All of a sudden, he realized what she was saying and released his grip from around Ashton's throat.

"We're clear," Ashton coughed, heaving in a huge breath, trying to hold himself up at the bar.

Garrett pushed a finger in the other man's face. "Just in case you didn't know who I am…my name is Reaper, and if you want something to do with her, you come through me. You apologize to her because you don't deserve to breathe the same air that she does. You hurt and embarrassed her. She didn't deserve that, you apologize right now."

"I wasn't thinking, Hannah. I'm sorry," he wheezed, his face red.

"It's fine," she told him, still holding onto Garrett's arm.

"It's not," Garrett argued.

She cupped his cheeks in her hands. "I love you for doing this for me, but it really is. There's no reason that you should get in trouble over him. Let's just go," she pleaded with him.

"I'm shitfaced, aren't I?" he asked her, stumbling now that the adrenaline was no longer flowing through his body.

She couldn't help the laugh that came out of her mouth. "You are, but we're gonna have to talk about this in the morning."

Garrett knew that sometime over the night he'd swallowed a lot of cotton. That had to be why his mouth was so dry. Cracking an eye open, he closed it quickly as he realized it was light outside and that light hurt. Hurt badly. He moaned, pulling the blanket up over his face, but even that hurt. His hands were killing him.

"What the fuck did I do?" His voice sounded wrecked, even to his own ears.

"You don't remember?"

That voice was Hannah, that he knew. "Not really," he admitted, sitting up and putting his hand over his eyes.

"Let's see if this rings a bell," she had a seat next to him and handed him a bottle of water, along with what looked like some Tylenol. "You and I had a huge argument about some pictures that Ashton released to the press. We yelled at each other, you were especially mean, but then you told me you loved me before you ran out of the room."

It was slowly coming back to him, and he felt like a piece of shit as he remembered their argument. "God, I am so sorry." He put his head in his hands. "I never meant for it to come out that way."

"I know." She ran her hand along his back. "I know that you meant what you said too."

"I did." He looked at her. "I swear to God, I did. I so wish I could have given you a better 'I love you' than that." His eyes were bloodshot and he licked his lips. "I'm so sorry. I am like him."

"No, no you're not. Not at all. You just had too much to drink, we were mad at each other, you saw him put his hand on me, and you flew off the handle. You protected me. Maybe not in the best of ways, but you did."

"Is that why my hands hurt?" He flexed both of them and for the first time noticed dried blood on them.

"Yeah, you beat the crap out of him. I thought you were going to choke him to death."

"Damn, I'm sorry," he apologized again. "I haven't lost control like that in a long time."

"I know. Jared told me that it had been a while since they saw you go crazy."

"It has been. I learned to control it for the most part. It takes a lot for me to snap, but I guess I hit that point last night." He ran his hand through his hair. Out of anything that could have happened, he hated that she had seen that. "I didn't want you to ever see that side of me," he whispered.

"This may surprise you," she told him softly. "But I liked it. It was hot."

He chuckled. "Are you kidding me?"

"No, I'm not. In fact, there are a lot of things that I love about you."

"Really?" Something about her was different. She looked at him openly; there was no tension around her eyes. He put his hands on her hips and scooted her closer to him. "I'd love to hear what they are."

Hannah was about to very honest. Seeing him defend her the night before and seeing how upset he'd gotten because of what Ashton had done flipped a switch inside her. Those insecurities that had always been at the forefront of every decision she made were now more towards the back of her mind, not right there glaring at her like they normally were. She felt more comfortable in her skin, more comfortable in the relationship. Garrett had risked a lot losing his temper like he had, but he had done it without a second thought for her.

"I love your earrings, your tattoos, the way you smile with just the corners of your mouth sometimes, then when you do smile with your whole mouth and your dimples show—it seriously makes my heart race. I love the fact that you call me, that you aren't scared to text me in front of your friends, that you aren't scared to wear a super small Harmony Stewart shirt in front of an arena full of people."

He cracked up at that and put his arms around her, pulling her to him. "I would kiss you, but I need to brush my teeth."

"That's totally sexy too," she told him dryly.

He dug his fingers into her sides, making her laugh before he threw her onto her back before he got up from the bed, making his way to the bathroom.

"That's another thing. I love that you can pick me up and throw me around. If I ever get too heavy for it, I'm gonna be so sad."

He looked over his shoulder at her. "If you ever get too heavy for me, I'll just pump some more iron."

"That's a nice sacrifice that you'll make for me."

Garrett turned around in the doorway of the bathroom. "I'd make whatever sacrifice I had to, and I hope that you would do the same for me."

She watched as he turned back around and went deeper into the room. After a minute she heard the shower crank on. She sat there for a few moments thinking about him, thinking about the things he had done for her, the sacrifices that he had already made. Making a snap decision, she stood up and started taking her clothes off. By the time she made it to the shower, she was naked. She pulled back the curtain, causing Garrett to jump. "Do you need some help washing your back?"

One of those smiles spread across his face, and he handed her the washrag that was in his hand. "I do, and if you need help, I would be more than willing to wash your front."

Her laugh echoed throughout the bathroom as he pulled her inside. That laugh died as he crowded her against the wall of the shower and lowered his head to hers. There she tasted the mint of his toothpaste as his tongue swept against the inside of her mouth. Reaching down her back, he put his hands around her thighs and lifted so that she could wrap her legs around his waist. Hannah put her arms around his neck and held on so that she could pull her mouth back from his. "Now you're just showing off," she used her teeth to nip at his neck.

"Whatever it takes, baby. Whatever it takes."

Chapter Thirty-Seven

This time when Garrett woke up, his mouth wasn't dry and his eyes didn't hurt from the bright light of the sun. Instead, he was warm, sated, and completely calm as he looked at the brown hair trailing over his right bicep. Hannah moaned as she buried her head deeper into his arm, wrapping her arm securely around his waist.

"We seriously need to get up," he told her as he looked at the clock sitting on the bedside table. It was well after two in the afternoon.

"We're on Vegas time though," she mumbled, running her nails along his side.

"As true as that statement is," he moved his hand to her neck and pushed against it, causing her to raise her eyes to his, "I need to find out if I'm gonna have to go to jail."

"What?" She was still in the warmth of their cocoon, not thinking about the series of events that had brought them to where they were right now.

He cleared his throat and moved her hair out of her face, before dropping a kiss on her forehead. "I'm willing to bet Ashton wasn't too impressed with the fact I beat his ass. I'm prepared to have to go jail today."

Hannah wrapped her arms tightly around his waist and buried her head in his bare chest. "If he does, I'll put him in jail."

The words were muffled, but he caught them and chuckled. "That's nice of you babe, but what has he done to you?"

"I have proof."

A cold dread settled in his stomach. With his hands, he pulled her face back. "Proof about what? What are you not telling me?"

She closed her eyes, shaking her head. Suddenly, he flashed back to when he had advanced on her in the suite the day before and how she had shrunk back. She had really been scared of him. "Christ, Hannah, did he hit you? Is that why you were so uneasy with me yesterday when I was stalking around like a dumbass?"

"I really don't want to talk about it and please respect that, but if he tries to put you in jail, I'll have him there faster than he can snap his fingers. Just trust me. Trust that this is something I can't talk about right now. It's not because I want to hide something from you, it's just because I can't handle it."

His green eyes searched her brown ones, and he could see the pain and hurt there. He realized looking there that it didn't matter if she told him what had happened—if it caused her that much pain, he didn't have to know. "Okay, whatever you want. You tell me when you want to, and I'll do my best to keep my hair-trigger temper under control."

She nodded. "Thank you."

"Know this though," he cupped her cheeks. "No matter how mad I am, I've *never* hit a woman. I'll never raise my hand to you—ever."

"I know that." And she did. Yesterday had been proof of that. When she put her hands on him, he had stopped, just with her asking him to.

"I'm not going to pretend that I don't want to know what happened to you, but I'll respect your wishes."

"Thank you." She squeezed his waist tightly and rested her head on his chest again. She could hear his heart beating as he stroked her hair. This had quickly become the safest place in the world to her, and she never wanted to give it up. "Shell doesn't even know what happened," she whispered. "Nobody does."

That gutted him. She kept so much to herself, and he wanted to tell her she didn't have to. At the same time, he hadn't grown up the way she had, in the public eye. His band didn't get popular until he was past that stage in his life. They weren't headlining until they were twenty-five or twenty-six. Hannah wasn't even that old yet, and she had already been around the world. "You don't have to handle things by yourself anymore, you have me. I love you, and I'm not gonna let anything happen to you."

"I've never believed anyone when they've said that to me before, but I believe it when you say it."

"Good," he smiled. "Don't damage my masculinity like that."

There were so many questions on the tip of his tongue that he wanted to ask. How had her parents not known what was going on with her? She seemed to be close to at least her mom. Had they just turned a blind eye? How had someone like her kept her life so private? It wasn't in his makeup to just leave things alone and not find out the answers that he wanted so badly to know, but he would do it for this woman.

"We need to get up," she told him, trailing a nail down his chest. Just like that the mood in the room and the air around them changed.

"Already there," he smirked.

"That's not what I meant, and you know it," she giggled.

He gripped her hips and tried to pull her over on top of him when they heard a knock at the suite door. "Let me go get it," she told him. "Just in case."

"I'm not scared, Hannah," he assured her.

"I know, but I think it would be better if I did it."

He didn't want to hide in the bedroom like he was scared, but again he would do what she asked. "If it's someone who wants me, I'll be out there."

She shushed him as she put on a pair of sweatpants and a large t-shirt. Hannah shut the door to the bedroom as she made her way into the living area. There was another knock.

"Coming," she said as she hurried to the door. Her hands shook as she gripped the handle and pulled the door slowly open. She never, not even in a million years, would have guessed who was on the other side of that door.

"Don't slam the door in my face." Ashton held his hands up to the door, pushing on it slightly.

"You need to back the fuck up," Garrett told him as he stalked out of the bedroom.

Hannah almost smiled at the imposing figure he made. He also wore a pair of sweatpants, but he wore no shirt. His tattoos were bright against his skin, his ab muscles tight, almost like he was holding himself back from launching at the other man.

"I can't pull the two of you off each other," Hannah warned. "You have to promise me you aren't going to beat each other up."

"He lays a hand on you or toward you, I can't promise what I'm going to do, babe."

"Ashton, its best you stay out there," Hannah told him, putting herself in between the two of them.

"No, you don't put yourself in between us, you come back here beside me," Garrett told her, pulling her back with his hand.

"Please don't fight," she begged. "Ashton, just tell us why you're here and then leave."

Ashton was quiet for so long, she thought that maybe he'd forgotten why he was there. It gave her a moment to study him. His left eye was swollen shut, there were marks around his neck from where Garrett had choked him, and he was hunched over, like his ribs were hurting.

"I'm sorry," Ashton finally said, pulling his one eye up to look at her.

"What?" she asked, disbelief in her voice. Was he serious?

He licked his cracked lips and looked past Garrett so that he could see her. "I'm sorry. I did a lot of things to you that I shouldn't have done. I don't expect you to accept my apology, but I have a problem that I need help with."

"When did you come to this conclusion?" She had heard this so many times from him, and she had always believed him. This time, she wouldn't make the same mistake. "You've said this before."

Garrett stood, his hand gripping the door tightly, to keep him from closing his hand around the bastard's neck in front of him. He really didn't want to hear the words they spoke to one another. He wanted to shove Ashton's face off his neck.

"I know I have, but this morning I woke up bloody, bruised, and sore. Nobody should have to wake up this way."

"I'm not fuckin' sorry I did it," Garrett interjected. "If it had been up to me, I would have given you even more than I did. You deserve every ache and pain I gave you. The only thing I'm sorry about is she had to see it."

"I do," he agreed. "I deserve what you wanted to give to me."

Hannah mulled over in her head what she should say to this. What did Ashton expect her to say? What did Garrett expect her to say? She was so tired.

"I wish you the best Ashton, and that's all I can tell you."

"Can you forgive me?" his voice was so weak and pleading that she wanted to tell him to man up.

"No, I can't," she told him. "Honestly, I don't know that I ever can forgive you, but I can thank you. You showed me what I don't want from a man, and you made it possible for me to appreciate the one I have standing in between the two of us."

"I need your forgiveness," he told her, his voice becoming harder.

"I'm not giving it to you."

He opened his mouth again, and Garrett held up his hand. "She told you that she's not giving you her forgiveness. Let it go."

"I want to hear her say it," he said again.

"You're not going to. This is over. You turn your ass around, tuck your tail between your legs, and run on home to mommy. Got it?"

It was obvious that Ashton wasn't happy, but he didn't want to scrap with Garrett again. "Fine, but I just wanted to let you know I'm sorry, and I'm not pressing charges against him."

"Thanks," Garrett bit out. "Really appreciate it, but if you don't leave right now, I'm gonna beat the shit out of you again." He slammed the door in Ashton's face and turned around, leaning against it. "You okay?"

Hannah nodded. "I just never realized how manipulative he is before that."

"Well then, thank God for that."

He walked over and enveloped her in his arms. She clung to him, needing to feel the closeness they had earlier. "He's never going to hurt me again."

"Damn right."

"Now, how about we get out of this hotel room and go have some fun? I only have a couple days left," she grinned up at him.

"Sounds good to me." He wanted to ask her to come home with him, but knew that she probably wanted to go to her own house and check on things there, see her parents and friends in Nashville. But what he wouldn't give to have her on the plane with him when they all left. It was just another reminder of the lives they led.

Chapter Thirty-Eight

"**D**id you see this?"

The two of them were relaxing in their own cabana on their last afternoon in Vegas. In a few hours it would be time for them to go, but they wanted to get as much time as they could away from all the obligations. She would have to go back to Nashville, and he would have to go to Huntington Beach.

Garrett glanced at the cell phone that Hannah held in front of his face and had to laugh. It looked as if Ashton was retracting his statement and issuing a public apology to not only Hannah, but him as well.

> *"Harmony is very happy with Reaper and it was wrong for me to try and mess that up. I met him, we talked. He's a really cool guy," Ashton said as he spoke with Country Daily.*

"Yeah, we talked alright," he snorted.

"Well at least he realized that he did wrong," Hannah shrugged. "That's the first time he's ever admitted to being wrong about anything. Ten bucks says his management saw his face, asked him what happened, he told them what an idiot he is, and then they had to do something to stop the true story from coming out. That's just how they work in our neck of the woods." She shook her head, disgusted with the whole thing.

For a moment, Garrett was quiet, and he struggled with what he wanted to say to her. While honesty was working with the two of them, he wasn't sure that she was ready to discuss what he wanted to ask her about. "You know that if you ever wanted to talk to me about what he did to you, I would listen with no judgment, right?"

"I know," she smiled softly over at him. "I've never told anybody about what he did to me. The hospital took the pictures, and I left with them before they could ask his name to press charges. That was probably the stupidest thing I could have done, but I was so embarrassed and still scared. He truly made me believe that it was all my fault, that it was something that I asked for. By that time, I was so interested in trying to be perfect for him, that I didn't want anyone to know what had been happening behind closed doors for months. Not the physical abuse, but the emotional abuse. I didn't want Shell to find out, or my parents, or my fans. I felt like it was my fault, and I didn't know how to deal with it. To be honest, I still don't."

He reached over and grabbed her hand in his. He really needed to know the answer to this question, but he knew that it would scare him to death if she said yes. "Serious question here, Han. Does my temper scare you?"

She was quiet for a long time, and he wondered if he'd overstepped some kind of invisible boundary. "It does," she admitted.

That crushed him. He never wanted to scare her—ever. At the same time, he couldn't change who he was or how he dealt with things, but he could try to be better. "Damn," he whispered. "I never wanted to scare you with the way I am."

"You're just so intense sometimes. You and Jared both. There are times when the both of you have scared me, but that's not on you two. That's on me. I know that neither one of you would ever hurt me, but that doesn't mean that I don't worry about it."

"I don't want to worry you."

"I can't change that part of my personality yet. Just know that you being here and being able to tell you little things about what happened with Ashton and you standing up for me the way you did, it helped things so much. I don't want you to change for me," she assured him.

"Will you at least be honest with me when I do it then? Will you say 'Garrett, you're scaring me' that way I can back my temper down. Believe it or not, I do have some control over it."

She knew that he did, and she wanted to prove to him that she could also learn a few things. "When I'm being too clingy and to self-deprecating, you have to call me out on it too. We both have flaws and faults that we need to work on. We'll do that together." The promise was implied in the tone of voice that she used.

Since they were alone in their own cabana, she got up and walked the short distance to where he lay on his own lounger. Without asking, she lay down beside him and made herself comfortable. When his arms went around her, she knew this was where she belonged, and the fear that it would change when she went home clogged up her throat. Would it still feel this way when half a continent stretched between them? "I love you," she told him softly as she listened to the steady beat of his heart.

"Love you too," he whispered back to her, as he kissed her on the forehead. "We've worked too hard at this to let a little distance get in our way," he tried to make joke of what she was thinking about.

"How did you know?"

"Because I'm thinking about it too, and it's killing me trying to figure out what we can do."

Neither one of them had an answer that would completely solve the issues they had with a long-distance relationship, so instead of talking about it, she let him hold her in his arms while the minutes and hours counted down until there were none left.

Epilogue

"You sure you won't come home with me?" Garrett asked as he and Hannah stood in the airport, getting ready to separate into two different directions.

"I need to go home and see my mom, sleep in my own bed, see my house. It's not that I don't want to, I do, but I feel like I should go do things there too."

He nodded, knowing that what she spoke was the truth. The fact that he was going home to do those things didn't escape him; it just made him sad to be leaving her. The past few days had been amazing. He had almost let himself believe that she would be there for him every day. What it would be like if they were married and living their lives together.

"I'm just going to miss you," he whispered against her ear as he pulled her hips flush with his.

"Now you sound like me," she laughed, throwing her arms around his neck.

Shell was leaving with Jared immediately for their vacation, and the rest of the Black Friday band was going back to California, leaving her as the only one leaving on the plane to Nashville.

"Can't help it, I got used to you."

"I got used to you too, but right now we have two separate lives," she reminded him.

"I know. I'll see you soon. Right?"

She raised her eyebrows. "You think I'm going to stay away from you for that long?"

"Well, I had hoped not."

"Then you truly don't understand what kind of hold you have on me, Garrett Thompson." She leaned in, brushing her lips against his neck.

It was late at night, and they were pretty sure no one of importance was around. It allowed them to be a little more open than they normally would have been in public. Moving his hand down, he cupped it around her thigh, caressing her lightly. "I hope it's the same kind of hold you have on me."

"I'm sure that it is."

The overhead announcement said that it was time for her to board her flight, and he groaned, pushing his forehead against hers. "You really gotta go?

"I really gotta go. But it won't be long until we see each other again."

"I wish that we weren't based on two separate coasts," he grumbled.

"Me too, but you can't make hard rock in Nashville, and I can't make country in California, so we're just going to have to work this out."

Again, she was right, but it didn't mean he had to like it. Gripping her around the neck, he pulled her mouth to his, kissing her lightly.

She wanted him to deepen it but knew if they got start-ed, they would never stop. She would miss her flight and then just fly on to California with him and probably never look back. "I love you," she said softly as she pulled her lips back from his.

"Love you too," he answered. "Just like we're on the road, huh?"

"Just like that. We'll do all the things we did before to keep up with each other," she promised.

"Why does this feel different?" he questioned, not wanting to let her go.

"We're much more invested in each other now. I mean you've beaten someone up for me," she smiled.

"And do it again in a heartbeat if you need me too." They called for her flight again, and he released his grip on her.

"I'll call you when I land."

"You better." He dug his hands into her hair one more time and pulled it slightly so that she tilted her head back to look at him. "I'm just a phone call, plane ride, Skype session away. Don't you forget that."

"You either." She leaned up and kissed him along his jaw line. "We'll see each other soon."

The side of his mouth tilted. "Not soon enough, but I'll let you go for now."

And he did, pushing her slightly towards her gate. When she looked back, he was already walking away. She couldn't take it, the view of his back as he walked away from her. Nashville would still be there in a month, in a day, in a year—whenever she decided to go home. Her parents would understand, her business could be conducted wherever she chose to do it, but Garrett would only be in one place. That was California.

"Garrett," she screamed as she left the gate, running towards him.

He turned around, surprise evident on his face. "Hannah?"

"I don't want to go home," she breathed heavily, tears pooling in her eyes. "I want to go with you, home is where you are. Nashville can wait, but these early days that we can spend together, they won't. I don't want to let this go," she told him.

He hugged her fiercely to his chest. "Then we won't. God, I didn't want to let you go," he whispered.

"I didn't want you to let me go either," she told him, reaching up to kiss his lips. Against them, she whispered, "We have our whole lives to finish what we've started here, but we only have one beginning to experience, and I want that experience with you."

The End

If you, or someone you know, is in an abusive relationship, there is help. Please contact http://www.thehotline.org/. There are no fees, no names, no judgment, just help.

Acknowledgements

Allison, who always believes in me enough for the both of us. I couldn't ever do any of this without you. I'm so blessed that we are close enough that you can be honest with me, because there were part of this I needed honesty about. I will always love this journey for how it brought our friendship back together.

Michael, thank you for letting me listen to hours and hours of Brantley Gilbert and Avenged Sevenfold. I know you love me, even if you make fun of me on a regular basis.

Thank you to the readers, bloggers, and authors that I've met this past year. I take a little piece of me with you in everything and you'll never know how much you all mean to me!

Connect

Facebook:
https://www.facebook.com/authorlaramiebriscoe

Twitter:
https://www.twitter.com/laramiebriscoe

Pinterest:
https://www.pinterest.com/laramiebriscoe

I love to hear from fans! Please drop me an email at:
laramie.briscoe@gmail.com.

Want to find out when I'm having a new release? Join my mailing list at Substance B!
http://substance-b.com/LaramieBriscoe.html

Sneak Peek of Rockin' Country 1.5

Coming July 2014

Chapter One

I t was after three o'clock in the morning when the two of them pulled into the garage of Garrett's Huntington Beach home.

"I hate that it's dark and I can't see the views I know you probably have," Hannah pouted as she stepped out of his sports car.

"Yeah, too bad we couldn't get a later flight. At least you'll be able to see what the inside of the house looks like."

He came around the car and grabbed her hand in his. Butterflies danced in her stomach and she wasn't sure why. It wasn't like this was the first time she was going to a boyfriend's house. She and Ashton had done it a couple of times, more so in the beginning than towards the end. Never had she felt at home with him, at his house. Hannah didn't ever want to feel that way with Garrett. Underlying fear had her nerves on edge. What if she stayed here with him and they realized that maybe they weren't as compatible as they seemed to be?

"You okay?" he asked as he let her hand go to separate keys on his key ring.

"Yeah, just nervous," she giggled.

"Why?" He grinned at her giggle. "It's just me here."

"I guess," she shrugged. "This is all still new to me."

"Never stayed at Ashton's?" he asked as they walked inside and he put a code into the security system.

"No, I did. This just feels different."

Hannah was having trouble articulating her feelings. She couldn't put into words just how important this was for her, for them, and for their relationship. With other people this was probably easy, with her, it felt like the rest of her life counted on how this visit went.

"It's supposed to," he told her as he walked into what she realized was a kitchen and began turning lights on. "When it's important and it means a lot, it feels different. We're not playing house here, Han. This is the real fuckin' deal."

She huffed and he stuck his tongue between his lips. "Knew that would get ya."

Just as she was about to ask him a question, she heard the clickety clack of nails and the unmistakable sound of a dog collar. Before she could say anything, Garrett was on his knees, his arms wide open for what looked like a gray Doberman pincher. The dog whined, running towards his owner and threw himself into Garrett's arms, yipping and whining, obviously excited.

"Hey Havock," he cooed, running his hands over the dog's head and using his fingers to scratch the hair there. "Did you miss me?"

Standing back, she watched as Garrett had a seat in the middle of the kitchen floor and let the dog pounce on him. Havock, as Garrett had called him, was so excited that he kept licking the man's face. His chest heaved until finally Garrett stuck his hand out and pointed his finger in the 'down' direction. "Sit," he commanded and the Doberman obeyed.

"You wanna come meet him?" he looked back at Hannah.

"I didn't want to interrupt your reunion," she smiled, slowly walking over to where the two sat.

Garrett's face burned. "It's been a little while since he's seen me for longer than a few days. He's my boy," he ruffled the hair on the dog's head again. "C'mere," he indicated, holding his hand out to her. "He needs to smell you first. He's a trained guard dog. He'll take you down if you aren't careful."

Dogs hadn't ever been something that she and her family had, so this did make her a little uncomfortable. Not so uncomfortable that she couldn't stay in the same home with them, but she wasn't sure how to act.

"Havock, this is your new roomie, Hannah," he introduced them.

Hannah snickered when he called her a roomie, but then forced herself to relax as she put her hand out to the dog. He sniffed her a few times and made a circle around her before sitting in front of her and licking her fingers. "Does he like me?"

"Yeah, he likes you," Garrett laughed as Havock licked her hand and then laid down on the ground on his back. "Nobody wants to see your junk, buddy," he clapped his hands. "C'mon, let's give her the tour."

If Hannah had ideas about what his house looked like, it didn't begin to compare to what the reality of it was.

"Do you really need all this room?" she asked as they entered the fourth bedroom. It was decorated the way she figured a typical bachelor pad looked. His basement was amazing—even to her. It had a fully stocked bar, a pool table, a lounge area and a huge set up for video games. He mentioned that he hosted tons of game nights and they sometimes went into the wee hours of the mornings.

"Nah, but when you're young and you have money...you have an image to uphold. Especially when you're out here on the West Coast. You're lucky you grew up in Nashville where it's so laid back."

"It's not as laid back as you think. There's a good 'ole boys club that it took me a long time to break into."

"But you weren't expected to drive an Escalade right outta the box now where you?"

He had her there. "No, I wasn't. But ya know, I think that comes from there being so many songwriters in Nashville. There's only really a select few that are making a ton of money. Most of the people who roll up outside of a recording or writing session are in a rusted out pick-up truck. I mean, most of the artists write music to make money. That's what a typical Nashville deal looks like. If I had no songwriting credits, I'd be living like a College Freshman and that's no lie."

"Even with touring?"

It was still so odd for her to be able to have these conversations with him. She'd never been this comfortable with Ashton to have these kinds of talks and nobody else really knew the business the way he did. "I got my butt kicked on my touring gig to tell you the truth. I make pretty good on the merchandising, but I should have held out for a bigger piece of the ticket pie. Shell and I wrote that down for next time. We both knew there would be a few things we didn't exactly do right, and that was one of them. Learned a lesson with that."

"That's good though, as long as you learn from your mistakes. There's not a damn thing wrong with that."

A silence encompassed them and she rocked back and forth on her heels. "So we've been all over this house and there are two things I'm wondering."

"What's that?"

"Number one, what's the backyard look like? Number two, what's your bedroom look like?"

"Well, I can answer one question right now," he grabbed her hand and pulled her in the direction of a closed door at the end of the hall. "This is my bedroom."

He opened the door and allowed her to walk in before him. She turned around to give him a little grin. It was exactly how she imagined it would look. The walls were a gunmetal gray, dark carpet covered the floor, all of the furniture was black and in the middle sat a huge bed. It was four-poster with again dark covers.

"You really are dark sometimes aren't you?"

Garrett shrugged. "It's all a part of my personality. Why should I get rid of one part to make the other part better? I am who I am."

She couldn't argue with that. He really was who he was and she realized that there wasn't anything she would ask him to change. There was no reason to ask him to change. Hannah loved him exactly the way he was.

"Come over here," he maneuvered her over to where a set of double doors sat in the wall.

She watched as he moved the curtains back and then opened them. It lead out onto a balcony that had all weather furniture. She loved it already.

"This is amazing."

"Believe it or not, this is where I do a lot of writing. It's so damn peaceful and you can just get inside your own head out here. I close those doors and in essence I close the world off and I escape into my own world. I get rid of everything that's bothering me or whatever I'm going through in my life. This is my own little piece of Heaven right here."

It was so special to her that he was showing her this part of him—this place that he obviously loved. "Ever brought anyone else here?" she asked on impulse.

"Nope, I've never seen myself being happy with anyone here. I get the feeling you already love it just as much as I do."

Grabbing his hand, she pulled him to her and then put her hands on his hips. "I'll reserve judgment on that until you show me the back yard."

"You're beautiful and smart. You reserve your opinions until you really know what you're dealing with. I'm gonna have to remember that about you, Hannah Stewart."

Slowly, he pulled her over to the edge of the balcony and then pointed down. "Take a look at the backyard."

When she looked down, she knew that this was the place for her. There was a huge pool—much bigger than hers. To the left of it was an outside dining area along with what looked like an outside fireplace. She had always wanted something like this, but Tennessee wasn't exactly conducive to it—with the summers being so hot and muggy—and the winters being a crapshoot. It was landscaped beautifully and she saw a volleyball net further back on the property as well as a gate.

"That gate leads to my own personal part of the beach."

"You were right," she told him as she looked up into his eyes. "This is a little slice of Heaven."

"It is," he agreed. "But it's been damn lonely. I think it's been waiting on you."

In little moments of truth, he could completely undo her. It was a part of his personality that she still wasn't used to and wasn't sure that she ever would be. Garrett had the habit of just throwing out little things like that in every day conversation.

"Maybe I was waiting on it," she corrected. "Maybe I need it even more than I thought I did."

For the first time in a very long time, she felt at peace. There was no one running her this way and that. No one asking for an autograph. She wasn't sitting at her Nashville home feeling bad that she wasn't hanging out with family or friends. That's what they expected her to do when she was in town and not working. Hannah was doing something for herself and she had a feeling she was going to enjoy every single minute of it. A jaw-popping yawn came out of her mouth at that moment and Garrett leisurely ran his hand down her back.

"Why don't we go to sleep? This will all be here in the morning. I can take you down to the beach and we can explore and then you can call your long lost friend Shell and the two of you can have lunch together."

That sounded so good to her. "Does anyone know I'm here?"

"Just my parents and Stacey. I haven't even shared it with the guys yet. So we can keep it quiet if you want."

"I just really want to enjoy myself and relax."

He framed her face with his hands. "You have nothing to explain to me. We'll do whatever you want to do. I'm just happy you're here."

And so was she.

Made in the USA
Charleston, SC
23 August 2014